The Peterkin Papers

LUCRETIA P. HALE

T H E

Peterkin Papers

With the original illustrations

THE NEW YORK REVIEW CHILDREN'S COLLECTION

New York

THIS IS A NEW YORK REVIEW BOOK
PUBLISHED BY THE NEW YORK REVIEW OF BOOKS
1755 Broadway, New York, NY 10019
www.nyrb.com

Library of Congress Cataloging–in–Publication Data

Hale, Lucretia P. (Lucretia Peabody), 1820–1900.
The Peterkin papers / by Lucretia P. Hale.
p. cm. — (New York Review children's collection)
Summary: The humorous adventures of a foolish family whose
problems are righted by the Lady from Philadelphia.
ISBN-13: 978-1-59017-212-4 (alk. paper)
ISBN-10: 1-59017-212-4 (alk. paper)
[1. Family life—Fiction. 2. Humorous stories.] I. Title. II. Series.
PZ7.H137Pe 2006
[Fic]—dc22
2006017647

ISBN-13: 978-1-59017-212-4
ISBN-10: 1-59017-212-4

Cover design by Louise Fili Ltd.
Cover illustration by Barbara McClintock

T O

Meggie

(The Daughter of The Lady from Philadelphia)

To whom these stories
were first
told

Contents

The Peterkin Papers

Contents ❦ *continued*

The Last of the Peterkins

The Peterkin Papers

Preface

How the Peterkins Came to Publish Their Adventures

THE PETERKIN family were discussing certain troubles of theirs that occurred one night when they had been to the Carnival of Authors in Boston. They were much distressed with the difficulty of making people understand about it. Their neighbors were constantly asking why it was they went in costume, and why they were kept out of their own house and obliged to spend the night at the station. Many strange stories were abroad, and it was not agreeable to be so talked over, certainly, without chance of explanation. Solomon John then suggested that a true account of their adventures should be written out, and published in all of the leading papers.

Mrs. Peterkin shrank from this; it would make the whole matter more public than ever.

Mr. Peterkin asked if she would prefer a book of their adventures; she declared that she would, for there would be the covers, which would seem to shut it up, and make the matter less public.

Mr. Peterkin thought a book might contain other adventures of the family. Solomon John would have written a book before now, if he had known what to write. Why not mention that fact? The history of their troubles with keys would explain in part the difficulty of getting into their own house the night of the Carnival, for if Agamemnon's invention of "one key alone necessary," had been patented, they would have been saved this perplexity.

Each one of the family recalled some event that might form the subject of a chapter. Mrs. Peterkin reminded them of their

Fourth of July explosion, and the fire. Elizabeth Eliza thought the worst day was, when there was no fire, but the engines insisted on coming and the engineer insisted there was. The little boys were enchanted with the idea of a book. They could remember such remarkable adventures: their going to the menagerie, and Solomon John's expedition for cider. If there were not enough adventures they would get up some new ones.

They could write some chapters themselves, only they were not sure about the spelling part. Mr. Peterkin shook his head. "Of what use were the common schools, if his boys could not spell?"

Elizabeth Eliza objected to a book. None of the neighbors had done anything of the sort. She would be glad to have some explanation of the affair of the Carnival, because such stories about it had gone abroad in the town Still, would it be safe to say all they felt about the policeman? She would not wish to offend him, but surely he was in fault.

Agamemnon, at last, suggested they should consult the lady from Philadelphia. She had always been interested in their adventures, and if she gave her consent it would be all right. Elizabeth Eliza agreed to this, and it was proposed she should write to the lady from Philadelphia for advice. Still Elizabeth Eliza was reluctant to send on the whole story of their sufferings the night of the Carnival. It would take a great deal of postage, and they might not get on the right stamps; and if so, it would go to the dead-letter office, and never be heard of again, and all the work of writing would be wasted. They were so particular now at the post-office. And perhaps the lady from Philadelphia would be away, perhaps they had better wait till she came on in the summer.

The whole family objected to this. Agamemnon was sure it would take a long time to get out the book anyhow, and there ought to be no delay.

Solomon John suggested a postal card. Everybody reads a postal, and everybody would read it as it came along, and see its importance, and help it on. If the lady from Philadelphia were away, her family and all her servants would read it, and send it after her, for answer.

Elizabeth Eliza thought the postal a bright idea. It would not take so long to write as a letter, and would not be so expensive. But could they get the whole subject on a postal?

The little boys suggested you might send two, and have it continued on the second postal.

But Mr. Peterkin believed there could be no difficulty, there was but one question:

Shall the Adventures of the Peterkin family be published?

This was decided upon, and there was room for each of the family to sign, the little boys contenting themselves with rough sketches of their india-rubber boots.

Mr. Peterkin, Agamemnon, and Solomon John took the postal card to the post office early one morning, and by the afternoon of that very day, and all the next day, and for many days, came streaming in answers on postals and in letters. Their card had been addressed to the lady from Philadelphia, with the number of her street. But it must have been read by their neighbors in their own town post-office before leaving; it must have been read along its way, for by each mail came piles of postals and letters from town after town, in answer to the question; and all in the same tone: "Yes, yes; publish the adventures of the Peterkin family."

"Publish them, of course."

And in time came the answer from the lady from Philadelphia:

"Yes, of course; publish them."

This is why they are now published.

The Lady Who Put Salt in Her Coffee

THIS was Mrs. Peterkin. It was a mistake. She had poured out a delicious cup of coffee, and, just as she was helping herself to cream, she found she had put in salt instead of sugar! It tasted bad. What should she do? Of course she couldn't drink the coffee; so she called in the family, for she was sitting at a late breakfast all alone. The family came in; they all tasted, and looked, and wondered what should be done, and all sat down to think.

At last Agamemnon, who had been to college, said, "Why don't we go over and ask the advice of the chemist?" (For the chemist lived over the way, and was a very wise man.)

Mrs. Peterkin said, "Yes," and Mr. Peterkin said, "Very well," and all the children said they would go too. So the little boys put on their india-rubber boots, and over they went.

Now the chemist was just trying to find out something which should turn everything it touched into gold; and he had a large glass bottle into which he put all kinds of gold and silver, and many other valuable things, and melted them all up over the fire, till he had almost found what he wanted. He could turn things into almost gold. But just now he had used up all the gold that he had round the house, and gold was high. He had used up his wife's gold thimble and his great-grandfather's gold-bowed spectacles; and he had melted up the gold head of his great-great-grandfather's cane; and, just as the Peterkin family came in, he was down on his knees before his wife, asking her to let him have her wedding-ring to melt up with all the rest, because this time he knew he should succeed, and should be able to turn everything into gold; and then she could have a new wedding-ring of diamonds, all set in emeralds and rubies and topazes, and all the furniture could be turned into the finest of gold.

Now his wife was just consenting when the Peterkin family burst in. You can imagine how mad the chemist was! He came near throwing his crucible — that was the name of his melting-pot — at their heads. But he didn't. He listened as calmly as he could to the story of how Mrs. Peterkin had put salt in her coffee.

At first he said he couldn't do anything about it; but when Agamemnon said they would pay in gold if he would only go, he packed up his bottles in a leather case, and went back with them all.

First he looked at the coffee, and then stirred it. Then he put in a little chlorate of potassium, and the family tried it all round; but it tasted no better. Then he stirred in a little bichlorate of magnesia. But Mrs. Peterkin didn't like

that. Then he added some tartaric acid and some hypersul-
phate of lime. But no; it was no better. "I have it!" exclaimed the chemist, — "a little ammonia is just the thing!"
No, it wasn't the thing at all.

Then he tried, each in turn, some oxalic, cyanic, acetic,
phosphoric, chloric, hyperchloric, sulphuric, boracic, silicic,
nitric, formic, nitrous nitric, and carbonic acids. Mrs. Peterkin tasted each, and said the flavor was pleasant, but not
precisely that of coffee. So then he tried a little calcium,
aluminum, barium, and strontium, a little clear bitumen,
and a half of a third of a sixteenth of a grain of arsenic. This

gave rather a pretty color; but still Mrs. Peterkin ungrate-
fully said it tasted of anything but coffee. The chemist was
not discouraged. He put in a little belladonna and atropine,
some granulated hydrogen, some potash, and a very little

antimony, finishing off with a little pure carbon. But still Mrs. Peterkin was not satisfied.

The chemist said that all he had done ought to have taken out the salt. The theory remained the same, although the experiment had failed. Perhaps a little starch would have some effect. If not, that was all the time he could give. He should like to be paid, and go. They were all much obliged to him, and willing to give him $1.37\frac{1}{2}$ in gold. Gold was now $2.69\frac{3}{4}$, so Mr. Peterkin found in the newspaper. This gave Agamemnon a pretty little sum. He sat himself down to do it. But there was the coffee! All sat and thought awhile, till Elizabeth Eliza said, "Why don't we go to the herb-woman?" Elizabeth Eliza was the only daughter. She was named after her two aunts, — Elizabeth, from the sister of her father; Eliza, from her mother's sister. Now, the herb-woman was an old woman who came round to sell herbs, and knew a great deal. They all shouted with joy at the idea of asking her, and Solomon John and the younger children agreed to go and find her too.

The herb-woman lived down at the very end of the street; so the boys put on their india-rubber boots again, and they set off. It was a long walk through the village, but they came at last to the herb-woman's house, at the foot of a high hill. They went through her little garden. Here she had marigolds and hollyhocks, and old maids and tall sun-flowers, and all kinds of sweet-smelling herbs, so that the air was full of tansy-tea and elder-blow. Over the porch grew a hop-vine, and a brandy-cherry tree shaded the door, and a luxuriant cranberry-vine flung its delicious fruit across the window. They went into a small parlor, which smelt very spicy. All around hung little bags full of catnip, and pepper-mint, and all kinds of herbs; and dried stalks hung from the ceiling; and on the shelves were jars of rhubarb, senna, manna, and the like.

But there was no little old woman. She had gone up into the woods to get some more wild herbs, so they all thought they would follow her, — Elizabeth Eliza, Solomon John, and the little boys. They had to climb up over high rocks, and in among huckleberry-bushes and blackberry-vines. But the little boys had their india-rubber boots. At last they discovered the little old woman. They knew her by her hat. It was steeple-crowned, without any vane. They saw her digging with her trowel round a sassafras bush. They told her their story, — how their mother had put salt in her coffee, and how the chem-ist had made it worse instead of better, and how their mother couldn't drink it, and wouldn't she come and see what she could do? And she said she would, and took up her little old apron, with pockets all round, all filled with everlasting and pennyroyal, and went back to her house.

There she stopped, and stuffed her huge pockets with some

of all the kinds of herbs. She took some tansy and peppermint, and caraway-seed and dill, spearmint and cloves, pennyroyal and sweet marjoram, basil and rosemary, wild thyme and some of the other time, — such as you have in clocks, — sappermint and oppermint, catnip, valerian, and hop; indeed, there isn't a kind of herb you can think of that the little old woman didn't have done up in her little paper bags, that had all been dried in her little Dutch-oven. She packed these all up, and then went back with the children, taking her stick.

Meanwhile Mrs. Peterkin was getting quite impatient for her coffee.

As soon as the little old woman came she had it set over the fire, and began to stir in the different herbs. First she put in a little hop for the bitter. Mrs. Peterkin said it tasted like hop-tea, and not at all like coffee. Then she tried a little flagroot and snakeroot, then some spruce gum, and some caraway and some dill, some rue and rosemary, some sweet marjoram and sour, some oppermint and sappermint, a little spearmint and peppermint, some wild thyme, and some of the other tame time, some tansy and basil, and catnip and valerian, and sassafras, ginger, and pennyroyal. The children tasted after each mixture, but made up dreadful faces. Mrs. Peterkin tasted, and did the same. The more the old woman stirred, and the more she put in, the worse it all seemed to taste.

So the old woman shook her head, and muttered a few words, and said she must go. She believed  the coffee was bewitched. She bundled up her packets of herbs, and took her trowel, and her basket, and her stick, and went back to her root of sassafras, that she had left half in the air and half out. And all she would take for pay was five cents in currency.

Then the family were in despair, and all sat and thought a great while. It was growing late in the day, and Mrs. Peterkin hadn't had her cup of coffee. At last Elizabeth Eliza said, "They say that the lady from Philadelphia, who is staying in town, is very wise. Suppose I go and ask her what is best to be done." To this they all agreed, it was a great thought, and off Elizabeth Eliza went.

She told the lady from Philadelphia the whole story, — how her mother had put salt in the coffee; how the chemist had been called in; how he tried everything but could make it no better; and how they went for the little old herb-woman,

and how she had tried in vain, for her mother couldn't drink the coffee. The lady from Philadelphia listened very attentively, and then said, "Why doesn't your mother make a fresh cup of coffee?" Elizabeth Eliza started with surprise. Solomon John shouted with joy; so did Agamemnon, who had just finished his sum; so did the little boys, who had followed on. "Why didn't we think of that?" said Elizabeth Eliza; and they all went back to their mother, and she had her cup of coffee.

About Elizabeth Eliza's Piano

LIZABETH ELIZA had a present of a piano, and she was to take lessons of the postmaster's daughter.

They decided to have the piano set across the window in the parlor, and the carters brought it in, and went away.

After they had gone the family all came in to look at the piano; but they found the carters had placed it with its back turned towards the middle of the room, standing close against the window.

How could Elizabeth Eliza open it? How could she reach the keys to play upon it?

Solomon John proposed that they should open the window, which Agamemnon could do with his long arms. Then Elizabeth Eliza should go round upon the piazza, and open the piano. Then she could have her music-stool on the piazza, and play upon the piano there.

So they tried this; and they all thought it was a very pretty sight to see Elizabeth Eliza playing on the piano, while she sat on the piazza, with the honeysuckle vines behind her.

It was very pleasant, too, moonlight evenings. Mr.

Peterkin liked to take a doze on his sofa in the room; but the rest of the family' liked to sit on the piazza. So did Elizabeth Eliza, only she had to have her back to the moon.

All this did very well through the summer; but, when the fall came, Mr. Peterkin thought the air was too cold from the open window, and the family did not want to sit out on the piazza.

Elizabeth Eliza practised in the mornings with her cloak on; but she was obliged to give up her music in the evenings, the family shivered so.

One day, when she was talking with the lady from Philadelphia, she spoke of this trouble.

The lady from Philadelphia looked surprised, and then said, "But why don't you turn the piano round?"

One of the little boys pertly said, "It is a square piano."

But Elizabeth Eliza went home directly, and, with the help of Agamemnon and Solomon John, turned the piano round.

"Why did we not think of that before?" said Mrs. Peterkin. "What shall we do when the lady from Philadelphia goes home again?"

Solomon John Goes for Apples and Cider

OLOMON JOHN agreed to ride to Farmer Jones's for a basket of apples, and he decided to go on horseback. The horse was brought round to the door. Now he had not ridden for a great while; and, though the little boys were there to help him, he had great trouble in getting on the horse.

He tried a great many times, but always found himself facing the wrong way, looking at the horse's tail. They turned the horse's head, first up the street, then down the street; it made no difference; he always made some mistake, and found himself sitting the wrong way.

"Well," said he, at last, "I don't know as I care. If the horse has his head in the right direction, that is the main thing. Sometimes I ride this way in the cars, because I like it better. I can turn my head easily enough, to see where we are going." So off he went, and the little boys said he looked like a circus-rider, and they were much pleased.

He rode along out of the village, under the elms, very quietly. Pretty soon he came to a bridge, where the road went across a little stream. There was a road at the side, leading down into the stream, because sometimes wagoners watered their horses there. Solomon John's horse turned off too, to drink of the water.

"Very well," said Solomon John, "I don't blame him

for wanting to wet his feet, and to take a drink, this hot day."

When they reached the middle of the stream, the horse bent over his head.

"How far his neck comes into his back!" exclaimed Solomon John; and at that very moment he found he had slid down over the horse's head, and was sitting on a stone, looking into the horse's face. There were two frogs, one on each side of him, sitting just as he was, which pleased Solomon John, so he began to laugh instead of to cry.

But the two frogs jumped into the water.

"It is time for me to go on," said Solomon John. So he gave a jump, as he had seen the frogs do; and this time he came all right on the horse's back, facing the way he was going.

"It is a little pleasanter," said he.

The horse wanted to nibble a little of the grass by the side of the way; but Solomon John remembered what a long neck he had, and would not let him stop.

At last he reached Farmer Jones's, who gave him his basket of apples.

Next he was to go on to a cider-mill, up a little lane by Farmer Jones's house, to get a jug of cider. But as soon as the horse was turned into the lane, he began to walk very slowly, — so slowly that Solomon John thought he would not get there before night. He whistled, and shouted, and thrust his knees into the horse, but still he would not go.

"Perhaps the apples are too heavy for him," said he. So he began by throwing one of the apples out of the basket. It hit the fence by the side of the road, and that started up the horse, and he went on merrily.

"That was the trouble," said Solomon John; "that apple was too heavy for him."

But very soon the horse began to go slower and slower. So Solomon John thought he would try another apple. This hit a large rock, and bounded back under the horse's feet, and sent him off at a great pace. But very soon he fell again into a slow walk.

Solomon John had to try another apple. This time it fell into a pool of water, and made a great splash, and set the horse out again for a little while; but he soon returned to a slow walk, — so slow that Solomon John thought it would be to-morrow morning before he got to the cider-mill.

"It is rather a waste of apples," thought he; "but I can pick them up as I come back, because the horse will be going home at a quick pace."

So he flung out another apple; that fell among a party of ducks, and they began to make such a quacking and a waddling, that it frightened the horse into a quick trot.

So the only way Solomon John could make his horse go was by flinging his apples, now on one side, now on the other. One time he frightened a cow, that ran along by the side of the road, while the horse raced with her. Another time he started up a brood of turkeys, that gobbled and strutted enough to startle twenty horses. In another place he came near hitting a boy, who gave such a scream that it sent the horse off at a furious rate.

And Solomon John got quite excited himself, and he did not stop till he had thrown away all his apples, and had reached the corner of the cider-mill.

"Very well," said he, "if the horse is so lazy, he won't mind my stopping to pick up the apples on the way home. And I am not sure but I shall prefer walking a little to riding the beast."

The man came out to meet him from the cider-mill, and reached him the jug. He was just going to take it, when he turned his horse's head round, and, delighted at the idea of going home, the horse set off at a full run, without waiting for the jug. Solomon John clung to the reins, and his knees held fast to the horse. He called out "Whoa! whoa!" but the horse would not stop.

He went galloping on past the boy, who stopped, and flung an apple at him; past the turkeys, that came and gobbled at him; by the cow, that turned and ran back in a race with them until her breath gave out; by the ducks, that came and quacked at him; by an old donkey, that brayed over the wall at him; by some hens, that ran into the road under the horse's feet, and clucked at him; by a great rooster, that stood up on a fence, and crowed at him; by Farmer Jones, who looked out to see what had become of him; down the village street, and he never stopped till he had reached the door of the house.

Out came Mr. and Mrs. Peterkin, Agamemnon, Elizabeth Eliza, and the little boys.

Solomon John got off his horse all out of breath.

"Where is the jug of cider?" asked Mrs. Peterkin.

"It is at the cider-mill," said Solomon John.

"At the mill!" exclaimed Mr. Peterkin.

"Yes," said Solomon John; "the little boys had better walk out for it; they will quite enjoy it; and they had better take a basket; for on the way they will find plenty of apples, scattered all along either side of the lane, and hens, and ducks, and turkeys, and a donkey."

The little boys looked at each other, and went: but they stopped first, and put on their india-rubber boots.

The Peterkins Try to Become Wise

THEY were sitting round the breakfast-table, and wondering what they should do because the lady from Philadelphia had gone away. "If," said Mrs. Peterkin, "we could only be more wise as a family!" How could they manage it? Agamemnon had been to college, and the children all went to school; but still as a family they were not wise. "It comes from books," said one of the family. "People who have a great many books are very wise." Then they counted up that there were very few books in the house, — a few schoolbooks and Mrs. Peterkin's cookbook were all.

"That's the thing!" said Agamemnon. "We want a library."

"We want a library!" said Solomon John. And all of them exclaimed, "We want a library!"

"Let us think how we shall get one," said Mrs. Peterkin. "I have observed that other people think a great deal of thinking."

So they all sat and thought a great while.

Then said Agamemnon, "I will make a library. There are some boards in the wood-shed, and I have a hammer and some nails, and perhaps we can borrow some hinges, and there we have our library!"

They were all very much pleased at the idea.

"That's the bookcase part," said Elizabeth Eliza; "but where are the books?"

So they sat and thought a little while, when Solomon John exclaimed, "I will make a book!"

They all looked at him in wonder.

"Yes," said Solomon John, "books will make us wise; but first I must make a book."

So they went into the parlor, and sat down to make a book. But there was no ink. What should he do for ink? Elizabeth Eliza said she had heard that nutgalls and vinegar made very good ink. So they decided to make some. The little boys said they could find some nutgalls up in the woods. So they all agreed to set out and pick some. Mrs. Peterkin put on her cape-bonnet, and the little boys got into their india-rubber boots, and off they went.

The nutgalls were hard to find. There was almost everything else in the woods, — chestnuts and walnuts, and small hazel-nuts, and a great many squirrels; and they had to walk a great way before they found any nutgalls. At last they came home with a large basket and two nutgalls in it. Then came the question of the vinegar. Mrs. Peterkin had used her very last on some beets they had the day before. "Suppose we go and ask the minister's wife," said Elizabeth Eliza.

So they all went to the minister's wife. She said if they wanted some good vinegar they had better set a barrel of cider down in the cellar, and in a year or two it would make very nice vinegar. But they said they wanted it that very afternoon. When the minister's wife heard this she said she should be very glad to let them have some vinegar, and gave them a cupful to carry home.

So they stirred in the nutgalls, and by the time evening came they had very good ink.

Then Solomon John wanted a pen. Agamemnon had a steel one, but Solomon John said, "Poets always used quills." Elizabeth Eliza suggested that they should go out to the poultry-yard  and get a quill. But it was already dark. They had, however, two lanterns, and the little boys borrowed the neighbors'. They set out in procession for the poultry-yard. When they got there the fowls were all at roost, so they could look at them quietly. But there were no geese! There were Shanghais, and Cochin-Chinas, and Guinea hens, and Barbary hens, and speckled hens, and Poland roosters, and bantams, and ducks, and turkeys, but not one goose! "No geese but ourselves," said Mrs. Peterkin, wittily, as they returned to the house. The sight of this procession roused up the village. "A torchlight procession!" cried all the boys of the town; and they gathered round the house, shouting for the flag; and Mr. Peterkin had to invite them in, and give them cider and gingerbread, before he could explain to them that it was only his family visiting his hens.

After the crowd had dispersed Solomon John sat down to think of his writing again. Agamemnon agreed to go over to the bookstore to get a quill. They all went over

with him. The bookseller was just shutting up his shop. However, he agreed to go in and get a quill, which he did, and they hurried home.

So Solomon John sat down again, but there was no paper. And now the bookstore was shut up. Mr. Peterkin suggested that the mail was about in, and perhaps he should have a letter, and then they could use the envelope to write upon. So they all went to the post-office, and the little boys had their india-rubber boots on, and they all shouted when they found Mr. Peterkin had a letter. The postmaster inquired what they were shouting about; and when they told him he said he would give Solomon John a whole sheet of paper for his book. And they all went back rejoicing.

So Solomon John sat down, and the family all sat round the table look- ing at him. He had his pen, his ink, and his paper. He dipped his pen into the  ink and held it over the paper, and thought a minute, and then said, "But I haven't got anything to say."

The Peterkins at the Menagerie

IT was a sad blow to the Peterkin family when they found Solomon John had nothing to say in the book which he tried once to write.

"I think it must happen often," said Elizabeth Eliza; "for everybody does not write a book, and this must be the reason."

"It is singular," said Mr. Peterkin. "To be wise enough to write a book, one must read books; and yet how can we read them until somebody is wise enough to write them?"

But nobody answered Mr. Peterkin.

"We ought to see more things," said Solomon John.

"We ought to go to the menagerie," said the little boys.

"Yes," said Mrs. Peterkin, "we might learn something at the menagerie."

"There is a giraffe at the menagerie," said the little boys.

"Well, my sons," said Mr. Peterkin, leaving the breakfast-table, "let every one learn something about the giraffe this morning, and we will go and see him in the afternoon!"

So the family all separated, and spent their morning trying to learn about the giraffe.

Mrs. Peterkin sat and thought. Agamemnon borrowed a book. And the rest went out and asked questions.

In the afternoon, all the family came together in the entry, ready to go to the menagerie, — the little boys in their india-rubber boots.

"The giraffe," said Mr. Peterkin, "is the same as the camelopard. Can any one tell me more about him?"

"The camel is sometimes called the ship of the desert," said one of the little boys.

"But this is the camelopard," interrupted Solomon John; "it is quite a different thing."

"Let Agamemnon speak first," said Mr. Peterkin; "he was a week in college, and ought to know."

"The fore legs of the camelopard," began Agamemnon, "are much longer than the hinder, which are very short."

"It must look like a rabbit," said Mrs. Peterkin.

"Yes, mamma," they all said.

"But, then," said Solomon John, "I think the fore legs of the rabbit are short, and the hinder ones long."

"We can easily see," said Mr. Peterkin; "we can go and look at our own rabbits."

"Yes," cried the little boys, "let us all go and see our rabbits."

So they went to the rabbit-hutch, at the very end of the garden, — Mr. and Mrs. Peterkin, Agamemnon and Elizabeth Eliza, Solomon John and the little boys in their india-rubber boots.

"You are right," said Mrs. Peterkin, "their hind legs are long. How very singular an animal must look made the other way!"

On the way back through the garden, Mr. Peterkin asked some more about the camelopard, or giraffe.

"The French call it the giraffe," said Elizabeth Eliza.

"Let us call it the giraffe, then," said Mr. Peterkin;

"then we shall learn a little French; and, to be wise, it is best to learn all we can."

"It feeds on the leaves of trees," said Solomon John. "It is tall enough to crop them."

Mrs. Peterkin stopped, and exclaimed, "An animal like a rabbit turned the other way, tall enough to feed on the leaves of trees! Solomon John, you must be mistaken!

"The trees in that country," said Elizabeth Eliza, "are not so high, perhaps."

"Do let us go and see," cried the little boys, impatiently.

"Well," said Mr. Peterkin, "perhaps we had better not wait any longer."

They all went out into the street, and walked along in a row, — Mr. and Mrs. Peterkin, Agamemnon and Elizabeth Eliza, Solomon John and the little boys.

It might have made people stare, but all the other families in the village were on their way to the menagerie, which was open for the first time that afternoon.

The little boys would have liked to stop outside to see the picture of the Two-Headed Woman, but Mr. and Mrs. Peterkin hurried them in.

There was a great crowd inside the tent, and Elizabeth Eliza thought she heard some bears roar. The little boys stopped the first thing to look at the monkeys.

"Papa," they asked, "do not monkeys usually have grinding organs?"

"I have seen them with grinding organs in the streets," said Mr. Peterkin, "but I should not expect it in a menagerie."

Mrs. Peterkin passed on to the ostrich.

"Is this the giraffe?" she asked of the keeper.

The family hurried her on. "That is the ostrich; don't you see it is a bird?" said Agamemnon.

"Let us stop and look at it," said Mr. Peterkin.

"It does look like a camel, ma'am," said the keeper, "and, like the camel, it inhabits the desert. It will eat leather, grass, hair, iron, stones, or anything that is given, and its large eggs weigh over fifteen pounds."

"Dear me, how useful!" said Mrs. Peterkin; "I think we might keep one to eat up the broken crockery, and one egg would last for a week; and what a treasure to have at Thanksgiving!"

But there were so many things to look at, the Peterkins had very little chance to talk or to ask questions.

There was a polar bear, walking up and down his cage, as if he were looking for the North Pole.

Then there were some porcupines with orange-colored teeth, and some owls whose eyes were very large and round.

"I should like an owl," said Mr. Peterkin to his wife; "they look very wise."

"Yes," said Mrs. Peterkin, "their wisdom must come from looking at things, their eyes are so very large."

So she opened her eyes wide, and went and looked at a jaguar.

They soon came to the giraffe. "It is a tall animal," exclaimed Mrs. Peterkin; "do they have many of them in the country this comes from?" she asked of the keeper.

"Half of him is a 'ship of the desert,'" cried one of the little boys, "the other half is a leopard."

But no one paid any attention to what he said.

"It must be hard to ride him," said Solomon John, "there is such a slope from his head to his tail."

"He is quite different from a rabbit," said Mrs. Peterkin; "there is such a difference in the length of the legs, and this animal is very much taller than a rabbit."

One of the little boys thought he should like to have a giraffe by a cherry-tree, then he could coast down his back when he wanted to come down the tree.

The Peterkins stayed at the menagerie till it was quite dark, wandering round, and asking questions, and wondering at the strange animals they saw.

At last, when they were outside the tent again, they counted up the children, and found the little boys were missing.

"They must have stayed in with the monkeys," said Elizabeth Eliza.

They all turned back to look for them; but the doorkeeper would not let them go in without paying again.

To this Mr. and Mrs. Peterkin objected, and Mrs. Peterkin begged and entreated the doorkeeper to let her in; how hard-hearted he was!

"Suppose his little boys should be left as food for lions," she cried. "Had not he any feelings?"

The doorkeeper was so moved, that at last he let in Mr. and Mrs. Peterkin, and Elizabeth Eliza, while Agamemnon and Solomon John waited outside.

But in vain they looked round; no little boys were found. Mrs. Peterkin stopped a long time in front of the tiger's cage; the tiger looked quite wicked enough to have eaten the little boys, but the keeper explained to her that they could not have got in between the wires, even if they had tried.

Elizabeth Eliza looked closely among the monkeys, but could not find the little boys; she could have told them by their india-rubber boots.

A number of stray little boys were brought to Mrs. Peterkin, but they were not the right ones.

The crowd was growing less, so it could be easily seen the little boys were not there, and they went sadly out.

Solomon John then suggested that perhaps they had gone in to see the Two-Headed Woman; so his father gave him a ticket to go in and see. He saw the Two-Headed Woman, but no little boys.

Mrs. Peterkin was filled with the blackest fears, and wanted to sit down and cry; but the postmaster and his daughter came along, and the daughter advised Mrs. Peterkin to go home; she thought they might find them there, and she agreed to go home with her and Elizabeth Eliza. Meanwhile the postmaster and Mr. Peterkin were to walk round the enclosure in one direction, and Agamemnon and Solomon John in another direction, and two policemen were to pass through the middle.

This was done, and all the parties met in a place behind the tent of the Two-Headed Woman. And just there, sitting on a log, were the little boys, each eating AN APPLE TART!

Mrs. Peterkin Wishes to Go to Drive

NE morning Mrs. Peterkin was feeling very tired, as she had been having a great many things to think of, and she said to Mr. Peterkin, "I believe I shall take a ride this morning!"

And the little boys cried out, "Oh, may we go too?"

Mrs. Peterkin said that Elizabeth Eliza and the little boys might go.

So Mr. Peterkin had the horse put into the carryall, and he and Agamemnon went off to their business, and Solomon John to school; and Mrs. Peterkin began to get ready for her ride.

She had some currants she wanted to carry to old Mrs. Twomly, and some gooseberries for somebody else, and Elizabeth Eliza wanted to pick some flowers to take to the minister's wife; so it took them a long time to prepare.

The little boys went out to pick the currants and the gooseberries, and Elizabeth Eliza went out for her flowers, and Mrs. Peterkin put on her cape-bonnet, and in time they were all ready. The little boys were in their india-rubber boots, and they got into the carriage.

Elizabeth Eliza was to drive; so she sat on the front seat, and took up the reins, and the horse started off merrily, and then suddenly stopped, and would not go any farther.

Elizabeth Eliza shook the reins, and pulled them, and

then she clucked to the horse; and Mrs. Peterkin clucked;
and the little boys whistled
and shouted; but still the
horse would not go.

"We shall have to whip
him," said Elizabeth Eliza.

Now Mrs. Peterkin never
liked to use the whip; but,
as the horse would not go,
she said she would get out
and turn her head the other
way, while Elizabeth Eliza

whipped the horse, and when he began to go she would hurry
and get in.

So they tried this, but the horse would not stir.

"Perhaps we have too heavy a load," said Mrs. Peterkin,
as she got in.

So they took out the currants and the gooseberries and
the flowers, but still the horse would not go.

One of the neighbors, from the opposite house, looking
out just then, called out to them to try the whip. There
was a high wind, and they could not hear exactly what
she said.

"I have tried the whip," said Elizabeth Eliza.

"She says 'whips,' such as you eat," said one of the little
boys.

"We might make those," said Mrs. Peterkin, thoughtfully.

"We have got plenty of cream," said Elizabeth Eliza.

"Yes, let us have some whips," cried the little boys,
getting out.

And the opposite neighbor cried out something about
whips; and the wind was very high.

So they went into the kitchen, and whipped up the cream,

and made some very delicious whips; and the little boys tasted all round, and they all thought they were very nice.

They carried some out to the horse, who swallowed it down very quickly.

"That is just what he wanted," said Mrs. Peterkin; "now he will certainly go!"

So they all got into the carriage again, and put in the currants, and the gooseberries, and the flowers; and Elizabeth Eliza shook the reins, and they all clucked; but still the horse would not go!

"We must either give up our ride," said Mrs. Peterkin, mournfully, "or else send over to the lady from Philadelphia, and see what she will say."

The little boys jumped out as quickly as they could; they were eager to go and ask the lady from Philadelphia. Elizabeth Eliza went with them, while her mother took the reins.

They found that the lady from Philadelphia was very ill that day, and was in her bed. But

when she was told what the trouble was she very kindly said they might draw up the curtain from the window at the foot of the bed, and open the blinds, and she would see. Then she asked for her opera-glass, and looked through it, across the way, up the street, to Mrs. Peterkin's door.

After she had looked through the glass she laid it down, leaned her head back against the pillow, for she was very tired, and then said, "Why don't you unchain the horse from the horse-post?"

Elizabeth Eliza and the little boys looked at one another, and then hurried back to the house and told their mother. The horse was untied, and they all went to ride.

7

The Peterkins at Home

AT DINNER

NOTHER little incident occurred in the Peterkin family. This was at dinner-time.

They sat down to a dish of boiled ham. Now it was a peculiarity of the children of the family that half of them liked fat, and half liked lean. Mr. Peterkin sat down to cut the ham. But the ham turned out to be a very remarkable one. The fat and the lean came in separate slices, — first one of lean, then one of fat, then two slices of lean, and so on. Mr. Peterkin began as usual by helping the children first, according to their age. Now Agamemnon, who liked lean, got a fat slice; and Elizabeth Eliza, who preferred fat, had a lean slice. Solomon John, who could eat nothing but lean,  was helped to fat, and so on. Nobody had what he could eat.

It was a rule of the Peterkin family that no one should eat any of the vegetables without some of the meat; so now, although the children saw upon their plates apple-sauce, and squash and tomato, and sweet potato and sour potato, not one of them could eat a mouthful, because not one was satisfied with the meat. Mr. and Mrs. Peterkin, however, liked both fat and lean, and were making a very good meal, when they looked up and saw the children all sitting eating nothing, and looking dissatisfied into their plates.

"What is the matter now?" said Mr. Peterkin.

But the children were taught not to speak at table. Agamemnon, however, made a sign of disgust at his fat, and Elizabeth Eliza at her lean, and so on; and they presently discovered what was the difficulty.

"What shall be done now?" said Mrs. Peterkin.

They all sat and thought for a little while.

At last said Mrs. Peterkin, rather uncertainly, "Suppose we ask the lady from Philadelphia what is best to be done."

But Mr. Peterkin said he didn't like to go to her for everything; let the children try and eat their dinner as it was.

And they all tried, but they couldn't. "Very well, then," said Mr. Peterkin, "let them go and ask the lady from Philadelphia."

"All of us?" cried one of the little boys, in the excitement of the moment.

"Yes," said Mrs. Peterkin, "only put on your india-rubber boots." And they hurried out of the house.

The lady from Philadelphia was just going in to her dinner; but she kindly stopped in the entry to hear what the trouble was. Agamemnon and Elizabeth Eliza told her all the difficulty, and the lady from Philadelphia said, "But why don't you give the slices of fat to those who like the fat, and the slices of lean to those who like the lean?"

They looked at one another. Agamemnon looked at Elizabeth Eliza, and Solomon John looked at the little boys. "Why didn't we think of that?" said they, and ran home to tell their mother.

8

Why the Peterkins Had a Late Dinner

HE trouble was in the dumb-waiter. All had seated themselves at the dinner-table, and Amanda had gone to take out the dinner she had sent up from the kitchen on the dumb-waiter. But something was the matter; she could not pull it up. There was the dinner, but she could not reach it. All the family, in turn, went and tried; all pulled together in vain; the dinner could not be stirred.

"No dinner!" exclaimed Agamemnon.

"I am quite hungry," said Solomon John.

At last Mr. Peterkin said, "I am not proud. I am willing to dine in the kitchen."

This room was below the dining-room. All consented to this. Each one went down, taking a napkin.

The cook laid the kitchen table, put on it her best table-cloth, and the family sat down. Amanda went to the dumb-waiter for the dinner, but she could not move it down.

The family were all in dismay. There was the dinner, half-way between the kitchen and dining-room, and there were they all hungry to eat it!

"What is there for dinner?" asked Mr. Peterkin.

"Roast turkey," said Mrs. Peterkin.

Mr. Peterkin lifted his eyes to the ceiling.

"Squash, tomato, potato, and sweet potato," Mrs. Peterkin continued.

"Sweet potato!" exclaimed both the little boys.

"I am very glad now that I did not have cranberry," said Mrs. Peterkin, anxious to find a bright point.

"Let us sit down and think about it," said Mr. Peterkin.

"I have an idea," said Agamemnon, after a while.

"Let us hear it," said Mr. Peterkin. "Let each one speak his mind."

"The turkey," said Agamemnon, "must be just above the kitchen door. If I had a ladder and an axe, I could cut away the plastering and reach it."

"That is a great idea," said Mrs. Peterkin.

"If you think you could do it," said Mr. Peterkin.

"Would it not be better to have a carpenter?" asked Elizabeth Eliza.

"A carpenter might have a ladder and an axe, and I think we have neither," said Mrs. Peterkin.

"A carpenter! A carpenter!" exclaimed the rest.

It was decided that Mr. Peterkin, Solomon John, and the little boys should go in search of a carpenter.

Agamemnon proposed that, meanwhile, he should go and borrow a book, for he had another idea.

"This affair of the turkey," he said, "reminds me of those buried cities that have been dug out, — Herculaneum, for instance."

"Oh, yes," interrupted Elizabeth Eliza, "and Pompeii."

"Yes," said Agamemnon. "They found there pots and kettles. Now, I should like to know how they did it; and I mean to borrow a book and read. I think it was done with a pickaxe."

So the party set out. But when Mr. Peterkin reached the carpenter's shop there was no carpenter to be found there.

"He must be at his house, eating his dinner," suggested Solomon John.

"Happy man," exclaimed Mr. Peterkin, "he has a dinner to eat!"

They went to the carpenter's house, but found he had gone out of town for a day's job. But his wife told them that he always came back at night to ring the nine-o'clock bell.

"We must wait till then," said Mr. Peterkin, with an effort at cheerfulness.

At home he found Agamemnon reading his book, and all sat down to hear of Herculaneum and Pompeii.

Time passed on, and the question arose about tea. Would it do to have tea when they had had no dinner? A part of the family thought it would not do; the rest wanted tea.

"I suppose you remember the wise lady of Philadelphia, who was here not long ago?" said Mr. Peterkin.

"Oh, yes," said Mrs. Peterkin.

"Let us try to think what she would advise us," said Mr. Peterkin.

"I wish she were here," said Elizabeth Eliza.

"I think," said Mr. Peterkin, "she would say, let them that want tea have it; the rest can go without."

So they had tea, and, as it proved, all sat down to it.

But not much was eaten, as there had been no dinner.

When the nine-o'clock bell was heard, Agamemnon, Solomon John, and the little boys rushed to the church and found the carpenter.

They asked him to bring a ladder, axe, and pickaxe. As he felt it might be a case of fire he brought also his fire-buckets.

When the matter was explained to him he went into the dining-room, looked into the dumb-waiter, untwisted a cord, and arranged the weight, and pulled up the dinner.

There was a family shout.

"The trouble was in the weight," said the carpenter.

"That is why it is called a dumb-waiter," Solomon John explained to the little boys.

The dinner was put upon the table.

Mrs. Peterkin frugally suggested that they might now keep it for next day, as to-day was almost gone, and they had had tea.

But nobody listened. All sat down to the roast turkey, and Amanda warmed over the vegetables.

"Patient waiters are no losers," said Agamemnon.

The Peterkins' Summer Journey

IN FACT, it was their last summer's journey, — for it had been planned then; but there had been so many difficulties it had been delayed.

The first trouble had been about trunks. The family did not own a trunk suitable for travelling. Agamemnon had his valise, that he had used when he stayed a week at a time at the academy; and a trunk had been bought for Elizabeth Eliza when she went to the seminary. Solomon John and Mr. Peterkin, each had his patent-leather hand-bag. But all these were too small for the family. And the little boys wanted to carry their kite.

Mrs. Peterkin suggested her grandmother's trunk. This was a hair-trunk, very large and capacious. It would hold everything they would want to carry except what would go in Elizabeth Eliza's trunk, or the valise and bags.

Everybody was delighted at this idea. It was agreed that the next day the things should be brought into Mrs. Peterkin's room for her to see if they could all be packed.

"If we can get along," said Elizabeth Eliza, "without having to ask advice I shall be glad!"

"Yes," said Mr. Peterkin, "it is time now for people to be coming to ask advice of us."

The next morning Mrs. Peterkin began by taking out the things that were already in the trunk. Here were last year's winter things, and not only these, but old clothes that had been put away, — Mrs. Peterkin's wedding-dress; the skirts the little boys used to wear before they put on jackets and trousers.

All day Mrs. Peterkin worked over the trunk, putting away the old things, putting in the new. She packed up all the clothes she could think of, both summer and winter ones, because you never can tell what sort of weather you will have.

Agamemnon fetched his books, and Solomon John his spy-glass. There were her own and Elizabeth Eliza's best bonnets in a bandbox; also Solomon John's hats, for he had an old one and a new one. He bought a new hat for fishing, with a very wide brim and deep crown; all of heavy straw.

Agamemnon brought down a large heavy dictionary, and an atlas still larger. This contained maps of all the countries in the world.

"I have never had a chance to look at them," he said; "but when one travels, then is the time to study geography."

Mr. Peterkin wanted to take his turning-lathe. So Mrs. Peterkin packed his tool-chest. It gave her some trouble, for it came to her just as she had packed her summer dresses. At first she thought it would help to smooth the dresses, and placed it on top; but she was forced to take all out, and set it at the bottom. This was not so much matter, as she had not yet the right dresses to put in. Both Mrs. Peterkin and Elizabeth Eliza would need new dresses for this occasion. The little boys' hoops went in; so did their india-rubber boots, in case it should not rain when they started. They each had a hoe and shovel, and some baskets, that were packed.

Mrs. Peterkin called in all the family on the evening of the second day to see how she had succeeded. Everything was packed, even the little boys' kite lay smoothly on the top.

"I like to see a thing so nicely done," said Mr. Peterkin.

The next thing was to cord up the trunk, and Mr. Peterkin tried to move it. But neither he, nor Agamemnon, nor Solomon John could lift it alone, or all together.

Here was a serious difficulty. Solomon John tried to make light of it.

"Expressmen could lift it. Expressmen were used to such things."

"But we did not plan expressing it," said Mrs. Peterkin, in a discouraged tone.

"We can take a carriage," said Solomon John.

"I am afraid the trunk would not go on the back of a carriage," said Mrs. Peterkin.

"The hackman could not lift it, either," said Mr. Peterkin.

"People do travel with a greal deal of baggage," said Elizabeth Eliza.

"And with very large trunks," said Agamemnon.

"Still they are trunks that can be moved," said Mr. Peterkin, giving another try at the trunk in vain. "I am afraid we must give it up," he said; "it would be such a trouble in going from place to place."

"We would not mind if we got it to the place," said Elizabeth Eliza.

"But how to get it there?" Mr. Peterkin asked, with a sigh.

"This is our first obstacle," said Agamemnon; "we must do our best to conquer it."

"What is an obstacle?" asked the little boys.

"It is the trunk," said Solomon John.

"Suppose we look out the word in the dictionary," said Agamemnon, taking the large volume from the trunk. "Ah, here it is" — And he read: —

"OBSTACLE, *an impediment.*"

"That is a worse word than the other," said one of the little boys.

"But listen to this," and Agamemnon continued: "*Impediment* is something that entangles the feet; *obstacle* something that stands in the way; *obstruction*, something that blocks up the passage; *hinderance*, something that holds back."

"The trunk is all these," said Mr. Peterkin, gloomily.

"It does not entangle the feet," said Solomon John, "for it can't move."

"I wish it could," said the little boys together.

Mrs. Peterkin spent a day or two in taking the things out of the trunk and putting them away.

"At least," she said, "this has given me some experience in packing."

And the little boys felt as if they had quite been a journey.

But the family did not like to give up their plan. It was suggested that they might take the things out of the trunk, and pack it at the station; the little boys could go and come with the things. But Elizabeth Eliza thought the place too public.

Gradually the old contents of the great trunk went back again to it.

At length a friend unexpectedly offered to lend Mr. Peterkin a good-sized family trunk. But it was late in the season, and so the journey was put off from that summer.

But now the trunk was sent round to the house, and a family consultation was held about packing it. Many things would have to be left at home, it was so much smaller than the grandmother's hair-trunk. But Agamemnon had been studying the atlas through the winter, and felt familiar with the more important places, so it would not be necessary to take it. And Mr. Peterkin decided to leave his turning-lathe at home, and his tool-chest.

Again Mrs. Peterkin spent two days in accommodating the things. With great care and discretion, and by borrowing two more leather bags, it could be accomplished. Everything of importance could be packed except the little boys' kite. What should they do about that?

The little boys proposed carrying it in their hands; but Solomon John and Elizabeth Eliza would not consent to this.

"I do think it is one of the cases where we might ask the advice of the lady from Philadelphia," said Mrs. Peterkin, at last.

"She has come on here," said Agamemnon, "and we have not been to see her this summer."

"She may think we have been neglecting her," suggested Mr. Peterkin.

The little boys begged to be allowed to go and ask her opinion about the kite. They came back in high spirits.

"She says we might leave this one at home, and make a new kite when we get there," they cried.

"What a sensible idea!" exclaimed Mr. Peterkin; "and I may have leisure to help you."

"We'll take plenty of newspapers," said Solomon John.

"And twine," said the little boys. And this matter was settled.

The question then was, "When should they go?"

The Peterkins' Journey Again Postponed

I T was very difficult for the Peterkin family to decide where to go.

Mrs. Peterkin did not want to go to the seashore, as she was a little afraid of the sea.

Elizabeth Eliza had no desire to go to the mountains.

"It tires you so to go up," said Mrs. Peterkin.

"I suppose one sees a great deal," said Mr. Peterkin.

"I don't know," said Elizabeth Eliza, who had been up Sundown Hill, "because, on the way up, your back is to the view all the time."

"I know it," said Solomon John; "and when you are on the top of the hill, you are too high up to see anything. You can't tell whether they are men or boys."

"And when you come down," continued Elizabeth Eliza, "you have to be looking at your feet all the time, to see where you are treading; so you don't get any view."

"I want to go where we shall really see something," said Mr. Peterkin.

"I should like to go up some of the burning mountains," said Agamemnon; "volcanoes, — I have read of them, — like Mount Aetna. I should like to go up one of those."

"I should rather come down," said Mrs. Peterkin.

"The ground is so hot," continued Agamemnon, "that you can roast eggs in it."

"That would be jolly," cried the little boys.

"It must make it inexpensive for fuel," said Mr. Peterkin.

"I suppose the inhabitants don't have to take in coal," said Mrs. Peterkin.

"Let's go," cried the little boys.

"Only our india-rubber boots would stick," said one of them.

"And then the inhabitants get buried up now and then," said Elizabeth Eliza.

"Oh, that was a great while ago," said Agamemnon. "You know I read about their being dug out."

"Still, I should not like to be buried up," said Mrs. Peterkin, "even if I were dug out."

"I suppose, by this time," said Mr. Peterkin, "the top of the mountain must have pretty much all come down, all there is to come down — so many years!"

"It must be the mountain that came down to Mahomet," said Solomon John. "Somebody told me about his not being able to go to it, so it came to him."

"I would not like to go among the Mahometans," said Mrs. Peterkin.

"Certainly not to the deserts of Arabia!" exclaimed Elizabeth Eliza.

The little boys would like to see the "Arabian Nights."

"I don't think we want to journey as far as that," said Mr. Peterkin.

Agamemnon was annoyed. The family did not understand. These volcanoes were not so far off as Arabia. Still, they were over the sea, and they would hardly care to travel so far.

"Yet I think we want to see something more than merely to go into the country," said Elizabeth Eliza.

Solomon John had been sitting in quiet for some time.

"What is it, Solomon John?" said Mr. Peterkin. "You have an idea —"

"Yes," said Solomon John, starting up and walking across the room, in excitement. "Why should we not go to — Philadelphia?"

"And see the place that the lady from Philadelphia came from," exclaimed Elizabeth Eliza.

"She is so wise," said Mrs. Peterkin; "she has had such opportunities."

"Let us go to-morrow; don't wait for the vacation," cried the little boys in delight.

"It would be a very poor time to go now," said Mrs. Peterkin, "when the only person we should know, the lady from Philadelphia, is here."

"She could tell us how to go," said Solomon John.

"It is very hot in Philadelphia in summer, I have heard," said Mr. Peterkin.

"That is why she comes away," said Elizabeth Eliza.

"It would be a pity to go when everybody is away," said Agamemnon.

"Everybody away!" exclaimed the little boys. "What fun! Then we could go into the shops and take what we wanted!"

"Don't be absurd," said Solomon John; "of course, the policemen stay."

"Why should we not go later?" said Agamemnon.

"Why not wait till the fall?" said Mr. Peterkin.

"We ought to go in the little boys' vacation," said Mrs. Peterkin.

The little boys thought this was no matter; they could do something else in the vacation.

"But then, it would not be a summer journey," said Mrs. Peterkin.

Elizabeth Eliza felt this was not a serious objection.

"We might wait till the Centennial," suggested Agamemnon.

Mrs. Peterkin was firm against this.

"No, I am old enough now," she said. "If I were to wait till I'm a hundred, I shouldn't enjoy anything!"

"There must be enough to see there now," said Mr. Peterkin.

"Benjamin Franklin came from Philadelphia, or else he went to it," said Agamemnon.

"Oh, yes, I know all about him," said Solomon John; "he made paint-brushes of his cat's tail!"

"Oh, no, that was another Benjamin, I am pretty sure," said Agamemnon.

"I don't know about that," said Solomon John; "but he became a famous artist, and painted the king and queen of England."

"You must have mixed up the Benjamins," said Agamemnon. "I will go and borrow an encyclopaedia, and look them out."

"And we will make paint-brushes out of Elizabeth Eliza's cat," exclaimed the little boys; "and we will become famous, and paint the king and queen of England."

"You must not use the whole cat," said Solomon John; "and there is no king of England now."

"And I cannot spare her tail," cried Elizabeth Eliza, starting up in agony for her cat.

"It is only Philadelphia cats that are used for paint-brushes," said Mr. Peterkin. "We will see about it when we go. I think it is a good plan to wait till autumn, and it will give us time to talk with the lady from Philadelphia and consult her about it.

The little boys were quite satisfied. "A vacation and a journey too!" It was raining a little; but they put on their india-rubber boots, and went out to chase some ducks from a neighboring mud-puddle.

11

The Peterkins Snowed-Up

RS. PETERKIN awoke one morning to find a heavy snow-storm raging. The wind had flung the snow against the windows, had heaped it up around the house, and thrown it into huge white drifts over the fields, covering hedges and fences.

Mrs. Peterkin went from one window to the other to look out; but nothing could be seen but the driving storm and the deep white snow. Even Mr. Bromwick's house, on the opposite side of the street, was hidden by the swift-falling flakes.

"What shall I do about it?" thought Mrs. Peterkin. "No roads cleared out! Of course there'll be no butcher and no milkman!"

The first thing to be done was to wake up all the family early; for there was enough in the house for breakfast, and there was no knowing when they would have anything more to eat.

It was best to secure the breakfast first.

So she went from one room to the other, as soon as it was

light, waking the family, and before long all were dressed and downstairs.

And then all went round the house to see what had happened.

All the water-pipes that there were were frozen. The milk was frozen. They could open the door into the wood-house; but the wood-house door into the yard was banked up with snow; and the front door, and the piazza door, and the side door stuck. Nobody could get in or out!

Meanwhile, Amanda, the cook, had succeeded in making the kitchen fire, but had discovered there was no furnace coal.

"The furnace coal was to have come to-day," said Mrs. Peterkin, apologetically.

"Nothing will come to-day," said Mr. Peterkin, shivering.

But a fire could be made in a stove in the dining-room.

All were glad to sit down to breakfast and hot coffee. The little boys were much pleased to have "ice-cream" for breakfast.

"When we get a little warm," said Mr. Peterkin, "we will consider what is to be done."

"I am thankful I ordered the sausages yesterday," said

Mrs. Peterkin. "I was to have had a leg of mutton to-day."

"Nothing will come to-day," said Agamemnon, gloomily.

"Are these sausages the last meat in the house?" asked Mr. Peterkin.

"Yes," said Mrs. Peterkin.

The potatoes also were gone, the barrel of apples empty, and she had meant to order more flour that very day.

"Then we are eating our last provisions," said Solomon John, helping himself to another sausage.

"I almost wish we had stayed in bed," said Agamemnon.

"I thought it best to make sure of our breakfast first," repeated Mrs. Peterkin.

"Shall we literally have nothing left to eat?" asked Mr. Peterkin.

"There's the pig!" suggested Solomon John.

Yes, happily, the pigsty was at the end of the wood-house, and could be reached under cover.

But some of the family could not eat fresh pork.

"We should have to 'corn' part of him," said Agamemnon.

"My butcher has always told me," said Mrs. Peterkin, "that if I wanted a ham I must keep a pig. Now we have the pig, but have not the ham!"

"Perhaps we could 'corn' one or two of his legs," suggested one of the little boys.

"We need not settle that now," said Mr. Peterkin. "At least the pig will keep us from starving."

The little boys looked serious; they were fond of their pig.

"If we had only decided to keep a cow," said Mrs. Peterkin.

"Alas! yes," said Mr. Peterkin, "one learns a great many things too late!"

"Then we might have had ice-cream all the time!" exclaimed the little boys.

Indeed, the little boys, in spite of the prospect of starving, were quite pleasantly excited at the idea of being snowed-up, and hurried through their breakfasts that they might go and try to shovel out a path from one of the doors.

"I ought to know more about the water-pipes," said Mr. Peterkin. "Now, I shut off the water last night in the bath-room, or else I forgot to; and I ought to have shut it off in the cellar."

The little boys came back. Such a wind at the front door, they were going to try the side door.

"Another thing I have learned to-day," said Mr. Peterkin, "is not to have all the doors on one side of the house, because the storm blows the snow against *all* the doors."

Solomon John started up.

"Let us see if we are blocked up on the east side of the house!" he exclaimed.

"Of what use," asked Mr. Peterkin, "since we have no door on the east side?"

"We could cut one," said Solomon John.

"Yes, we could cut a door," exclaimed Agamemnon.

"But how can we tell whether there is any snow there?" asked Elizabeth Eliza, — "for there is no window."

In fact, the east side of the Peterkins' house formed a blank wall. The owner had originally planned a little block of semi-detached houses. He had completed only one, very semi and very detached.

"It is not necessary to see," said Agamemnon, profoundly; "of course, if the storm blows against this side of the house, the house itself must keep the snow from the other side."

"Yes," said Solomon John, "there must be a space clear of snow on the east side of the house, and if we could open a way to that" —

"We could open a way to the butcher," said Mr. Peterkin, promptly.

Agamemnon went for his pick-axe. He had kept one in the house ever since the adventure of the dumb-waiter.

"What part of the wall had we better attack?" asked Mr. Peterkin.

Mrs. Peterkin was alarmed.

"What will Mr. Mudge, the owner of the house, think of it?" she exclaimed. "Have we a right to injure the wall of the house?"

"It is right to preserve ourselves from starving," said Mr. Peterkin. "The drowning man must snatch at a straw!"

"It is better that he should find his house chopped a little when the thaw comes," said Elizabeth Eliza, "than that he should find us lying about the house, dead of hunger, upon the floor."

Mrs. Peterkin was partially convinced.

The little boys came in to warm their hands. They had not succeeded in opening the side door, and were planning trying to open the door from the wood-house to the garden.

"That would be of no use," said Mrs. Peterkin, "the butcher cannot get into the garden."

"But we might shovel off the snow," suggested one of the little boys, "and dig down to some of last year's onions."

Meanwhile, Mr. Peterkin, Agamemnon, and Solomon John had been bringing together their carpenter's tools, and Elizabeth Eliza proposed using a gouge, if they would choose the right spot to begin.

The little boys were delighted with the plan, and hastened to find, — one, a little hatchet, and the other a gimlet. Even Amanda armed herself with a poker.

"It would be better to begin on the ground floor," said Mr. Peterkin.

"Except that we may meet with a stone foundation," said Solomon John.

"If the wall is thinner upstairs," said Agamemnon, "it will do as well to cut a window as a door, and haul up anything the butcher may bring below in his carts."

Everybody began to pound a little on the wall to find a favorable place, and there was a great deal of noise. The little boys actually cut a bit out of the plastering with their hatchet and gimlet. Solomon John confided to Elizabeth Eliza that it reminded him of stories of prisoners who cut themselves free, through stone walls, after days and days of secret labor.

Mrs. Peterkin, even, had come with a pair of tongs in her hand. She was interrupted by a voice behind her.

"Here's your leg of mutton, marm!"

It was the butcher. How had he got in?

"Excuse me, marm, for coming in at the side door, but the back gate is kinder blocked up. You were making such a pounding I could not make anybody hear me knock at the side door."

"But how did you make a path to the door?" asked Mr. Peterkin. "You must have been working at it a long time. It must be near noon now."

"I'm about on regular time," answered the butcher. "The town team has cleared out the high road, and the wind has been down the last half-hour. The storm is over."

True enough! The Peterkins had been so busy inside the house they had not noticed the ceasing of the storm outside.

"And we were all up an hour earlier than usual," said Mr. Peterkin, when the butcher left. He had not explained to the butcher why he had a pickaxe in his hand.

"If we had lain abed till the usual time," said Solomon John, "we should have been all right."

"For here is the milkman!" said Elizabeth Eliza, as a knock was now heard at the side door.

"It is a good thing to learn," said Mr. Peterkin, "not to get up any earlier than is necessary."

12

The Peterkins Decide to Keep a Cow

NOT that they were fond of drinking milk, nor that they drank very much. But for that reason Mr. Peterkin thought it would be well to have a cow, to encourage the family to drink more, as he felt it would be so healthy.

Mrs. Peterkin recalled the troubles of the last cold winter, and how near they came to starving, when they were shut up in a severe snowstorm, and the water-pipes burst, and the milk was frozen. If the cow-shed could open out of the wood-shed such trouble might be prevented.

Tony Larkin was to come over and milk the cow every morning, and Agamemnon and Solomon John agreed to learn how to milk, in case Tony should be "snowed up," or have the whooping-cough in the course of the winter. The little boys thought they knew how already.

But if they were to have three or four pailfuls of milk every day it was important to know where to keep it.

"One way will be," said Mrs. Peterkin, "to use a great deal every day. We will make butter."

"That will be admirable," thought Mr. Peterkin.

"And custards," suggested Solomon John.

"And syllabub," said Elizabeth Eliza.

"And cocoa-nut cakes," exclaimed the little boys.

"We don't need the milk for cocoa-nut cakes," said Mrs. Peterkin.

The little boys thought they might have a cocoa-nut tree instead of a cow. You could have the milk from the cocoa-nuts, and it would be pleasant climbing the tree, and you would not have to feed it.

"Yes," said Mr. Peterkin, "we shall have to feed the cow."

"Where shall we pasture her?" asked Agamemnon.

"Up on the hills, up on the hills," exclaimed the little boys, "where there are a great many bars to take down, and huckleberry-bushes!"

Mr. Peterkin had been thinking of their own little lot behind the house.

"But I don't know," he said, "but the cow might eat off all the grass in one day, and there would not be any left for to-morrow, unless the grass grew fast enough every night."

Agamemnon said it would depend upon the season. In a rainy season the grass would come up very fast, in a drought it might not grow at all.

"I suppose," said Mrs. Peterkin, "that is the worst of having a cow, — there might be a drought."

Mr. Peterkin thought they might make some calculation from the quantity of grass in the lot.

Solomon John suggested that measurements might be made by seeing how much grass the Bromwicks' cow, opposite them, eat up in a day.

The little boys agreed to go over and spend the day on the Bromwicks' fence, and take an observation.

"The trouble would be," said Elizabeth Eliza, "that cows walk about so, and the Bromwicks' yard is very large. Now she would be eating in one place and then she would walk

to another. She would not be eating all the time; a part of the time she would be chewing."

The little boys thought they should like nothing better than to have some sticks, and keep the cow in one corner of the yard till the calculations were made.

But Elizabeth Eliza was afraid the Bromwicks would not like it.

"Of course, it would bring all the boys in the school about the place, and very likely they would make the cow angry."

Agamemnon recalled that Mr. Bromwick once wanted to hire Mr. Peterkin's lot for his cow.

Mr. Peterkin started up.

"That is true; and of course Mr. Bromwick must have known there was feed enough for one cow."

"And the reason you didn't let him have it," said Solomon John, "was that Elizabeth Eliza was afraid of cows."

"I did not like the idea," said Elizabeth Eliza, "of their cow's looking at me over the top of the

fence, perhaps, when I should be planting the sweet peas in the garden. I hope our cow would be a quiet one. I should not like her jumping over the fence into the flower-beds."

Mr. Peterkin declared that he should buy a cow of the quietest kind.

"I should think something might be done about covering her horns," said Mrs. Peterkin; "that seems the most dangerous part. Perhaps they might be padded with cotton."

Elizabeth Eliza said cows were built so large and clumsy that if they came at you they could not help knocking you over.

The little boys would prefer having the pasture a great way off. Half the fun of having a cow would be going up on the hills after her.

Agamemnon thought the feed was not so good on the hills.

"The cow would like it ever so much better," the little boys declared, "on account of the variety. If she did not like the rocks and the bushes she could walk round and find the grassy places."

"I am not sure," said Elizabeth Eliza, "but it would be less dangerous to keep the cow in the lot behind the house, because she would not be coming and going, morning and night, in that jerky way the Larkins' cows come home. They don't mind which gate they rush in at. I should hate to have our cow dash into our front yard just as I was coming home of an afternoon."

"That is true," said Mr. Peterkin; "we can have the door of the cow-house open directly into the pasture, and save the coming and going."

The little boys were quite disappointed. The cow would miss the exercise, and they would lose a great pleasure.

Solomon John suggested that they might sit on the fence and watch the cow.

It was decided to keep the cow in their own pasture; and, as they were to put on an end kitchen, it would be perfectly easy to build a dairy.

The cow proved a quiet one. She was a little excited when all the family stood round at the first milking, and watched her slowly walking into the shed.

Elizabeth Eliza had her scarlet sack dyed brown a fortnight before. It was the one she did her gardening in, and it might have infuriated the cow. And she kept out

of the garden the first day or two.

Mrs. Peterkin and Elizabeth Eliza bought the best kind of milk-pans, of every size.

But there was a little disappointment about the taste of the milk.

The little boys liked it, and drank large mugs of it. Elizabeth Eliza said she could never learn to love milk warm from the cow, though she would like to do her best to patronize the cow.

Mrs. Peterkin was afraid Amanda did not understand about taking care of the milk; yet she had been down to overlook her, and she was sure the pans and the closet were all clean.

"Suppose we send a pitcher of cream over to the lady from Philadelphia to try," said Elizabeth Eliza; "it will be a pretty attention before she goes."

"It might be awkward if she didn't like it," said Solomon John. "Perhaps something is the matter with the grass."

"I gave the cow an apple to eat yesterday," said one of the little boys, remorsefully.

Elizabeth Eliza went over, and Mrs. Peterkin, too, and explained all to the lady from Philadelphia, asking her to taste the milk.

The lady from Philadelphia tasted, and said the truth was that the milk was sour.

"I was afraid it was so," said Mrs. Peterkin; "but I didn't know what to expect from these new kinds of cows."

The lady from Philadelphia asked where the milk was kept.

"In the new dairy," answered Elizabeth Eliza.

"Is that in a cool place?" asked the lady from Philadelphia.

Elizabeth Eliza explained it was close by the new kitchen.

"Is it near the chimney?" inquired the lady from Philadelphia.

"It is directly back of the chimney and the new kitchen range," replied Elizabeth Eliza. "I suppose it is too hot!"

"Well, well!" said Mrs. Peterkin, "that is it! Last winter the milk froze, and now we have gone to the other extreme! Where shall we put our dairy?"

13

The Peterkins' Christmas-Tree

ARLY in the autumn the Peterkins began to prepare for their Christmas-tree. Everything was done in great privacy, as it was to be a surprise to the neighbors, as well as to the rest of the family. Mr. Peterkin had been up to Mr. Bromwick's wood-lot, and with his consent, selected the tree. Agamemnon went to look at it occasionally after dark, and Solomon John made frequent visits to it mornings, just after sunrise. Mr. Peterkin drove Elizabeth Eliza and her mother that way, and pointed furtively to it with his whip; but none of them ever spoke of it aloud to each other. It was suspected that the little boys had been to see it Wednesday and Saturday afternoons. But they came home with their pockets full of chestnuts, and said nothing about it.

At length Mr. Peterkin had it cut down and brought secretly into the Larkins' barn. A week or two before Christmas a measurement was made of it with Elizabeth Eliza's yard-measure. To Mr. Peter-

kin's great dismay it was discovered that it was too high
to stand in the back parlor.

This fact was brought out at a secret council of Mr. and
Mrs. Peterkin, Elizabeth Eliza,
and Agamemnon.

Agamemnon suggested that
it might be set up slanting;
but Mrs. Peterkin was very
sure it would make her dizzy,
and the candles would drip.

But a brilliant idea came
to Mr. Peterkin. He pro-
posed that the ceiling of the parlor should be raised to
make room for the top of the tree.

Elizabeth Eliza thought the space would need to be
quite large. It must not be like a small box, or you could
not see the tree.

"Yes," said Mr. Peterkin, "I should have the ceiling
lifted all across the room; the effect would be finer."

Elizabeth Eliza objected to having the whole ceiling
raised, because her room was over the back parlor, and
she would have no floor while the alteration was going on,
which would be very awkward. Besides, her room was not
very high now, and, if the floor were raised, perhaps she
could not walk in it upright.

Mr. Peterkin explained that he didn't propose altering
the whole ceiling, but to lift up a ridge across the room
at the back part where the tree was to stand. This would
make a hump, to be sure, in Elizabeth Eliza's room; but
it would go across the whole room.

Elizabeth Eliza said she would not mind that. It would
be like the cuddy thing that comes up on the deck of a

ship, that you sit against, only here you would not have the sea-sickness. She thought she should like it, for a rarity. She might use it for a divan.

Mrs. Peterkin thought it would come in the worn place of the carpet, and might be a convenience in making the carpet over.

Agamemnon was afraid there would be trouble in keeping the matter secret, for it would be a long piece of work for a carpenter; but Mr. Peterkin proposed having the carpenter for a day or two, for a number of other jobs.

One of them was to make all the chairs in the house of the same height, for Mrs. Peterkin had nearly broken her spine by sitting down in a chair that she had supposed was her own rocking-chair, and it had proved to be two inches lower. The little boys were now large enough to sit in any chair; so a medium was fixed upon to satisfy all the family, and the chairs were made uniformly of the same height.

On consulting the carpenter, however, he insisted that the tree could be cut off at the lower end to suit the height of the parlor, and demurred at so great a change as altering the ceiling. But Mr. Peterkin had set his mind upon the improvement, and Elizabeth Eliza had cut her carpet in preparation for it.

So the folding-doors into the back parlor were closed, and for nearly a fortnight before Christmas there was great litter of fallen plastering, and laths, and chips, and shavings; and Elizabeth Eliza's carpet was taken up, and the furniture had to be changed, and one night she had to sleep at the Bromwicks', for there was a long hole in her floor that might be dangerous.

All this delighted the little boys. They could not understand what was going on. Perhaps they suspected a Christmas-tree, but they did not know why a Christmas-tree should have so many chips, and were still more astonished at the hump that appeared in Elizabeth Eliza's room. It must be a Christmas present, or else the tree in a box.

Some aunts and uncles, too, arrived a day or two before Christmas, with some small cousins. These cousins occupied the attention of the little boys, and there was a great deal of whispering and mystery, behind doors, and under the stairs, and in the corners of the entry.

Solomon John was busy, privately making some candles for the tree. He had been collecting some bayberries, as he understood they made very nice candles, so that it would not be necessary to buy any.

The elders of the family never all went into the back parlor together, and all tried not to see what was going on. Mrs. Peterkin would go in with Solomon John, or Mr. Peterkin with Elizabeth Eliza, or Elizabeth Eliza and Agamemnon and Solomon John. The little boys and the small cousins were never allowed even to look inside the room.

Elizabeth Eliza meanwhile went into town a number of times. She wanted to consult Amanda as to how much ice-cream they should need, and whether they could make it at home, as they had cream and ice. She was pretty busy in her own room; the furniture had to be changed, and the carpet altered. The "hump" was higher than she expected. There was danger of bumping her own head whenever she crossed it. She had to nail some padding on the ceiling for fear of accidents.

The afternoon before Christmas, Elizabeth Eliza, Solomon John, and their father collected in the back parlor for a council. The carpenters had done their work, and the tree stood at its full height at the back of the room, the top stretching up into the space arranged for it. All the chips and shavings were cleared away, and it stood on a neat box.

But what were they to put upon the tree?

Solomon John had brought in his supply of candles; but they proved to be very "stringy" and very few of them.

 It was strange how many bay-berries it took to make a few candles! The little boys had helped him, and he had gathered as much as a bushel of bay-berries. He had put them in water, and skimmed off the wax, according to the directions; but there was so little wax!

Solomon John had given the little boys some of the bits sawed off from the legs of the chairs. He had suggested that they should cover them with gilt paper, to answer for gilt apples, without telling them what they were for.

These apples, a little blunt at the end, and the candles, were all they had for the tree!

After all her trips into town Elizabeth Eliza had forgotten to bring anything for it.

"I thought of candies and sugar-plums," she said; "but I concluded if we made caramels ourselves we should not need them. But, then, we have not made caramels. The fact is, that day my head was full of my carpet. I had bumped it pretty badly, too."

Mr. Peterkin wished he had taken, instead of a fir-tree, an apple-tree he had seen in October, full of red fruit.

"But the leaves would have fallen off by this time," said Elizabeth Eliza.

"And the apples, too," said Solomon John.

"It is odd I should have forgotten, that day I went in on purpose to get the things," said Elizabeth Eliza, musingly. "But I went from shop to shop, and didn't know exactly what to get. I saw a great many gilt things for Christmas-trees; but I knew the little boys were making the gilt apples; there were plenty of candles in the shops, but I knew Solomon John was making the candles."

Mr. Peterkin thought it was quite natural.

Solomon John wondered if it were too late for them to go into town now.

Elizabeth Eliza could not go in the next morning, for there was to be a grand Christmas dinner, and Mr. Peterkin could not be spared, and Solomon John was sure he and Agamemnon would not know what to buy. Besides, they would want to try the candles to-night.

Mr. Peterkin asked if the presents everybody had been preparing would not answer. But Elizabeth Eliza knew they would be too heavy.

A gloom came over the room. There was only a flickering gleam from one of Solomon John's candles that he had lighted by way of trial.

Solomon John again proposed going into town. He

lighted a match to examine the newspaper about the trains. There were plenty of trains coming out at that hour, but none going in except a very late one. That would not leave time to do anything and come back.

"We could go in, Elizabeth Eliza and I," said Solomon John, "but we should not have time to buy anything."

Agamemnon was summoned in. Mrs. Peterkin was entertaining the uncles and aunts in the front parlor. Agamemnon wished there was time to study up something about electric lights. If they could only have a calcium light! Solomon John's candle sputtered and went out.

At this moment there was a loud knocking at the front door. The little boys, and the small cousins, and the uncles and aunts, and Mrs. Peterkin, hastened to see what was the matter.

The uncles and aunts thought somebody's house must be on fire. The door was opened, and there was a man, white with flakes, for it was beginning to snow, and he was pulling in a large box.

Mrs. Peterkin supposed it contained some of Elizabeth Eliza's purchases, so she ordered it to be pushed into the back parlor, and hastily called back her guests and the little boys into the other room. The little boys and the small cousins were sure they had seen Santa Claus himself.

Mr. Peterkin lighted the gas. The box was addressed to Elizabeth Eliza. It was from the lady from Philadelphia! She had gathered a hint from Elizabeth Eliza's letters that there was to be a Christmas-tree, and had filled this box with all that would be needed.

It was opened directly. There was every kind of gilt hanging-thing, from gilt pea-pods to butterflies on springs. There were shining flags and lanterns, and bird-cages, and nests with birds sitting on them, baskets of fruit, gilt apples and bunches of grapes, and, at the bottom of the whole, a large box of candles and a box of Philadelphia bonbons!

Elizabeth Eliza and Solomon John could scarcely keep from screaming. The little boys and the small cousins knocked on the folding-doors to ask what was the matter.

Hastily Mr. Peterkin and the rest took out the things and hung them on the tree, and put on the candles.

When all was done, it looked so well that Mr. Peterkin exclaimed: —

"Let us light the candles now, and send to invite all the neighbors to-night, and have the tree on Christmas Eve!"

And so it was that the Peterkins had their Christmas-tree the day before, and on Christmas night could go and visit their neighbors.

14

The Peterkins at the Centennial

THEY went.

The lady from Philadelphia had invited Mr. and Mrs. Peterkin and Elizabeth Eliza and the little boys to her own house, promising to find rooms for Agamemnon and Solomon John in the neighborhood, asking them to take their meals at her house.

But she lived far down in the city, and Mrs. Peterkin felt she would not want to go such a distance every day to the exhibition. Agamemnon and Solomon John proposed stopping at the Great Atlas Hotel, just outside the grounds. The little boys wished they could spend the night inside.

Meanwhile, a friend told them of lodgings they could have up-town, on the same side of the river as the Centennial grounds, and Mrs. Peterkin decided for this. She was afraid of fire in one of the lath-and-plaster hotels, and Mr. Peterkin agreed with her.

So a kind and respectful letter was written to the lady from Philadelphia, declining her invitation, but hoping to be able to call upon her often during their visit.

They did not reach their lodgings till late at night, between eleven and twelve o'clock, so were scarcely ready for an early start the next morning. Then they had to hold consultation as to the best method of proceeding, and to ask their fellow-boarders how to reach the horse-cars, for they were shocked to find that they were nearly two miles from the nearest entrance to the grounds. Mr. Peterkin, Agamemnon, and Solomon John would not mind walking; but Mrs. Peterkin declared it would be too much for her, and the first day they all wished to go together. Mrs. Peterkin had brought with her, all the way, a camp-stool, as she knew she should want to sit down often and it might be difficult to find a seat.

Elizabeth Eliza had an extra shawl, Mr. Peterkin his umbrella, and the little boys their india-rubber boots; they found it something of a walk to Lancaster Avenue, and they were obliged to take it slowly. By the time they reached it, every car that passed was so crowded there was not even a foot-hold. But the cars going south were all empty. Agamemnon had heard from one of the returned Centennial visitors that it was a good plan to take a car going down to the starting-point of the upward-bound cars. This they decided to do; it would give them also a view of the city. They were about an hour going down, and a little while finding the right car, but did reach one with plenty of seats. This soon became crowded, and was slow in its progress, and it was a long time before they reached the grounds. They were then some time in deciding whether to follow the people who were going into the Main Building, or those who went in at the principal gate. Then Mrs. Peterkin, who carried her camp-stool, did not like to have the family separated in going in, so she wanted to manage that all should go through the turnstile together, which was difficult to do and to pay their separate fifty-cent pieces. So when they were all inside, and Mr. Peterkin looked at his watch, he found it was already nearly three o'clock! Now some of their fellow-boarders had earnestly advised them to come back early, as the cars were so crowded at a later hour. And

Mrs. Peterkin had made up her mind it would be best, as it was her first day, to return at three o'clock. At the same time they discovered they were all very hungry, and Mr. Peterkin proposed they should go back to some of the numerous restaurants he had seen outside of the grounds, and then go home. But they all exclaimed against this. They were now in the broad space between the Main Building and Machinery Hall when, as they walked on, Elizabeth Eliza espied the sign of the "House of Public Comfort."

"This is exactly what we want," said Mr. Peterkin. "We will get our lunch there."

But, unfortunately, there was a very large crowd by the lunch counter. It was impossible for the whole family to press up together, and very difficult to find anything to eat. Solomon John did find some popped-corn balls, in magenta-colored paper, for the little boys, and Agamemnon secured some doughnuts for his mother and Elizabeth Eliza, while his father succeeded in eating a few raw oysters. The crowd was so great that Mrs. Peterkin could not even open her camp-stool.

"I think now," said she, "we had better go back, we have had enough for one day, and everybody says we ought not overtire ourselves at the beginning, and I am sure I was overtired when I got here."

Agamemnon thought they had not yet fairly looked at things. They could hardly say when they went back to their boarding-house what they had seen. So they all went to the centre of the large square of entrances by the fountain, and looked at the Main Building on one side, and Machinery Hall on the other, and decided that would do for the first day.

They found a car with plenty of seats, and Mrs. Peterkin felt herself rested for the walk home from the avenue.

The next day they started early, and were among the first to reach the grounds.

They proposed to take the tour of the grounds in one of the railroad cars. In this way they could get an idea of the whole. They joined a crowd of people rushing to one of the platforms to secure seats as a train came along. Mrs. Peterkin was near being left behind, it was so hard for her to decide which seat to take; and the hurry was so great, the rest of the family, thinking she was going to be left, all got out again and were obliged to hustle in the minute the train was starting.

The little boys were anxious to get out at the first stopping-place, but Mr. and Mrs. Peterkin preferred to make the whole tour and see everything first. In and out they went among the various buildings. Mrs. Peterkin said she would ask nothing better than to spend the day in this way. Agamemnon had a map, and tried to point out the several buildings as they came to them, but it was difficult to discover the numbers attached to them in the map. Meanwhile Solomon John studied the different colors of the flags. After some time Elizabeth Eliza said:

"I did not know they had so many of these 'Woman's Pavilions.'"

"I think they must have one for each State," said Mr. Peterkin.

"It is astonishing how much they are alike," said Mrs. Peterkin.

"With so many buildings," said Mr. Peterkin, "you could not expect to have them all different."

"Still," said Agamemnon, "I should not think they would have so many of these statues of horses with wings."

"They are very fine," said Mr. Peterkin. "No wonder

they repeat them so often."

"They come in pairs," said Solomon John.

"We have seen them five times. I counted," said one of the little boys.

Elizabeth Eliza started: "We must have made the tour at least five times! I have seen five Woman's Pavilions!"

"This is the very place where we got in," said Solomon John.

The whole family made a rush to get out, for they had just reached a platform, and the time for stopping was very short. Mrs. Peterkin stooped to extricate her camp-stool, which she had put under the seat, and getting it out with trouble, she looked up to find that the car was taking her on, and all the family behind on the platform! She wished to get out, but was held back by the other passengers, who declared she would break her neck if she jumped from the car in motion.

But at the next stopping-place she felt so flustered she hardly knew what to do, so she kept on and on till she felt she must somehow make up her mind to leave that car, and with a desperate resolution she stepped out on the platform. She found herself in a deserted part of the grounds, a few gentlemen only getting out to go to the Brewers' Hall. Though there was a crowd everywhere else, it seemed very solitary here. Mrs. Peterkin went round and round the Brewers' Hall, uncertain where to go. At last a gentleman noticed her, and asked if he could help her. When she told her case, he asked if her family had appointed any place of meeting in case of accident. Mrs. Peterkin thought she remembered their talking of the Main Building as a rendezvous. The gentleman advised her taking the train directly for the Main Building. She shook her head; she had already spent the morning in the cars. The gentleman smiled, but asked her to go on with him and he would show her where to get out.

Mrs. Peterkin joined him gratefully, and they took a train at a neighboring platform. But they had not gone very far, and were making another stop, when Mrs. Peterkin gave a scream! There was her family, standing in a row, ready to receive her! She was so agitated she could hardly get out, and almost fainted with delight at the meeting.

It appeared that a ticket-seller on the platform had advised the family to take a train back, and wait on some platform till they should see their mother passing. Mrs. Peterkin shuddered to think how she might have been walking round and round the Brewers' Hall all day, if it had not been for meeting the kindly gentleman.

The next thing was to get something to eat, though Mrs. Peterkin was too agitated to think of it; they went to the Vienna Bakery, not far away, and found an immense crowd. Only one or two places could be obtained in the veranda outside, and the family took turns in sitting. Then it was that Mrs. Peterkin found she had left her camp-stool in the car! The family in general did not regret it, for it was heavy and inconvenient to carry, and Mrs. Peterkin confessed she found it difficult to use it, as it always tumbled over when she went to sit down. It was one of the three-legged ones.

It seemed now time to go home, but Agamemnon, who had been studying the map, proposed they should pass through the Main Building on their way out, for a glimpse of it, as they had not yet been inside one of the buildings, and it was their second day.

They hastened on with this plan, and went in at the grand middle entrance. And here they felt as if they were really at the Exhibition. The high pillars, the crowded aisles, filled them with wonder.

A seat was found for Mrs. Peterkin near the very middle. Mr. Peterkin, Agamemnon, Solomon John, and Elizabeth Eliza ventured to leave her for a moment while they looked at the famous Elkington display, and the little boys stood at her side finishing some popped-corn balls. Suddenly Mrs. Peterkin saw the rest disappear from her sight. She sent the little boys to call them back. She directly left her seat to follow, but she lost sight of the little boys. There was a seething crowd going up and down. She tried to return to her seat, but could not find it. Her head was bewildered. She was sure she must have turned the wrong way. It all looked so much alike, stairways going up to the dome at each corner, and no signs of her family. The strains arose from the immense organ of "Home, Sweet Home." She felt that now she should never see that home again! She sat down, she got up again! A kindly lady asked if she could help her, and Mrs. Peterkin was forced to explain, for the second time that day, that she had lost her family! The lady turned to one of the guards, who asked Mrs. Peterkin many questions. She described Elizabeth Eliza with a brown dress and cock's feather in her hat and note-book in her hand. The guard pointed out seven ladies in sight, wearing brown dresses, hats with cock's feathers, and note-books in their hands, — neither of them Elizabeth Eliza.

He advised Mrs. Peterkin to wait awhile in the same place and then go home, as it was growing late. But how could she go? She did not have the address of her boarding-place, and never could remember those numbered streets. It might be one number just as well as another. The policeman asked where she came from? If anybody at home knew her address? Mrs. Peterkin thought the Bromwicks knew; the Bromwicks planned coming to the same place. He then told Mrs. Peterkin not to stir from her seat till he returned. She ventured scarcely to look to the right or the left. Indeed, she was almost sure the eye of another policeman was upon her. How she hoped the Bromwicks would never know her position! It seemed an age that the policeman was gone, yet she was surprised when he returned with her address, for which he had telegraphed to the Bromwicks. Mrs. Peterkin looked at him in dumb surprise, but he hurried her toward the main exit, promising to show her to the right cars. Slowly and sadly she followed to the door, when what was her astonishment to find, across the door-way in a straight row, her family awaiting her!

They too were under the care of a friendly policeman, who had advised them to await their mother there. Eager to leave, they all hurried away, passed the difficult turnstile, and hastened to the cars.

"Let us get home! Let us get home!" exclaimed Mrs. Peterkin, unwilling to listen to any explanations.

A crowd was pursuing the Lancaster Avenue car, and the family joined in the rush. Mr. Peterkin succeeded in lifting in Mrs. Peterkin, Elizabeth Eliza, and the little boys; the rest had to stand all the way on the edges of the cars.

Mrs. Peterkin reached the boarding-place in hysterics. She passed a restless night, disturbed by dreams of walking round and round the Brewers' Hall, of Mr. Peterkin falling from the steps of the cars and being run over, of policemen watching her, and she declared they must go home, she could not stay a day longer.

But all the family exclaimed against this. They had seen nothing as yet.

They decided to stay, and transfer their quarters the next night to one of the hotels by the grounds. According to the advice of one of their fellow-boarders, after depositing and checking their baggage at the House of Public Comfort, they went to the Massachusetts Building. Mrs. Peterkin was enchanted with the parlor and its cheery wood fire, and declared she would prefer to spend the day there, instead of going into the crowded buildings. She had some rolls and sandwiches that she had brought from the boarding-house that would serve for her luncheon, and it was agreed she should be left there for the day, and that the family would return for her at half-past four, in time for a little walk afterward in the grounds.

The family left her, relieved to think of her comfort. The heart of Mr. Peterkin swelled as he thought she was under the protection of the shield of Massachusetts.

They decided to separate. Mr. Peterkin and Agamemnon would take the little boys to the Agricultural Building, and to the American Restaurant for lunch, while Elizabeth Eliza and Solomon John planned the Art Gallery and Les Trois Frères Provençaux; for Elizabeth Eliza had been studying the French grammar, and wanted to try talking a little French. They had heard of all these places from their fellow-boarders. They were to meet in the Main Building, in front of Egypt, at half-past three.

They did all assemble there, to their surprise, but not until much after that hour. Mr. Peterkin and his party were wild with enthusiasm. They had been through Agricultural Hall, and had seen "Old Abe," looking so much like a stuffed eagle, that they were astonished when he moved his head. The little boys had bought chocolates and candies at every refreshment stand, and had eaten the bread which they had seen made by the baker of the queen, and apples cored by the apple-corer, and had bought little tin pails of the leaf-lard man, and had lunched at the banqueting-hall of the American Restaurant, and were now eager to try the restaurants in the Main Building.

Elizabeth Eliza and Solomon John had not so much to report. They were so crushed in the Art Gallery by the mass of people, that Elizabeth Eliza could not even lift her note-book, or examine her catalogue. She believed they had been into every room in the Art Gallery and in the Annex, but she could only look at the upper pictures, and could not stop at any. She was sure there must be more United States pictures than from any other country. The only work of art which she could remember enough to describe was the large bust of Washington, sitting on the eagle. They had found a seat near this, where they could examine it closely, and wondered why the eagle was not crushed.

Both Solomon John and Elizabeth Eliza agreed with the little boys that they would like another lunch, for their expedition to the Trois Frères was not satisfactory, and Elizabeth Eliza fancied their waiter could hardly have been a Frenchman, as he did not understand her French.

The little boys were now impatient for the restaurant, and they found seats in one of the galleries, where it was so pleasant looking down upon the crowd below, that Mr. Peterkin decided to go and bring Mrs. Peterkin to join them, while Elizabeth Eliza and Solomon John were to order their oysters. He looked at his watch, and found, to his horror, it was now five o'clock! And he hastened away. He did not seem to be gone long, for he came back breathless, to say that Mrs. Peterkin was no longer in the parlor of the Massachusetts Building!

Mrs. Peterkin, meanwhile, had enjoyed a comfortable nap in the quiet room, had walked about to look at the pictures, had eaten her luncheon, and when the chimes rung twelve, she was surprised to find the day was not farther gone. Still, she sat awhile, and looked out of the window; but she grew weary and restless, and when a party set forth from the room to go to the Main Building, she decided to join them.

They made a little tour first by St. George's Hill, the Japanese Dwelling, the Canada Log-house, and at last entered the Main Building, and Mrs. Peterkin found herself in Italy. The party whom she had joined took her to see the Norwegian groups, where they left her to meet other of their friends.

She stayed awhile in Norway and Sweden, then went on to China. Here everything was so strange that she sank into a seat bewildered. She felt she was in the midst of a weird dream, — strange figures on screens and vases, a mandarin nodding at her, idols glaring at her. She wished herself back in the safe parlor; she was sorry she ever had left it.

Ah! did she but know that at that moment the little boys were trying some ice-cream soda at a stand near by! Wearily she rose again and inquired the time, to find it was after half-past four! In her agitation, she went out in front of the building, and took the wrong direction. A kindly lady set her right again, but it was half-past five when she reached the shelter of the Massachusetts Building, going up the steps at the very moment Mr. Peterkin was announcing the terrible fact of her disappearance to the astounded family.

Mrs. Peterkin went in, to find every one gathering bags and parcels, preparing to leave. Where should she go? She rushed madly towards the door, and there stood the lady from Philadelphia, who directly declared that she would take Mrs. Peterkin home with her.

Mrs. Peterkin hardly knew how to leave her family behind in this uncertainty, but she followed mechanically the lady from Philadelphia and her party. As they went down the steps, they saw in front of them Mr. Peterkin and all the family in a row. Again they had consulted a policeman, who advised them to visit the Massachusetts Building once more.

Mrs. Peterkin spent the next day quietly with the lady from Philadelphia. The rest of the family went to the Exhibition. They went through Machinery Hall, stopping, as the day before, at every confectionery stand and refreshment room, wasting some time in the middle of the day, because Agamemnon preferred seeing the Corliss engine stop, and Solomon John wanted to wait and see it set going. But they had seen a great deal, and, to please the little boys, they had even visited the Fat Woman outside the grounds.

The next day, the lady from Philadelphia and her daughters assisted the party to the station. It was difficult for all to get through the crowd as a family, but Mr. and Mrs. Peterkin did cling together, and met Elizabeth Eliza, the little boys, Solomon John, and Agamemnon outside the barrier.

The last the lady from Philadelphia saw of them, the family were standing in a row, ready to enter the waiting train.

15

Mrs. Peterkin's Tea-Party

T WAS important to have a tea-party, as they had all been invited by everybody, — the Bromwicks, the Tremletts, and the Gibbonses. It would be such a good chance to pay off some of their old debts, now that the lady from Philadelphia was back again, and her two daughters, who would be sure to make it all go off well.

But as soon as they began to make out the list they saw there were too many to have at once, for there were but twelve cups and saucers in the best set.

"There are seven of *us*, to begin with," said Mr. Peterkin.

"We need not all drink tea," said Mrs. Peterkin.

"I never do," said Solomon John. The little boys never did.

"And we could have coffee, too," suggested Elizabeth Eliza.

"That would take as many cups," objected Agamemnon.

"We could use the every-day set for the coffee," answered Elizabeth Eliza; "they are the right shape. Besides," she went on, "they would not all come. Mr. and Mrs. Bromwick, for instance; they never go out."

"There are but six cups in the everyday set," said Mrs. Peterkin.

The little boys said there were plenty of saucers; and Mr. Peterkin agreed with Elizabeth Eliza that all would not come. Old Mr. Jeffers never went out.

"There are three of the Tremletts," said Elizabeth Eliza; "they never go out together. One of them, if not two, will be sure to have the headache. Ann Maria Bromwick would come, and the three Gibbons boys, and their sister Juliana; but the other sisters are out West, and there is but one Osborne."

It really did seem safe to ask "everybody." They would be sorry, after it was over, that they had not asked more.

"We have the cow," said Mrs. Peterkin, "so there will be as much cream and milk as we shall need."

"And our own pig," said Agamemnon. "I am glad we had it salted; so we can have plenty of sandwiches."

"I will buy a chest of tea," exclaimed Mr. Peterkin, "I have been thinking of a chest for some time."

Mrs. Peterkin thought a whole chest would not be needed; it was as well to buy the tea and coffee by the pound. But Mr. Peterkin determined on a chest of tea and a bag of coffee.

So they decided to give the invitations to all. It might be a stormy evening, and some would be prevented.

The lady from Philadelphia and her daughters accepted. And it turned out a fair day, and more came than were expected. Ann Maria Bromwick had a friend staying with her, and brought her over, for the Bromwicks were opposite neighbors. And the Tremletts had a niece, and Mary Osborne an aunt, that they took the liberty to bring.

The little boys were at the door, to show in the guests, and as each set came to the front gate they ran back to tell their mother that more were coming. Mrs. Peterkin had grown dizzy with counting those who had come, and trying to calculate how many were to come, and wondering why there were always more and never less, and whether the cups would go round.

The three Tremletts all came, with their niece. They all had had their headaches the day before, and were having that banged feeling you always have after a headache; so they all sat at the same side of the room on the long sofa.

All the Jefferses came, though they had sent uncertain answers. Old Mr. Jeffers had to be helped in, with his cane, by Mr. Peterkin.

The Gibbons boys came, and would stand just outside the parlor door. And Juliana appeared afterward, with the two other sisters, unexpectedly home from the West.

"Got home this morning!" they said. "And so glad to be in time to see everybody, — a little tired, to be sure, after forty-eight hours in a sleeping-car!"

"Forty-eight!" repeated Mrs. Peterkin; and wondered if there were forty-eight people, and why they were all so glad to come, and whether all could sit down.

Old Mr. and Mrs. Bromwick came. They thought it would not be neighborly to stay away. They insisted on getting into the most uncomfortable seats.

Yet there seemed to be seats enough while the Gibbons boys preferred to stand. But they never could sit round a tea-table. Elizabeth Eliza had thought they all might have room at the table, and Solomon John and the little boys could help in the waiting.

It was a great moment when the lady from Philadelphia arrived with her daughters. Mr. Peterkin was talking to Mr. Bromwick, who was a little deaf. The Gibbons boys retreated a little farther behind the parlor door. Mrs. Peterkin hastened forward to shake hands with the lady from Philadelphia, saying: —

"Four Gibbons girls and Mary Osborne's aunt, — that makes nineteen; and now" —

It made no difference what she said; for there was such

a murmuring of talk that any words suited. And the lady from Philadelphia wanted to be introduced to the Bromwicks.

It was delightful for the little boys. They came to Elizabeth Eliza, and asked: —

"Can't we go and ask more? Can't we fetch the Larkins?"

"Oh, dear, no!" answered Elizabeth Eliza. "I can't even count them."

Mrs. Peterkin found time to meet Elizabeth Eliza in the side entry, to ask if there were going to be cups enough.

"I have set Agamemnon in the front entry to count," said Elizabeth Eliza, putting her hand to her head.

The little boys came to say that the Maberlys were coming.

"The Maberlys!" exclaimed Elizabeth Eliza. "I never asked them."

"It is your father's doing," cried Mrs. Peterkin. "I do believe he asked everybody he saw!" And she hurried back to her guests.

"What if father really has asked everybody?" Elizabeth Eliza said to herself, pressing her head again with her hand.

There were the cow and the pig. But if they all took tea or coffee, or both, the cups could *not* go round.

Agamemnon returned in the midst of her agony.

He had not been able to count the guests, they moved about so, they talked so; and it would not look well to appear to count.

"What shall we do?" exclaimed Elizabeth Eliza.

"We are not a family for an emergency," said Agamemnon.

"What do you suppose they did in Philadelphia at the Exhibition, when there were more people than cups and saucers?" asked Elizabeth Eliza. "Could not you go and inquire? I know the lady from Philadelphia is talking about the Exhibition, and telling how she stayed at home to receive friends. And they must have had trouble there! Could not you go in and ask, just as if you wanted to know?"

Agamemnon looked into the room, but there were too many talking with the lady from Philadelphia.

"If we could only look into some book," he said, — "the encyclopaedia or the dictionary; they are such a help sometimes!"

At this moment he thought of his "Great Triumphs of Great Men," that he was reading just now. He had not reached the lives of the Stephensons, or any of the men of modern times. He might skip over to them, — he knew they were men for emergencies.

He ran up to his room, and met Solomon John coming down with chairs.

"That is a good thought," said Agamemnon. "I will bring down more upstairs chairs."

"No," said Solomon John, "here are all that can come down; the rest of the bedroom chairs match bureaus, and they never will do!"

Agamemnon kept on to his own room, to consult his books. If only he could invent something on the spur of the moment, — a set of bedroom furniture, that in an emergency could be turned into parlor chairs! It seemed an idea; and he sat himself down to his table and pencils, when he was interrupted by the little boys, who came to tell him that Elizabeth Eliza wanted him.

The little boys had been busy thinking. They proposed that the tea-table, with all the things on, should be pushed into the front room, where the company were; and those could take cups who could find cups.

But Elizabeth Eliza feared it would not be safe to push so large a table; it might upset, and break what china they had.

Agamemnon came down to find her pouring out tea, in the back room. She called to him: —

"Agamemnon, you must bring Mary Osborne to help, and perhaps one of the Gibbons boys would carry round some of the cups."

And so she began to pour out, and to send round the sandwiches, and the tea, and the coffee. Let things go as far as they would!

The little boys took the sugar and cream.

"As soon as they have done drinking bring back the cups and saucers to be washed," she said to the Gibbons boys and the little boys.

This was an idea of Mary Osborne's.

But what was their surprise that the more they poured out the more cups they seemed to have! Elizabeth Eliza took the coffee, and Mary Osborne the tea. Amanda brought fresh cups from the kitchen.

"I can't understand it," Elizabeth Eliza said to Amanda. "Do they come back to you round through the piazza? Surely there are more cups than there were!"

Her surprise was greater when some of them proved to be coffee-cups that matched the set! And they never had had coffee-cups.

Solomon John came in at this moment, breathless with triumph.

"Solomon John!" Elizabeth Eliza exclaimed; "I cannot understand the cups!"

"It is my doing," said Solomon John, with an elevated air. "I went to the lady from Philadelphia, in the midst of her talk. 'What do you do in Philadelphia, when you haven't enough cups?' 'Borrow of my neighbors,' she answered, as quick as she could."

"She must have guessed," interrupted Elizabeth Eliza.

"That may be," said Solomon John. "But I whispered to Ann Maria Bromwick, — she was standing by, — and she took me straight over into their closet, and old Mr. Bromwick bought this set just where we bought ours. And they had a coffee-set, too" —

"You mean where our father and mother bought them. We were not born," said Elizabeth Eliza.

"It is all the same," said Solomon John. "They match exactly."

So they did, and more and more came in.

Elizabeth Eliza exclaimed: —

"And Agamemnon says we are not a family for emergencies!"

"Ann Maria was very good about it," said Solomon John; "and quick, too. And old Mrs. Bromwick has kept all her set of two dozen coffee and tea cups!"

Elizabeth Eliza was ready to faint with delight and relief. She told the Gibbons boys, by mistake, instead of Agamemnon and the little boys. She almost let fall the cups and saucers she took in her hand.

"No trouble now!"

She thought of the cow, and she thought of the pig, and she poured on.

No trouble, except about the chairs. She looked into the room; all seemed to be sitting down, even her mother. No, her father was standing, talking to Mr. Jeffers. But he was drinking coffee, and the Gibbons boys were handing things around.

The daughters of the lady from Philadelphia were sitting on shawls on the edge of the window that opened upon the piazza. It was a soft, warm evening, and some of the young people were on the piazza. Everybody was talking and laughing, except those who were listening.

Mr. Peterkin broke away, to bring back his cup and another for more coffee.

"It's a great success, Elizabeth Eliza," he whispered.

"The coffee is admirable, and plenty of cups. We asked none too many. I should not mind having a tea-party every week."

Elizabeth Eliza sighed with relief as she filled his cup. It was going off well. There were cups enough, but she was not sure she could live over another such hour of anxiety; and what was to be done after tea?

16

The Peterkins Too Late for the Exhibition

Dramatis Personae. — Amanda (friend of Elizabeth Eliza), Amanda's mother, girls of the graduating class, Mrs. Peterkin, Elizabeth Eliza.

AMANDA [*coming in with a few graduates*].

MOTHER, the exhibition is over, and I have brought the whole class home to the collation.

MOTHER. — The whole class! But I only expected a few.

AMANDA. — The rest are coming. I brought Julie, and Clara, and Sophie with me. [*A voice is heard.*] Here are the rest.

MOTHER. — Why, no. It is Mrs. Peterkin and Elizabeth Eliza!

AMANDA. — Too late for the exhibition. Such a shame! But in time for the collation.

MOTHER [*to herself*]. — If the ice-cream will go round.

AMANDA. — But what made you so late? Did you miss the train? This is Elizabeth Eliza, girls, — you have heard me speak of her. What a pity you were too late!

MRS. PETERKIN. — We tried to come; we did our best.

MOTHER. — Did you miss the train? Didn't you get my postal-card?

MRS. PETERKIN. — We had nothing to do with the train.

AMANDA. — You don't mean you walked?

MRS. PETERKIN. — Oh, no, indeed!

ELIZABETH ELIZA. — We came in a horse and carryall.

JULIA. — I always wondered how anybody could come in a horse!

AMANDA. — You are too foolish, Julie. They came in the carryall part. But didn't you start in time?

MRS. PETERKIN. — It all comes from the carryall being so hard to turn. I told Mr. Peterkin we should get into trouble with one of those carryalls that don't turn easy.

ELIZABETH ELIZA. — They turn easy enough in the stable, so you can't tell.

MRS. PETERKIN. — Yes; we started with the little boys and Solomon John on the back seat, and Elizabeth Eliza on the front. She was to drive, and I was to see to the driving. But the horse was not faced toward Boston.

MOTHER. — And you tipped over in turning round! Oh, what an accident!

AMANDA. — And the little boys, — where are they? Are they killed?

ELIZABETH ELIZA. — The little boys are all safe. We left them at the Pringles', with Solomon John.

MOTHER. — But what did happen?

MRS. PETERKIN. — We started the wrong way.

MOTHER. — You lost your way, after all?

ELIZABETH ELIZA. — No; we knew the way well enough.

AMANDA. — It's as plain as a pikestaff!

MRS. PETERKIN. — No; we had the horse faced in the wrong direction, — toward Providence.

ELIZABETH ELIZA. — And mother was afraid to have me turn, and we kept on and on till we should reach a wide place.

MRS. PETERKIN. — I thought we should come to a road that would veer off to the right or left, and bring us back to the right direction.

MOTHER. — Could not you all get out and turn the thing round?

Mrs. Peterkin. — Why, no; if it had broken down we should not have been in anything, and could not have gone anywhere.

Elizabeth Eliza. — Yes, I have always heard it was best to stay in the carriage, whatever happens.

Julia. — But nothing seemed to happen.

Mrs. Peterkin. — Oh, yes; we met one man after another, and we asked the way to Boston.

Elizabeth Eliza. — And all they would say was, "Turn right round, — you are on the road to Providence."

Mrs. Peterkin. — As if we could turn right round! That was just what we couldn't.

Mother. — You don't mean you kept on all the way to Providence?

Elizabeth Eliza. — Oh, dear no! We kept on and on, till we met a man with a black hand-bag, — black leather, I should say.

Julia. — He must have been a book-agent.

Mrs. Peterkin. — I dare say he was; his bag seemed heavy. He set it on a stone.

Mother. — I dare say it was the same one that came here the other day. He wanted me to buy the "History of the Aborigines, Brought up from Earliest Times to the Present Date," in four volumes. I told him I hadn't time to read so much. He said that was no matter, few did, and it wasn't much worth it; they bought books for the look of the thing.

Amanda. — Now, that was illiterate; he never could have graduated. I hope, Elizabeth Eliza, you had nothing to do with that man.

Elizabeth Eliza. — Very likely it was not the same one.

MOTHER. — Did he have a kind of pepper-and-salt suit with one of the buttons worn?

MRS. PETERKIN. — I noticed one of the buttons was off.

AMANDA. — We're off the subject. Did you buy his book?

ELIZABETH ELIZA. — He never offered us his book.

MRS. PETERKIN. — He told us the same story, — we were going to Providence; if we wanted to go to Boston we must turn directly round.

ELIZABETH ELIZA. — I told him I couldn't; but he took the horse's head, and the first thing I knew —

AMANDA. — He had yanked you round!

MRS. PETERKIN. — I screamed; I couldn't help it!

ELIZABETH ELIZA. — I was glad when it was over!

MOTHER. — Well, well; it shows the disadvantage of starting wrong.

MRS. PETERKIN. — Yes, we came straight enough when the horse was headed right; but we lost time.

ELIZABETH ELIZA. — I am sorry enough I lost the exhibition, and seeing you take the diploma, Amanda. I never got the diploma myself. I came near it.

MRS. PETERKIN. — Somehow, Elizabeth Eliza never succeeded. I think there was partiality about the promotions.

ELIZABETH ELIZA. — I never was good about remembering things. I studied well enough, but when I came to say off my lesson I couldn't think what it was. Yet I could have answered some of the other girls' questions.

JULIA. — It's odd how the other girls always have the easiest questions.

ELIZABETH ELIZA. — I never could remember poetry. There was only one thing I could repeat.

AMANDA. — Oh, do let us have it now; and then we'll recite to you some of our exhibition pieces.

ELIZABETH ELIZA. — I'll try.

MRS. PETERKIN. — Yes, Elizabeth Eliza, do what you can to help entertain Amanda's friends.

[*All stand looking at* ELIZABETH ELIZA, *who remains silent and thoughtful.*]

ELIZABETH ELIZA. — I'm trying to think what it is about. You all know it. You remember, Amanda, — the name is rather long.

AMANDA. — It can't be Nebuchadnezzar, can it? — that is one of the longest names I know.

ELIZABETH ELIZA. Oh, dear, no!

JULIA. — Perhaps it's Cleopatra.

ELIZABETH ELIZA. — It does begin with a "C," — only he was a boy.

AMANDA. — That's a pity, for it might be "We are seven," only that is a girl. Some of them were boys.

ELIZABETH ELIZA. — It begins about a boy — if I could only think where he was. I can't remember.

AMANDA. — Perhaps he "stood upon the burning deck"?

ELIZABETH ELIZA. — That's just it; I knew he stood somewhere.

AMANDA. — Casabianca! Now begin — go ahead.

ELIZABETH ELIZA. —

> "*The boy stood on the burning deck,*
> *When — When*" —

I can't think who stood there with him.

JULIA. — If the deck was burning, it must have been on fire. I guess the rest ran away, or jumped into boats.

AMANDA. — That's just it: —

> "*Whence all but him had fled.*"

ELIZABETH ELIZA. — I think I can say it now.

> "*The boy stood on the burning deck,*
> *Whence all but him had fled*" —

[*She hesitates.*] Then I think he went —

JULIA. — Of course, he fled after the rest.

AMANDA. — Dear, no! That's the point. He didn't.

> "*The flames rolled on, he would not go*
> *Without his father's word.*"

ELIZABETH ELIZA. — Oh, yes. Now I can say it.

> "*The boy stood on the burning deck,*
> *Whence all but him had fled;*
> *The flames rolled on, he would not go*
> *Without his father's word.*"

But it used to rhyme. I don't know what has happened to it.

MRS. PETERKIN. — Elizabeth Eliza is very particular about the rhymes.

ELIZABETH ELIZA. — It must be "without his father's *head*," or, perhaps, "without his father *said*" he should.

JULIA. — I think you must have omitted something.

AMANDA. — She has left out ever so much!

MOTHER. — Perhaps it's as well to omit some, for the ice-cream has come, and you must all come down.

AMANDA. — And here are the rest of the girls; and let us all unite in a song!

[*Exeunt omnes singing.*]

17

The Peterkins Celebrate the Fourth of July

HE day began early.

A compact had been made with the little boys the evening before.

They were to be allowed to usher in the glorious day by the blowing of horns exactly at sunrise. But they were to blow them for precisely five minutes only, and no sound of the horns should be heard afterward till the family were downstairs.

It was thought that a peace might thus be bought by a short, though crowded, period of noise.

The morning came. Even before the morning, at half-past three o'clock, a terrible blast of the horns aroused the whole family.

Mrs. Peterkin clasped her hands to her head and exclaimed: "I am thankful the lady from Philadelphia is not here!" For she had been invited to stay a week, but had declined to come before the Fourth of July, as she was not well, and her doctor had prescribed quiet.

And the number of the horns was most remarkable! It was as though every cow in the place had arisen and was blowing through both her own horns!

"How many little boys are there? How many have we?" exclaimed Mr. Peterkin, going over their names one by one mechanically, thinking he would do it, as he might count imaginary sheep jumping over a fence, to put himself to sleep. Alas! the counting could not put him to sleep now, in such a din.

And how unexpectedly long the five minutes seemed! Elizabeth Eliza was to take out her watch and give the signal for the end of the five minutes, and the ceasing of the horns. Why did not the signal come? Why did not Elizabeth Eliza stop them?

And certainly it was long before sunrise; there was no dawn to be seen!

"We will not try this plan again," said Mrs. Peterkin.

"If we live to another Fourth," added Mr. Peterkin, hastening to the door to inquire into the state of affairs.

Alas! Amanda, by mistake, had waked up the little boys an hour too early. And by another mistake the little boys had invited three or four of their friends to spend the night with them. Mrs. Peterkin had given them permission to have the boys for the whole day, and they understood the day as beginning when they went to bed the night before. This accounted for the number of horns.

It would have been impossible to hear any explanation; but the five minutes were over, and the horns had ceased, and there remained only the noise of a singular leaping of feet, explained perhaps by a possible pillow-fight, that kept the family below partially awake until the bells and cannon made known the dawning of the glorious day, — the sunrise, or "the rising of the sons," as Mr. Peterkin jocosely called it when they heard the little boys and their friends clattering down the stairs to begin the outside festivities.

They were bound first for the swamp, for Elizabeth Eliza, at the suggestion of the lady from Philadelphia, had advised them to hang some flags around the pillars of the piazza. Now the little boys knew of a place in the swamp where they had been in the habit of digging for "flag-root," and where they might find plenty of flag flowers. They did bring away all they could, but they were a little out of bloom. The boys were in the midst of nailing up all they had on the pillars of the piazza, when the procession of the Antiques and Horribles passed along. As the procession saw the festive arrangements on the piazza, and the crowd of boys, who cheered them loudly, it stopped to salute the house with some especial strains of greeting.

Poor Mrs. Peterkin! They were directly under her windows! In a few moments of quiet, during the boys' absence from the house on their visit to the swamp, she had been trying to find out whether she had a sick-headache, or whether it was all the noise, and she was just deciding it was the sick-headache, but was falling into a light slumber, when the fresh noise outside began.

There were the imitations of the crowing of cocks, and braying of donkeys, and the sound of horns, encored and increased by the cheers of the boys. Then began the torpedoes, and the Antiques and Horribles had Chinese crackers also.

And, in despair of sleep, the family came down to breakfast.

Mrs. Peterkin had always been much afraid of fireworks, and had never allowed the boys to bring gunpowder into the house. She was even afraid of torpedoes; they looked so much like sugar-plums she was sure some of the children would swallow them, and explode before anybody knew it.

She was very timid about other things. She was not sure even about pea-nuts. Everybody exclaimed over this: "Surely there was no danger in pea-nuts!" But Mrs. Peterkin declared she had been very much alarmed at the Centennial Exhibition, and in the crowded corners of the streets in Boston, at the pea-nut stands, where they had machines to roast the pea-nuts. She did not think it was safe. They might go off any time, in the midst of a crowd of people, too!

Mr. Peterkin thought there actually was no danger, and he should be sorry to give up the pea-nut. He thought it an American institution, something really belonging to the Fourth of July. He even confessed to a quiet pleasure in crushing the empty shells with his feet on the sidewalks as he went along the streets.

Agamemnon thought it a simple joy.

In consideration, however, of the fact that they had had no real celebration of the Fourth the last year, Mrs. Peterkin had consented to give over the day, this year, to the amusement of the family as a Centennial celebration. She would prepare herself for a terrible noise, — only she did not want any gunpowder brought into the house.

The little boys had begun by firing some torpedoes a few days beforehand, that their mother might be used to the sound, and had selected their horns some weeks before.

Solomon John had been very busy in inventing some fireworks. As Mrs. Peterkin objected to the use of gunpowder, he found out from the dictionary what the different parts of gunpowder are, — saltpetre, charcoal, and sulphur. Charcoal, he discovered, they had in the wood-house; saltpetre they would find in the cellar, in the beef barrel; and sulphur they could buy at the apothecary's. He explained to his mother that these materials had never yet exploded in the house, and she was quieted.

Agamemnon, meanwhile, remembered a recipe he had read somewhere for making a "fulminating paste" of iron-

filings and powder of brimstone. He had written it down on a piece of paper in his pocket-book. But the iron filings must be finely powdered. This they began upon a day or two before, and the very afternoon before laid out some of the paste on the piazza.

Pin-wheels and rockets were contributed by Mr. Peterkin for the evening. According to a programme drawn up by Agamemnon and Solomon John, the reading of the Declaration of Independence was to take place in the morning, on the piazza, under the flags.

The Bromwicks brought over their flag to hang over the door.

"That is what the lady from Philadelphia meant," explained Elizabeth Eliza.

"She said the flags of our country," said the little boys. "We thought she meant 'in the country.'"

Quite a company assembled; but it seemed nobody had a copy of the Declaration of Independence.

Elizabeth Eliza said she could say one line, if they each could add as much. But it proved they all knew the same line that she did, as they began: —

"When, in the course of — when, in the course of — when, in the course of human — when in the course of human events — when, in the course of human events, it becomes — when, in the course of human events, it becomes necessary — when, in the course of human events, it becomes necessary for one people" —

They could not get any farther. Some of the party decided that "one people" was a good place to stop, and the little boys sent off some fresh torpedoes in honor of the people. But Mr. Peterkin was not satisfied. He invited the assembled party to stay until sunset, and meanwhile he would find a copy, and torpedoes were to be saved to be fired off at the close of every sentence.

And now the noon bells rang and the noon bells ceased.

Mrs. Peterkin wanted to ask everybody to dinner. She should have some cold beef. She had let Amanda go, because it was the Fourth, and everybody ought to be free that one day; so she could not have much of a dinner. But when she went to cut her beef she found Solomon had taken it to soak, on account of the saltpetre, for the fireworks!

Well, they had a pig; so she took a ham, and the boys had bought tamarinds and buns and a cocoa-nut. So the company stayed on, and when the Antiques and Horribles passed again they were treated to pea-nuts and lemonade.

They sung patriotic songs, they told stories, they fired torpedoes, they frightened the cats with them. It was a warm afternoon; the red poppies were out wide, and the hot sun poured down on the alley-ways in the garden.

There was a seething sound of a hot day in the buzzing of insects, in the steaming heat that came up from the ground. Some neighboring boys were firing a toy cannon. Every time it went off Mrs. Peterkin started, and looked to see if one of the little boys was gone. Mr. Peterkin had set out to find a copy of the "Declaration." Agamemnon had disappeared. She had not a moment to decide about her headache. She asked Ann Maria if she were not anxious

about the fireworks, and if rockets were not dangerous. They went up, but you were never sure where they came down.

And then came a fresh tumult! All the fire-engines in town rushed toward them, clanging with bells, men and boys yelling! They were out for a practice, and for a Fourth-of-July show.

Mrs. Peterkin thought the house was on fire, and so did some of the guests. There was great rushing hither and thither. Some thought they would better go home; some thought they would better stay. Mrs. Peterkin hastened into the house to save herself, or see what she could save. Elizabeth Eliza followed her, first proceeding to collect all the pokers and tongs she could find, because they could be thrown out of the window without breaking. She had read of people who had flung looking-glasses out of the window by mistake, in the excitement of the house being on fire, and had carried the pokers and tongs carefully

into the garden. There was nothing like being prepared. She had always determined to do the reverse. So with calmness she told Solomon John to take down the looking-glasses.

But she met with a difficulty, — there were no pokers and tongs, as they did not use them. They had no open fires; Mrs. Peterkin had been afraid of them. So Elizabeth Eliza took all the pots and kettles up to the upper windows, ready to be thrown out.

But where was Mrs. Peterkin? Solomon John found she had fled to the attic in terror. He persuaded her to come down, assuring her it was the most unsafe place; but she insisted upon stopping to collect some bags of old pieces, that nobody would think of saving from the general wreck, she said, unless she did. Alas! this was the result of fireworks on Fourth of July! As they

came downstairs they heard the the voices of all the company declaring there was no fire; the danger was past. It was long before Mrs. Peterkin could believe it. They told her the fire company was only out for show, and to celebrate the Fourth of July. She thought it already too much celebrated.

Elizabeth Eliza's kettles and pans had come down through the windows with a crash, that had only added to the festivities, the little boys thought.

Mr. Peterkin had been roaming about all this time in search of a copy of the Declaration of Independence. The public library was shut, and he had to go from house to house; but now, as the sunset bells and cannon began, he returned with a copy, and read it, to the pealing of the bells and sounding of the cannon. Torpedoes and crackers were fired at every pause. Some sweet-marjoram pots, tin cans filled with crackers which were lighted, went off with great explosions.

At the most exciting moment, near the close of the reading, Agamemnon, with an expression of terror, pulled Solomon John aside.

"I have suddenly remembered where I read about the 'fulminating paste' we made. It was in the preface to 'Woodstock,' and I have been round to borrow the book, to read the directions over again, because I was afraid about the 'paste' going off. READ THIS QUICKLY! and tell me, *Where is the fulminating paste?*"

Solomon John was busy winding some covers of paper over a little parcel. It contained chlorate of potash and sulphur mixed. A friend had told him of the composition. The more thicknesses of paper you put round it the louder it would go off. You must pound it with a hammer. Solomon John felt it must be perfectly safe, as his mother had taken potash for a medicine.

He still held the parcel as he read from Agamemnon's book: "This paste, when it has lain together about twenty-six hours, will *of itself* take fire, and burn all the sulphur away with a blue flame and a bad smell."

"Where is the paste?" repeated Solomon John, in terror.

"We made it just twenty-six hours ago," said Agamemnon.

"We put it on the piazza,". exclaimed Solomon John, rapidly recalling the facts, "and it is in front of our mother's feet!"

He hastened to snatch the paste away before it should take fire, flinging aside the packet in his hurry. Agamemnon, jumping upon the piazza at the same moment, trod upon the paper parcel, which exploded at once with the shock, and he fell to the ground, while at the same moment the paste "fulminated" into a blue flame directly in front of Mrs. Peterkin!

It was a moment of great confusion. There were cries and screams. The bells were still ringing, the cannon firing, and Mr. Peterkin had just reached the closing words: "Our lives, our fortunes, and our sacred honor."

"We are all blown up, as I feared we should be," Mrs. Peterkin at length ventured to say, finding herself in a lilac-bush by the side of the piazza.

She scarcely dared to open her eyes to see the scattered limbs about her.

It was so with all. Even Ann Maria Bromwick clutched a pillar of the piazza, with closed eyes.

At length Mr. Peterkin said, calmly, "Is anybody killed?"

There was no reply. Nobody could tell whether it was because everybody was killed, or because they were too wounded to answer. It was a great while before Mrs. Peterkin ventured to move.

But the little boys soon shouted with joy, and cheered the success of Solomon John's fireworks, and hoped he had some more. One of them had his face blackened by an unexpected cracker, and Elizabeth Eliza's muslin dress was burned here and there. But no one was hurt; no one had lost any limbs, though Mrs. Peterkin was sure she had seen some flying in the air. Nobody could understand how, as she had kept her eyes firmly shut.

No greater accident had occurred than the singeing of the tip of Solomon John's nose. But there was an unpleasant and terrible odor from the "fulminating paste."

Mrs. Peterkin was extricated from the lilac-bush. No one knew how she got there. Indeed, the thundering noise had stunned everybody. It had roused the neighborhood even more than before. Answering explosions came on every side, and, though the sunset light had not faded away, the little boys hastened to send off rockets under cover of the confusion. Solomon John's other fireworks would not go. But all felt he had done enough.

Mrs. Peterkin retreated into the parlor, deciding she really did have a headache. At times she had to come out when a rocket went off, to see if it was one of the little boys. She was exhausted by the adventures of the day, and almost thought it could not have been worse if the boys had been allowed gunpowder. The distracted lady was thankful there was likely to be but one Centennial Fourth in her lifetime, and declared she should never more keep anything in the house as dangerous as saltpetred beef, and she should never venture to take another spoonful of potash.

18

The Peterkins' Picnic

HERE was some doubt about the weather. Solomon John looked at the "Probabilities"; there were to be "areas of rain" in the New England States.

Agamemnon thought if they could only know where the areas of rain were to be they might go to the others. Mr. Peterkin proposed walking round the house in a procession, to examine the sky. As they returned they met Ann Maria Bromwick, who was to go, much surprised not to find them ready.

Mr. and Mrs. Peterkin were to go in the carryall, and take up the lady from Philadelphia, and Ann Maria, with the rest, was to follow in a wagon, and to stop for the daughters of the lady from Philadelphia. The wagon arrived, and so Mr. Peterkin had the horse put into the carryall.

A basket had been kept on the back piazza for some days, where anybody could put anything that would be needed for the picnic as soon as it was thought of. Agamemnon had already decided to take a thermometer; somebody was always complaining of being too hot or too cold at a picnic, and it would be a great convenience to see if she really were so. He thought now he might take a barometer, as "Probabilities" was so uncertain. Then, if it went down in a threatening way, they could all come back.

The little boys had tied their kites to the basket. They had never tried them at home; it might be a good chance on the hills. Solomon John had put in some fishing-poles;

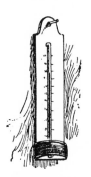

Elizabeth Eliza, a book of poetry. Mr. Peterkin did not like sitting on the ground, and proposed taking two chairs, one for himself and one for anybody else. The little boys were perfectly happy; they jumped in and out of the wagon a dozen times, with new india-rubber boots, bought for the occasion.

Before they started, Mrs. Peterkin began to think she had already had enough of the picnic, what with going and coming, and trying to remember things. So many mistakes were made. The things that were to go in the wagon were put in the carryall, and the things in the carryall had to be taken out for the wagon! Elizabeth Eliza forgot her water-proof, and had to go back for her veil, and Mr. Peterkin came near forgetting his umbrella.

Mrs. Peterkin sat on the piazza and tried to think. She felt as if she must have forgotten something; she knew she must. Why could not she think of it now, before it was too late? It seems hard any day to think what to have for dinner, but how much easier now it would be to stay at home quietly and order the dinner, — and there was the butcher's cart! But now they must think of everything.

At last she was put into the carryall, and Mr. Peterkin in front to drive. Twice they started, and twice they found something was left behind, — the loaf of fresh brown bread on the back piazza, and a basket of sandwiches on the front porch. And, just as the wagon was leaving, the little boys shrieked, "The basket of things was left behind!"

Everybody got out of the wagon. Agamemnon went back into the house, to see if any-thing else were left. He looked into the closets; he shut the front door, and was so busy that he forgot to get into the wagon him-self. It started off and went down the street without him!

He was wondering what he should do if he were left behind (why had they not thought to arrange a telegraph wire to the back wheel of the wagon, so that he might have sent a mes-sage in such a case!), when the Bromwicks drove out of their yard, in their buggy, and took him in.

They joined the rest of the party at Tatham Corners where they were all to meet and consult where they were to go. Mrs. Peterkin called to Aga-memnon, as soon as he appeared. She had been holding the barom-eter and the thermometer, and they waggled so that it troubled her. It was hard keeping the thermometer out of the sun, which would make it so warm. It really took away her pleasure, holding the things. Agamemnon decided to get into the carryall, on the seat with his father, and take the barometer and thermometer.

The consultation went on. Should they go to Cherry

Swamp, or Lonetown Hill? You had the view if you went
to Lonetown Hill, but maybe the drive to Cherry Swamp
was prettier.

Somebody suggested asking the lady from Philadelphia,
as the picnic was got up for her.

But where was she?

"I declare," said Mr. Peterkin, "I forgot to stop for her!"
The whole picnic there, and no lady from Philadelphia!

It seemed the horse had twitched his head in a threatening manner as they passed the house, and Mr. Peterkin
had forgotten to stop, and Mrs. Peterkin had been so busy
managing the thermometers that she had not noticed, and
the wagon had followed on behind.

Mrs. Peterkin was in despair. She knew they had forgotten something! She did not like to have Mr. Peterkin

make a short turn, and it was
getting late, and what would the
lady from Philadelphia think of
it, and had they not better give
it all up?

But everybody said "No!" and
Mr. Peterkin said he could make
a wide turn round the Lovejoy
barn. So they made the turn,
and took up the lady from Philadelphia, and the wagon
followed behind and took up her daughters, for there was
a driver in the wagon besides Solomon John.

Ann Maria Bromwick said it was so late by this time
they might as well stop and have the picnic on the Common! But the question was put again, Where should
they go?

The lady from Philadelphia decided for Strawberry Nook,
—it sounded inviting. There were no strawberries, and

there was no nook, it was said, but there was a good place to tie the horses.

Mrs. Peterkin was feeling a little nervous, for she did not know what the lady from Philadelphia would think of their having forgotten her, and the more she tried to explain it the worse it seemed to make it. She supposed they never did such things in Philadelphia; she knew they had invited all the world to a party, but she was sure she would never want to invite anybody again. There

was no fun about it till it was all over. Such a mistake, —to have a party for a person, and then go without her; but she knew they would forget something! She wished they had not called it their picnic.

There was another bother! Mr. Peterkin stopped. "Was

anything broke?" exclaimed Mrs. Peterkin. "Was something forgotten?" asked the lady from Philadelphia.

No! But Mr. Peterkin didn't know the way; and here he was leading all the party, and a long row of carriages following.

They all stopped, and it seemed nobody knew the way to Strawberry Nook, unless it was the Gibbons boys, who were far behind. They were made to drive up, and said that Strawberry Nook was in quite a different direction, but they could bring the party round to it through the meadows.

The lady from Philadelphia thought they might stop anywhere, such a pleasant day; but Mr. Peterkin said they were started for Strawberry Nook, and had better keep on.

So they kept on. It proved to be an excellent place, where they could tie the horses to a fence. Mrs. Peterkin did not like their all heading different ways; it seemed as if any of them might come at her, and tear up the fence, especially as the little boys had their kites flapping round. The Tremletts insisted upon the whole party going up on

the hill; it was too damp below. So the Gibbons boys, and the little boys, and Agamemnon, and Solomon John, and all the party, had to carry everything up to the rocks. The large basket of "things" was very heavy. It had been difficult to lift it into the wagon, and it was harder to take it out. But, with the help of the driver, and Mr. Peterkin, and old Mr. Bromwick, it was got up the hill.

And at last all was arranged. Mr. Peterkin was seated in his chair. The other was offered to the lady from Philadelphia, but she preferred the carriage cushions; so did old Mr. Bromwick. And the table-cloth was spread, — for they did bring a table-cloth, — and the baskets were opened, and the picnic really began. The pickles had tumbled into the butter, and the spoons had been forgotten, and the Tremletts' basket had been left on their front door-step. But nobody seemed to mind. Everybody was hungry, and everything they ate seemed of the best. The little boys were perfectly happy, and ate of all the kinds of cake. Two of the Tremletts would stand while they were eating, because they were afraid of the ants and the spiders that seemed to be crawling round. And Elizabeth Eliza had to keep poking with a fern-leaf to drive the insects out of the plates. The lady from Philadelphia was made comfortable with the cushions and shawls, leaning against a rock. Mrs. Peterkin wondered if she forgot she had been forgotten.

John Osborne said it was time for conundrums, and asked, "Why is a pastoral musical play better than the music we have here? Because one is a grasshopper, and the other is a grass-opera!"

Elizabeth Eliza said she knew a conundrum, a very funny one, one of her friends in Boston had told her. It was, "Why is ———" It began, "Why is something like ———" —— no, "Why are they different?" It was something about an old woman, or else it was something about a young one. It was very funny, if she could only think what it was about, or whether it was alike or different.

The lady from Philadelphia was proposing they should guess Elizabeth Eliza's conundrum, first the question, and then the answer, when one of the Tremletts came running down the hill, and declared she had just discovered a very threatening cloud, and she was sure it was going to rain down directly. Everybody started up, though no cloud was to be seen.

There was a great looking for umbrellas and water-proofs. Then it appeared that Elizabeth Eliza had left hers, after all, though she had gone back for it twice. Mr. Peterkin knew he had not forgotten his umbrella, because he had put the whole umbrella-stand into the wagon, and it had been brought up the hill, but it proved to hold only the family canes!

There was a great cry for the "emergency basket," that

had not been opened yet. Mrs. Peterkin explained how for days the family had been putting into it what might be needed, as soon as anything was thought of. Everybody stopped to see its contents. It was carefully covered with

newspapers. First came out a backgammon-board. "That would be useful," said Ann Maria, "if we have to spend the afternoon in anybody's barn." Next, a pair of andirons. "What were they for?" "In case of needing a fire in the woods," explained Solomon John. Then came a volume of the Encyclopaedia. But it was the first volume, Agamemnon now regretted, and contained only A and a part of B, and nothing about rain or showers. Next, a bag of pea-nuts, put in by the little boys, and Elizabeth Eliza's book of poetry, and a change of boots for Mr. Peterkin; a small foot-rug in case the ground should be damp; some paint-boxes of the little boys'; a box of fish-hooks for Solomon John; an ink-bottle, carefully done up in a great deal of newspaper, which was fortunate, as the ink was oozing out; some old magazines, and a blacking-bottle; and at the bottom a sun-dial. It was all very entertaining, and there seemed to

be something for every occasion but the present. Old Mr. Bromwick did not wonder the basket was so heavy. It was all so interesting that nobody but the Tremletts went down to the carriages.

The sun was shining brighter than ever, and Ann Maria insisted on setting up the sun-dial. Certainly there was no danger of a shower, and they might as well go on with the picnic. But when Solomon John and Ann Maria had arranged the sun-dial they asked everybody to look at their watches, so that they might see if it was right. And then came a great exclamation at the hour; it was time they were all going home!

The lady from Philadelphia had been wrapping her shawl about her, as she felt the sun was low. But nobody had any idea it was so late! Well, they had left late, and went back a great many times, had stopped sometimes to consult, and had been long on the road, and it had taken a long time to fetch up the things; so it was no wonder it was time to go away. But it had been a delightful picnic, after all.

19

The Peterkins' Charades

EVER since the picnic the Peterkins had been wanting to have "something" at their house in the way of entertainment. The little boys wanted to get up a "great Exposition," to show to the people of the place. But Mr. Peterkin thought it too great an effort to send to foreign countries for "exhibits," and it was given up.

There was, however, a new water-trough needed on the town common, and the ladies of the place thought it ought to be something handsome, — something more than a common trough, — and they ought to work for it.

Elizabeth Eliza had heard at Philadelphia how much women had done, and she felt they ought to contribute to such a cause. She had an idea, but she would not speak of it at first, not until after she had written to the lady from Philadelphia. She had often thought, in many cases, if they had asked her advice first, they might have saved trouble.

Still how could they ask advice before they themselves knew what they wanted? It was very easy to ask advice, but you must first know what to ask about. And again: Elizabeth Eliza felt you might have ideas, but you could not always put them together. There was this idea of the water-trough, and then this idea of getting some money for it. So she began with writing to the lady from Phila-delphia. The little boys believed she spent enough for it in postage-stamps before it all came out.

But it did come out at last that the Peterkins were to have some charades at their own house for the benefit of the needed water-trough, — tickets sold only to especial friends. Ann Maria Bromwick was to help act, because she could bring some old bonnets and gowns that had been worn by an aged aunt years ago, and which they had  always kept. Elizabeth Eliza said that Solomon John would have to be a Turk, and they must borrow all the red things and cashmere scarfs in the place. She knew people would be willing to lend things.

Agamemnon thought you ought to get in something about the Hindoos, they were such an odd people. Elizabeth Eliza said you must not have it too odd, or people would not understand it, and she did not want anything to frighten her mother. She had one word suggested by the lady from Philadelphia in her letters, — the one that had "Turk" in it, — but they ought to have two words.

"Oh, yes," Ann Maria said, "you must have two words; if the people paid for their tickets they would want to get their money's worth."

Solomon John thought you might have "Hindoos"; the little boys could color their faces brown, to look like Hindoos. You could have the first scene an Irishman catching a hen, and then paying the water-taxes for "dues," and then have the little boys for Hindoos.

A great many other words were talked of, but nothing seemed to suit. There was a curtain, too, to be thought of, because the folding-doors stuck when you tried to open and shut them. Agamemnon said that the Pan-Elocutionists

had a curtain they would probably lend John Osborne, and so it was decided to ask John Osborne to help.

If they had a curtain they ought to have a stage. Solomon John said he was sure he had boards and nails enough, and it would be easy to make a stage if John Osborne would help put it up.

All this talk was the day before the charades. In the midst of it Ann Maria went over for her old bonnets and dresses and umbrellas, and they spent the evening in trying on the various things, — such odd caps and remarkable bonnets! Solomon John said they ought to have plenty of bandboxes; if you only had bandboxes enough a charade was sure to go off well; he had seen charades in Boston. Mrs. Peterkin said there were plenty in their attic, and the little boys brought down piles of them, and the back parlor was filled with costumes.

Ann Maria said she could bring over more things if she only knew what they were going to act. Elizabeth Eliza told her to bring anything she had, — it would all come of use.

The morning came, and the boards were collected for the stage. Agamemnon and Solomon John gave themselves to the work, and John Osborne helped zealously. He said the Pan-Elocutionists would lend a scene also. There was a great clatter of bandboxes, and piles of shawls in corners, and such a piece of work in getting up the curtain! In the midst of it came in the little boys, shouting, "All the tickets are sold, at ten cents each!"

"Seventy tickets sold!" exclaimed Agamemnon.

"Seven dollars for the water-trough!" said Elizabeth Eliza.

"And we do not know yet what we are going to act!" exclaimed Ann Maria.

But everybody's attention had to be given to the scene that was going up in the background, borrowed from the Pan-Elocutionists. It was magnificent, and represented a forest.

"Where are we going to put seventy people?" exclaimed Mrs. Peterkin, venturing, dismayed, into the heaps of shavings, and boards, and litter.

The little boys exclaimed that a large part of the audience consisted of boys, who would not take up much room. But how much clearing and sweeping and moving of chairs was necessary before all could be made ready! It was late, and some of the people had already come to secure good seats, even before the actors had assembled.

"What are we going to act?" asked Ann Maria.

"I have been so torn with one thing and another," said Elizabeth Eliza, "I haven't had time to think!"

"Haven't you the word yet?" asked John Osborne, for the audience was flocking in, and the seats were filling up rapidly.

"I have got one word in my pocket," said Elizabeth Eliza, "in the letter from the lady from Philadelphia. She sent me the parts of the word. Solomon John is to be a Turk, but I don't yet understand the whole of the word."

"You don't know the word, and the people are all here!" said John Osborne, impatiently.

"Elizabeth Eliza!" exclaimed Ann Maria, "Solomon John says I'm to be a Turkish slave, and I'll have to wear a veil. Do you know where the veils are? You know I brought them over last night."

"Elizabeth Eliza! Solomon John wants you to send him the large cashmere scarf!" exclaimed one of the little boys, coming in. "Elizabeth Eliza! you must tell us what kind of faces to make up!" cried another of the boys.

And the audience were heard meanwhile taking their seats on the other side of the thin curtain.

"You sit in front, Mrs. Bromwick; you are a little hard of hearing; sit where you can hear."

"And let Julia Fitch come where she can see," said another voice.

"And we have not any words for them to hear or see!" exclaimed John Osborne, behind the curtain.

"Oh, I wish we'd never determined to have charades!" exclaimed Elizabeth Eliza. "Can't we return the money?"

"They are all here; we must give them something!" said John Osborne, heroically.

"And Solomon John is almost dressed," reported Ann Maria, winding a veil around her head.

"Why don't we take Solomon John's word 'Hindoos' for the first?" said Agamemnon.

John Osborne agreed to go in the first, hunting the "hin," or anything, and one of the little boys took the part of the hen, with the help of a feather duster. The bell rang, and the first scene began.

It was a great success. John Osborne's Irish was perfect. Nobody guessed the word, for the hen crowed by mistake; but it received great applause.

Mr. Peterkin came on in the second scene to receive the water-rates, and made a long speech on taxation. He was interrupted by Ann Maria as an old woman in a huge bonnet. She persisted in turning her back to the audience, speaking so low nobody heard her; and Elizabeth Eliza, who appeared in a more remarkable bonnet, was so alarmed she went directly back, saying she had forgotten something. But this was supposed to be the effect intended, and it was loudly cheered.

Then came a long delay, for the little boys brought out a number of their friends to be browned for Hindoos. Ann Maria played on the piano till the scene was ready. The curtain rose upon five brown boys done up in blankets and turbans.

"I am thankful that is over," said Elizabeth Eliza, "for

now we can act my word. Only I don't myself know the whole."

"Never mind, let us act it," said John Osborne, "and the audience can guess the whole."

"The first syllable must be the letter P," said Elizabeth Eliza, "and we must have a school."

Agamemnon was master, and the little boys and their friends went on as scholars. All the boys talked and shouted at once, acting their idea of a school by flinging pea-nuts about, and scoffing at the master.

"They'll guess that to be 'row,'" said John Osborne, in despair; "they'll never guess 'P'!"

The next scene was gorgeous. Solomon John, as a Turk, re-clined on John Osborne's army-blanket. He had on a turban, and a long beard, and all the family shawls. Ann Maria and Elizabeth Eliza were brought in to him, veiled, by the little boys in their Hindoo costumes.

This was considered the great scene of the evening, though Elizabeth Eliza was sure she did not know what to do, — whether to kneel or sit down; she did not know whether Turkish women did sit down, and she could not help laugh-ing whenever she looked at Solomon John. He, however, kept his solemnity. "I suppose I need not say much," he had said, "for I shall be the 'Turk who was dreaming of the hour.'" But he did order the little boys to bring sherbet, and when they brought it without ice insisted they must have their heads cut off, and Ann Maria fainted, and the scene closed.

"What are we to do now?" asked John Osborne, warming up to the occasion.

"We must have an 'inn' scene," said Elizabeth Eliza, consulting her letter; "two inns, if we can."

"We will have some travellers disgusted with one inn, and going to another," said John Osborne.

"Now is the time for the bandboxes," said Solomon John, who, since his Turk scene was over, could give his attention to the rest of the charade.

Elizabeth Eliza and Ann Maria went on as rival hostesses, trying to draw Solomon John, Agamemnon, and John Osborne into their several inns. The little boys carried valises, hand-bags, umbrellas, and bandboxes. Bandbox after bandbox appeared, and when Agamemnon sat down upon his the applause was immense. At last the curtain fell.

"Now for the whole," said John Osborne, as he made his way off the stage over a heap of umbrellas.

"I can't think why the lady from Philadelphia did not send me the whole," said Elizabeth Eliza, musing over the letter.

"Listen, they are guessing," said John Osborne. "'*D-ice-box*.' I don't wonder they get it wrong."

"But we know it can't be that!" exclaimed Elizabeth Eliza, in agony. "How can we act the whole if we don't know it ourselves?"

"Oh, I see it!" said Ann Maria, clapping her hands. "Get your whole family in for the last scene."

Mrs. and Mrs. Peterkin were summoned to the stage, and formed the background, standing on stools; in front were Agamemnon and Solomon John, leaving room for

Elizabeth Eliza between; a little in advance, and in front of all, half kneeling, were the little boys, in their india-rubber boots.

The audience rose to an exclamation of delight, "The Peterkins!" "P-Turk-Inns!"

It was not until this moment that Elizabeth Eliza guessed the whole.

"What a tableau!" exclaimed Mr. Bromwick; "the Peterkin family guessing their own charade."

20

The Peterkins Are Obliged to Move

AGAMEMNON had long felt it an impropriety to live in a house that was called a "semi-detached" house, when there was no other "semi" to it. It had always remained wholly detached, as the owner had never built the other half. Mrs. Peterkin felt this was not a sufficient reason for undertaking the terrible process of a move to another house, when they were fully satisfied with the one they were in.

But a more powerful reason forced them to go. The track of a new railroad had to be carried directly through the place, and a station was to be built on that very spot.

Mrs. Peterkin so much dreaded moving that she questioned whether they could not continue to live in the upper part of the house and give up the lower part to the station. They could then dine at the restaurant, and it would be very convenient about travelling, as there would be no danger of missing the train, if one were sure of the direction.

But when the track was actually laid by the side of the house, and the steam-engine of the construction train puffed and screamed under the dining-room windows, and the engineer calmly looked in to see what the family had for dinner, she felt, indeed, that they must move.

But where should they go? It was difficult to find a house that satisfied the whole family. One was too far off, and looked into a tan-pit; another was too much in the middle of the town, next door to a machine-shop. Elizabeth Eliza wanted a porch covered with vines, that should face the sunset; while Mr. Peterkin thought it would not be convenient to sit there looking towards the west in the late afternoon (which was his only leisure time), for the sun would shine in his face. The little boys wanted a house with a great many doors, so that they could go in and out often. But Mr. Peterkin did not like so much slamming, and felt there was more danger of burglars with so many doors. Agamemnon wanted an observatory, and Solomon John a shed for a workshop. If he could have carpenters' tools and a workbench he could build an observatory, if it were wanted.

But it was necessary to decide upon something, for they must leave their house directly. So they were obliged to take Mr. Finch's, at the Corners. It satisfied none of the family. The porch was a piazza, and was opposite a barn. There were three other doors, — too many to please Mr. Peterkin, and not enough for the little boys. There was

no observatory, and nothing to observe if there were one, as the house was too low, and some high trees shut out any view. Elizabeth Eliza had hoped for a view; but Mr. Peterkin consoled her by deciding it was more healthy to have to walk for a view, and Mrs. Peterkin agreed that they might get tired of the same every day.

And everybody was glad a selection was made, and the little boys carried their india-rubber boots the very first afternoon.

Elizabeth Eliza wanted to have some system in the moving, and spent the evening in drawing up a plan. It would be easy to arrange everything beforehand, so that there should not be the confusion that her mother dreaded, and the discomfort they had in their last move. Mrs. Peterkin shook her head; she did not think it possible to move with any comfort. Agamemnon said a great deal could be done with a list and a programme.

Elizabeth Eliza declared if all were well arranged a programme would make it perfectly easy. They were to have new parlor carpets, which could be put down in the new house the first thing. Then the parlor

furniture could be moved in, and there would be two comfortable rooms, in which Mr. and Mrs. Peterkin could sit while the rest of the move went on. Then the old parlor carpets could be taken up for the new dining-room and the downstairs bedroom, and the family could meanwhile dine at the old house. Mr. Peterkin did not object to this, though the distance was considerable, as he felt exercise would be good for them all. Elizabeth Eliza's programme then arranged that the dining-room furniture should be moved the third day, by which time one of the old parlor carpets would be down in the new dining-room, and they could still sleep in the old house. Thus there would always be a quiet, comfortable place in one house or the other. Each night, when Mr. Peterkin came home, he would find some place for quiet thought and rest, and each day there should be moved only the furniture needed for a certain room. Great confusion would be avoided and nothing misplaced. Elizabeth Eliza wrote these last words at the head of her programme, — "Misplace nothing." And Agamemnon made a copy of the programme for each member of the family.

The first thing to be done was to buy the parlor carpets. Elizabeth Eliza had already looked at some in Boston, and the next morning she went, by an early train, with her father, Agamemnon, and Solomon John, to decide upon them.

They got home about eleven o'clock, and when they reached the house were dismayed to find two furniture wagons in front of the gate, already partly filled! Mrs. Peterkin was walking in and out of the open door, a large book in one hand, and a duster in the other, and she came to meet them in an agony of anxiety. What should they do? The furniture carts had appeared soon after the rest had left for Boston, and the men insisted upon beginning to move the things. In vain had she shown Elizabeth Eliza's programme; in vain had she insisted they must take only the parlor furniture. They had declared they must put the heavy pieces in the bottom of the cart, and the lighter furniture on top. So she had seen them go into every room in the house, and select one piece of furniture after another, without even looking at Elizabeth Eliza's programme; she doubted if they could read it if they had looked at it.

Mr. Peterkin had ordered the carters to come; but he had no idea they would come so early, and supposed it would take them a long time to fill the carts.

But they had taken the dining-room sideboard first, —

a heavy piece of furniture, — and all its contents were now on the dining-room tables. Then, indeed, they selected the parlor book-case, but had set every book on the floor. The men had told Mrs. Peterkin they would put the books in the bottom of the cart, very much in the order they were taken from the shelves. But by this time Mrs. Peterkin was considering the carters as natural enemies, and dared not trust them; besides, the books ought all to be dusted. So she was now holding one of the volumes of Agamemnon's Encyclopaedia, with difficulty, in one hand, while she was dusting it with the other. Elizabeth Eliza was in dismay. At this moment four men were bringing down a large chest of drawers from her father's room, and they called to her to stand out of the way. The parlors were a scene of confusion. In dusting the books Mrs. Peterkin neglected to restore them to the careful rows in which they were left by the men, and they lay in hopeless masses in different parts of the room. Elizabeth Eliza sunk in despair upon the end of a sofa.

"It would have been better to buy the red and blue carpet," said Solomon John.

"Is not the carpet bought?" exclaimed Mrs. Peterkin. And then they were obliged to confess they had been unable to decide upon one, and had come back to consult Mrs. Peterkin.

"What shall we do?" asked Mrs. Peterkin.

Elizabeth Eliza rose from the sofa and went to the door, saying, "I shall be back in a moment."

Agamemnon slowly passed round the room, collecting the scattered volumes of his Encyclopaedia. Mr. Peterkin offered a helping hand to a man lifting a wardrobe.

Elizabeth Eliza soon returned. "I did not like to go and ask her. But I felt that I must in such an emergency. I explained to her the whole matter, and she thinks we should take the carpet at Makillan's."

"Makillan's" was a store in the village, and the carpet was the only one all the family had liked without any doubt; but they had supposed they might prefer one from Boston.

The moment was a critical one. Solomon John was sent directly to Makillan's to order the carpet to be put down that very day. But where should they dine? where should they have their supper? and where was Mr. Peterkin's "quiet hour"? Elizabeth Eliza was frantic; the dining-room floor and table were covered with things.

It was decided that Mr. and Mrs. Peterkin should dine at the Bromwicks, who had been most neighborly in their offers, and the rest should get something to eat at the baker's.

Agamemnon and Elizabeth Eliza hastened away to be ready to receive the carts at the other house, and direct the furniture as they could. After all there was something exhilarating in this opening of the new house, and in deciding where things should go. Gaily Elizabeth Eliza stepped down the front garden of the new home and across the piazza, and to the door. But it was locked, and she had no keys!

"Agamemnon, did you bring the keys?" she exclaimed.

No, he had not seen them since the morning, — when — ah! — yes, the little boys were allowed to go to the house for their india-rubber boots, as there was a threatening of rain. Perhaps they had left some door unfastened — perhaps they had put the keys under the door-mat. No, each door, each window, was solidly closed, and there was no mat!

"I shall have to go to the school to see if they took the keys with them," said Agamemnon; "or else go home to see if they left them there." The school was in a different direction from the house, and far at the other end of the town; for Mr. Peterkin had not yet changed the boys' school, as he proposed to do after their move.

"That will be the only way," said Elizabeth Eliza, for it had been arranged that the little boys should take their lunch to school, and not come home at noon.

She sat down on the steps to wait, but only for a moment, for the carts soon appeared, turning the corner. What should be done with the furniture? Of course the carters must wait for the keys, as she should need them to set the furniture up in the right places. But they could not stop for this. They put it down upon the piazza, on the steps, in the garden, and Elizabeth Eliza saw how incongruous it was! There was something from every room in the house! Even the large family chest, which had proved too heavy for them to travel with, had come down from the attic, and stood against the front door.

And Solomon John appeared with the carpet-woman, and a boy with a wheelbarrow, bringing the new carpet. And all stood and waited. Some opposite neighbors appeared to offer advice and  look on, and Elizabeth Eliza groaned inwardly that only the shabbiest of their furniture appeared to be standing full in view.

It seemed ages before Agamemnon returned, and no wonder; for he had been to the house, then to the school, then back to the house, for one of the little boys had left the keys at home, in the pocket of his clothes. Meanwhile the carpet-woman had waited, and the boy with the wheelbarrow had waited, and when they got in they found the parlor must be swept and cleaned. So the carpet-woman went off in dudgeon, for she was sure there would not be time enough to do anything.

And one of the carts came again, and in their hurry the men set the furniture down anywhere. Elizabeth Eliza was hoping to make a little place in the dining-room, where they might have their supper, and go home to sleep. But she looked out, and there were the carters bringing the bedsteads, and proceeding to carry them upstairs.

In despair Elizabeth Eliza went back to the old house. If she had been there she might have prevented this. She found Mrs. Peterkin in an agony about the entry oil-cloth. It had been made in the house, and how could it be taken out of the house? Agamemnon made measurements; it certainly could not go out of the front door! He suggested it might be left till the house was pulled down, when it could easily be moved out of one side. But Elizabeth Eliza reminded him that the whole house was to be moved without being taken apart. Perhaps it could be cut in strips narrow enough to go out. One of the men loading the remaining cart disposed of the question by coming in and rolling up the oil-cloth and carrying it off on top of his wagon.

Elizabeth Eliza felt she must hurry back to the new house. But what should they do? — no beds here, no carpets there! The dining-room table and sideboard were at the other house, the plates, and forks, and spoons here. In vain she looked at her programme. It was all reversed; everything was misplaced. Mr. Peterkin would suppose they were to eat here and sleep here, and what had become of the little boys?

Meanwhile the man with the first cart had returned. They fell to packing the dining-room china.

They were up in the attic, they were down in the cellar. Every one suggested to take the tacks out of the parlor carpets, as they should want to take them next. Mrs. Peterkin sunk upon a kitchen chair.

"Oh, I wish we had decided to stay and be moved in the house!" she exclaimed.

Solomon John urged his mother to go to the new house, for Mr. Peterkin would be there for his "quiet hour." And when the carters at last appeared, carrying the parlor carpets on their shoulders, she sighed and said, "There is nothing left," and meekly consented to be led away.

They reached the new house to find Mr. Peterkin sitting calmly in a rocking-chair on the piazza, watching the oxen coming into the opposite barn. He was waiting for the keys, which Solomon John had taken back with him. The little boys were in a horse-chestnut tree, at the side of the house.

Agamemnon opened the door. The passages were crowded with furniture, the floors were strewn with books; the bureau was upstairs that was to stand in a lower bedroom; there was not a place to lay a table, — there was nothing to lay upon it; for the knives and plates and spoons had not come, and although the tables were there they were covered with chairs and boxes.

At this moment came a covered basket from the lady from Philadelphia. It contained a choice supper, and forks and spoons, and at the same moment appeared a pot of hot tea from an opposite neighbor. They placed all this on the back of a bookcase lying upset, and sat around it. Solomon John came rushing in from the gate.

"The last load is coming! We are all moved!" he exclaimed; and the little boys joined in a chorus, "We are
moved! we are moved!"

Mrs. Peterkin looked sadly round; the kitchen utensils
were lying on the parlor lounge, and an old family gun on
Elizabeth Eliza's hat-box. The parlor clock stood on a
barrel; some coal-scuttles had been placed on the parlor
table, a bust of Washington stood in the door-way, and the
looking-glasses leaned against the pillars of the piazza. But
they were moved! Mrs. Peterkin felt, indeed, that they
were very much moved.

21

The Peterkins Decide to Learn the Languages

ERTAINLY now was the time to study the languages. The Peterkins had moved into a new house, far more convenient than their old one, where they would have a place for everything and everything in its place. Of course they would then have more time.

Elizabeth Eliza recalled the troubles of the old house; how for a long time she was obliged to sit outside of the window upon the piazza, when she wanted to play on her piano.

Mrs. Peterkin reminded them of the difficulty about the table-cloths. The upper table-cloth was kept in a trunk that had to stand in front of the door to the closet under the stairs. But the under table-cloth was kept in a drawer in the closet. So, whenever the cloths were changed, the trunk had to be pushed away under some projecting shelves to make room for opening the closet-door (as the under table-cloth must be taken out first), then the trunk was pushed back to make room for it to be opened for the upper table-cloth, and, after all, it was necessary to push the trunk away again to open the closet-door for the knife-tray. This always consumed a great deal of time.

Now that the china-closet was large enough, everything could find a place in it.

Agamemnon especially enjoyed the new library. In the old house there was no separate room for books. The dictionaries were kept upstairs, which was very inconvenient, and the volumes of the Encyclopaedia could not be together. There was not room for all in one place. So from A to P were to be found downstairs, and from Q to Z were scattered in different rooms upstairs. And the worst of it was, you could never remember whether from A to P included P. "I always went upstairs after P," said Agamemnon, "and then always found it downstairs, or else it was the other way."

Of course, now there were more conveniences for study. With the books all in one room there would be no time wasted in looking for them.

Mr. Peterkin suggested they should each take a separate language. If they went abroad this would prove a great convenience. Elizabeth Eliza could talk French with the Parisians; Agamemnon, German with the Germans; Solomon John, Italian with the Italians; Mrs. Peterkin, Spanish in Spain; and perhaps he could himself master all the Eastern languages and Russian.

Mrs. Peterkin was uncertain about undertaking the Spanish; but all the family felt very sure they should not go to Spain (as Elizabeth Eliza dreaded the Inquisition), and Mrs. Peterkin felt more willing.

Still she had quite an objection to going abroad. She had always said she would not go till a bridge was made across the Atlantic, and she was sure it did not look like it now.

Agamemnon said there was no knowing. There was something new every day, and a bridge was surely not harder to invent than a telephone, for they had bridges in the very earliest days.

Then came up the question of the teachers. Probably these could be found in Boston. If they could all come the same day three could be brought out in the carryall. Agamemnon could go in for them, and could learn a little on the way out and in.

Mr. Peterkin made some inquiries about the Oriental languages. He was told that Sanscrit was at the root of all. So he proposed they should all begin with Sanscrit. They would thus require but one teacher, and could branch out into the other languages afterward.

But the family preferred learning the separate languages. Elizabeth Eliza already knew something of the French. She had tried to talk it, without much success, at the Centennial Exhibition, at one of the side-stands. But she found she had been talking with a Moorish gentleman who did not understand French. Mr. Peterkin feared they might need more libraries if all the teachers came at the same hour; but Agamemnon reminded him that they would be using different dictionaries. And Mr. Peterkin thought something might be learned by having them all at once. Each one might pick up something beside the language he was studying, and it was a great thing to learn to talk a foreign language while others were talking about you. Mrs. Peterkin was afraid it would be like the Tower of Babel, and hoped it was all right.

Agamemnon brought forward another difficulty. Of course they ought to have foreign teachers, who spoke only their native languages. But, in this case, how could they engage them to come, or explain to them about the carryall, or arrange the proposed hours? He did not understand how anybody ever began with a foreigner, because he could not even tell him what he wanted.

Elizabeth Eliza thought a great deal might be done by signs and pantomime. Solomon John and the little boys began to show how it might be done. Elizabeth Eliza explained how "*langues*" meant both "languages" and "tongues," and they could point to their tongues. For practice, the little boys represented the foreign teachers talking in their different languages, and Agamemnon and Solomon John went to invite them to come out and teach the family by a series of signs.

Mr. Peterkin thought their success was admirable, and that they might almost go abroad without any study of the languages, and trust to explaining themselves by signs. Still, as the bridge was not yet made, it might be as well to wait and cultivate the languages.

Mrs. Peterkin was afraid the foreign teachers might imagine they were invited out to lunch. Solomon John had constantly pointed to his mouth as he opened it and shut it, putting out his tongue; and it looked a great deal more as if he were inviting them to eat than asking them to teach. Agamemnon suggested that they might carry the separate dictionaries when they went to see the teachers, and that would show that they meant lessons, and not lunch.

Mrs. Peterkin was not sure but she ought to prepare a lunch for them, if they had come all that way; but she certainly did not know what they were accustomed to eat.

Mr. Peterkin thought this would be a good thing to learn of the foreigners. It would be a good preparation for going abroad, and they might get used to the dishes before starting. The little boys were delighted at the idea of having new things cooked. Agamemnon had heard that beer-soup was a favorite dish with the Germans, and he would inquire how it was made in the first lesson. Solomon John had heard they were all very fond of garlic, and thought it would be a pretty attention to have some in the house the first day, that they might be cheered by the odor.

Elizabeth Eliza wanted to surprise the lady from Philadelphia by her knowledge of French, and hoped to begin on her lessons before the Philadelphia family arrived for their annual visit.

There were still some delays. Mr. Peterkin was very anxious to obtain teachers who had been but a short time in this country. He did not want to be tempted to talk any English with them. He wanted the latest and freshest languages, and at last came home one day with a list of "brand-new foreigners."

They decided to borrow the Bromwicks' carryall to use, beside their own, for the first day, and Mr. Peterkin and Agamemnon drove into town to bring all the teachers out. One was a Russian gentleman, travelling, who came with no idea of giving lessons, but perhaps he would consent to do so. He could not yet speak English.

Mr. Peterkin had his card-case, and the cards of the several gentlemen who had recommended the different teachers, and he went with Agamemnon from hotel to hotel collecting them. He found them all very polite, and ready to come, after the explanation by signs agreed upon. The dictionaries had been forgotten, but Agamemnon had a directory, which looked the same, and seemed to satisfy the foreigners.

Mr. Peterkin was obliged to content himself with the

Russian instead of one who could teach Sanscrit, as there was no new teacher of that language lately arrived.

But there was an unexpected difficulty in getting the Russian gentleman into the same carriage with the teacher of Arabic, for he was a Turk, sitting with a fez on his head, on the back seat! They glared at each other, and began to assail each other in every language they knew, none of which Mr. Peterkin could understand. It might be Russian; it might be Arabic. It was easy to understand that they would never consent to sit in the same carriage. Mr. Peterkin was in despair; he had forgotten about the Russian war! What a mistake to have invited the Turk!

Quite a crowd collected on the sidewalk in front of the hotel. But the French gentleman politely, but stiffly, invited the Russian to go with him in the first carryall. Here was another difficulty. For the German professor was quietly ensconced on the back seat! As soon as the French gentleman put his foot on the step and saw him he addressed him in such forcible language that the German professor got out of the door the other side, and came round on the sidewalk and took him by the collar. Certainly the German and French gentlemen could not be put together, and more crowd collected!

Agamemnon, however, had happily studied up the German word "Herr," and he applied it to the German, inviting him by signs to take a seat in the other carryall. The German consented to sit by the Turk, as they neither of them could understand the other; and at last they started, Mr. Peterkin with the Italian by his side, and the French and Russian teachers behind, vociferating to each other in languages unknown to Mr. Peterkin, while he feared they were not perfectly in harmony; so he drove home as fast as possible. Agamemnon had a silent party. The Spaniard by his side was a little moody, while the Turk and the German behind did not utter a word.

At last they reached the house, and were greeted by Mrs. Peterkin and Elizabeth Eliza, Mrs. Peterkin with her llama lace shawl over her shoulders, as a tribute to the Spanish teacher. Mr. Peterkin was careful to take his party in first, and deposit them in a distant part of the library, far from the Turk or the

German, even putting the Frenchman and Russian apart.

Solomon John found the Italian dictionary, and seated himself by his Italian; Agamemnon, with the German dictionary, by the German. The little boys took their copy of the "Arabian Nights" to the Turk. Mr. Peterkin attempted to explain to the Russian that he had no Russian dictionary, as he had hoped to learn Sanscrit of him, while Mrs. Peterkin was trying to inform her teacher that she had no books in Spanish. She got over all fears of the Inquisition, he looked so sad, and she tried to talk a little, using English words, but very slowly, and altering the accent as far as she knew how. The Spaniard bowed, looked gravely interested, and was very polite.

Elizabeth Eliza, meanwhile, was trying her grammar phrases with the Parisian. She found it easier to talk French than to understand him. But he understood perfectly her sentences. She repeated one of her

vocabularies, and went on with, "*J'ai le livre.*" "*As-tu le pain?*" "*L'enfant a une poire.*" He listened with great attention, and replied slowly. Suddenly she started after making out one of his sentences, and went to her mother to whisper, "They have made the mistake you feared. They think they are invited to lunch! *He* has just been thanking me for our politeness in inviting them to *déjeuner*, — that means breakfast!"

"They have not had their breakfast!" exclaimed Mrs. Peterkin, looking at her Spaniard; "he does look hungry! What shall we do?"

Elizabeth Eliza was consulting her father. What should they do? How should they make them understand that they invited them to teach, not lunch. Elizabeth Eliza begged Agamemnon to look out "*apprendre*" in the dictionary. It must mean to teach. Alas, they

found it means both to teach and to learn! What should they do? The foreigners were now sitting silent in their different corners. The Spaniard grew more and more sallow. What if he should faint? The Frenchman was rolling up each of his mustaches to a point as he gazed at the German. What if the Russian should fight the Turk? What if the

German should be exasperated by the airs of the Parisian?

"We must give them something to eat," said Mr. Peterkin, in a low tone. "It would calm them."

"If I only knew what they were used to eating," said Mrs. Peterkin.

Solomon John suggested that none of them knew what the others were used to eating, and they might bring in anything.

Mrs. Peterkin hastened out with hospitable intents. Amanda could make good coffee. Mr. Peterkin had suggested some

American dish. Solomon John sent a little boy for some olives.

It was not long before the coffee came in, and a dish of baked beans. Next, some olives and a loaf of bread, and some boiled eggs, and some bottles of beer. The effect was astonishing. Every man spoke his own tongue, and fluently. Mrs. Peterkin poured out coffee for the Spaniard, while he bowed to her. They all liked beer; they all liked olives. The Frenchman was fluent about "*les moeurs Améri-caines.*" Elizabeth Eliza supposed he alluded to their not having set any table. The Turk smiled; the Russian was voluble. In the midst of the clang of the different languages, just as Mr. Peterkin was again repeating, under cover of the noise of many tongues, "How shall we make them understand that we want them to teach?" — at this very moment the door was flung open, and there came in the lady from Philadelphia, that day arrived, her first call of the season.

She started back in terror at the tumult of so many different languages. The family, with joy, rushed to meet her. All together they called upon her to explain for them. Could she help them? Could she tell the foreigners they wanted to take lessons? Lessons? They had no sooner uttered the word than their guests all started up with faces beaming with joy. It was the one English word they all knew! They had come to Boston to give lessons! The Russian traveller had hoped to learn English in this way. The thought pleased them more than the *déjeuner*. Yes, gladly would they give lessons. The Turk smiled at the idea. The first step was taken. The teachers knew they were expected to teach.

22

Modern Improvements at the Peterkins'

AGAMEMNON felt that it became necessary for him to choose a profession. It was important on account of the little boys. If he should make a trial of several different professions he could find out which would be the most likely to be successful, and it would then be easy to bring up the little boys in the right direction. Elizabeth Eliza agreed with this. She thought the family occasionally made mistakes, and had come near disgracing themselves. Now was their chance to avoid this in future by giving the little boys a proper education.

Solomon John was almost determined to become a doctor. From earliest childhood he had practised writing recipes on little slips of paper. Mrs. Peterkin, to be sure, was afraid of infection. She could not bear the idea of his bringing one disease after the other into the family circle. Solomon John, too, did not like sick people. He thought he might manage it if he should not have to see his patients while they were sick. If he could only visit them when they were recovering, and when the danger of infection was over, he would really enjoy making calls.

He should have a comfortable doctor's chaise, and take one of the little boys to hold his horse while he went in, and he thought he could get through the conversational part very well, and feeling the pulse, perhaps looking at the tongue. He should take and read all the newspapers, and so be thoroughly acquainted with the news of the day to

talk of. But he should not like to be waked up at night to visit. Mr. Peterkin thought that would not be necessary. He had seen signs on doors of "Night Doctor," and certainly it would be as convenient to have a sign of "Not a Night Doctor."

Solomon John thought he might write his advice to those of his patients who were dangerously ill, from whom there was danger of infection. And then Elizabeth Eliza agreed that his prescriptions would probably be so satisfactory that they would keep his patients well, — not too well to do without a doctor, but needing his recipes.

Agamemnon was delayed, however, in his choice of a profession, by a desire he had to become a famous inventor. If he could only invent something important, and get out a patent, he would make himself known all over the country. If he could get out a patent he would be set up for life, or at least as long as the patent lasted, and it would be well to be sure to arrange it to last through his natural life.

Indeed, he had gone so far as to make his invention. It had been suggested by their trouble with a key, in their late moving to their new house. He had studied the matter over a great deal. He looked it up in the Encyclopaedia, and had spent a day or two in the Public Library, in reading about Chubb's Lock and other patent locks.

But his plan was more simple. It was this: that all keys should be made alike! He wondered it had not been thought of before; but so it was, Solomon John said, with all inventions, with Christopher Columbus, and everybody. Nobody knew the invention till it was invented, and then it looked very simple. With Agamemnon's plan you need have but one key, that should fit everything! It should be a medium-sized key, not too  large to carry. It ought to answer for a house door, but you might open a portmanteau with it. How much less danger there would be of losing one's keys if there were only one to lose!

Mrs. Peterkin thought it would be inconvenient if their father were out, and she wanted to open the jam-closet for the little boys. But Agamemnon explained that he did not mean there should be but one key in the family, or in a town, — you might have as many as you pleased, only they should all be alike.

 Elizabeth Eliza felt it would be a great convenience, — they could keep the front door always locked, yet she could open it with the key of her upper drawer; that she was sure to have with her. And Mrs. Peterkin felt it might be a convenience if they had one on each story, so that they need not go up and down for it.

Mr. Peterkin studied all the papers and advertisements, to decide about the lawyer whom they should consult, and at last, one morning, they went into town to visit a patent-agent.

Elizabeth Eliza took the occasion to make a call upon the lady from Philadelphia, but she came back hurriedly to her mother.

"I have had a delightful call," she said; "but — perhaps I was wrong — I could not help, in conversation, speaking of Agamemnon's proposed patent. I ought not to have mentioned it, as such things are kept profound secrets; they say women always do tell things; I suppose that is the reason."

"But where is the harm?" asked Mrs. Peterkin. "I'm sure you can trust the lady from Philadelphia."

Elizabeth Eliza then explained that the lady from Philadelphia had questioned the plan a little when it was told her, and had suggested that "if everybody had the same key there would be no particular use in a lock."

"Did you explain to her," said Mrs. Peterkin, "that we were not all to have the same keys?"

"I couldn't quite understand her," said Elizabeth Eliza, "but she seemed to think that burglars and other people might come in if the keys were the same."

"Agamemnon would not sell his patent to burglars!" said Mrs. Peterkin, indignantly.

"But about other people," said Elizabeth Eliza; "there is my upper drawer; the little boys might open it at Christmas-time, — and their presents in it!"

"And I am not sure that I could trust Amanda," said Mrs. Peterkin, considering.

Both she and Elizabeth Eliza felt that Mr. Peterkin ought to know what the lady from Philadelphia had suggested. Elizabeth Eliza then proposed going into town, but it would take so long she might not reach them in time. A telegram would be better, and she ventured to suggest using the Telegraph Alarm.

For, on moving into their new house, they had discovered

it was provided with all the modern improvements. This had been a disappointment to Mrs. Peterkin, for she was afraid of them, since their experience the last winter, when their water-pipes were frozen up. She had been originally attracted to the house by an old pump at the side, which had led her to believe there were no modern improvements. It had pleased the little boys, too. They liked to pump the handle up and down, and agreed to pump all the water needed, and bring it into the house.

There was an old well, with a picturesque well-sweep, in a corner by the barn. Mrs. Peterkin was frightened by this at first. She was afraid the little boys would be falling in every day. And they showed great fondness for pulling the bucket up and down. It proved, however, that the well was dry. There was no water in it; so she had some  moss thrown down, and an old feather-bed, for safety, and the old well was a favorite place of amusement.

The house, it had proved, was well furnished with bathrooms, and "set-waters" everywhere. Water-pipes and gas-pipes all over the house; and a hack-, telegraph-, and fire-alarm, with a little knob for each.

Mrs. Peterkin was very anxious. She feared the little boys would be summoning somebody all the time, and it was decided to conceal from them the use of the knobs, and the card of directions at the side was destroyed. Agamemnon had made one of his first inventions to help thus. He had arranged a number of similar knobs to be put in rows in different parts of the house, to appear as if they were intended for ornament, and had added some to the original knobs. Mrs. Peterkin felt more secure, and Agamemnon thought of taking out a patent for this invention.

It was, therefore, with some doubt that Elizabeth Eliza proposed sending a telegram to her father. Mrs. Peterkin, however, was pleased with the idea. Solomon John was out, and the little boys were at school, and she herself would touch the knob, while Elizabeth Eliza should write the telegram.

"I think it is the fourth knob from the beginning," she said, looking at one of the rows of knobs.

Elizabeth Eliza was sure of this. Agamemnon, she believed, had put three extra knobs at each end.

"But which is the end, and which is the beginning, — the top or the bottom?" Mrs. Peterkin asked hopelessly.

Still she bravely selected a knob, and Elizabeth Eliza hastened with her to look out for the messenger. How soon should they see the telegraph boy?

They seemed to have scarcely reached the window, when a terrible noise was heard, and down the shady street the white horses of the fire-brigade were seen rushing at a fatal speed!

It was a terrific moment!

"I have touched the fire-alarm," Mrs. Peterkin exclaimed.

Both rushed to open the front door in agony. By this time the fire-engines were approaching.

"Do not be alarmed," said the chief engineer; "the furniture shall be carefully covered, and we will move all that is necessary."

"Move again!" exclaimed Mrs. Peterkin, in agony.

Elizabeth Eliza strove to explain that she was only sending a telegram to her father, who was in Boston.

"It is not important," said the head engineer; "the fire will all be out before it could reach him."

And he ran upstairs, for the engines were beginning to play upon the roof.

Mrs. Peterkin rushed to the knobs again hurriedly; there was more necessity for summoning Mr. Peterkin home.

"Write a telegram to your father," she said to Elizabeth Eliza, "to 'come home directly.'"

"That will take but three words," said Elizabeth Eliza, with presence of mind, "and we need ten. I was just trying to make them out."

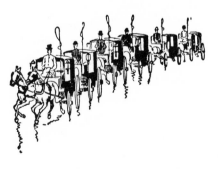

"What has come now?" exclaimed Mrs. Peterkin, and they hurried again to the window, to see a row of carriages coming down the street.

"I must have touched the carriage-knob," cried Mrs. Peterkin, "and I pushed it half-a-dozen times I felt so anxious!"

Six hacks stood before the door. All the village boys were assembling. Even their own little boys had returned from school, and were showing the firemen the way to the well.

Again Mrs. Peterkin rushed to the knobs, and a fearful sound arose. She had touched the burglar-alarm!

The former owner of the house, who had a great fear of burglars, had invented a machine of his own, which he had  connected with a knob. A wire attached to the knob moved a spring that could put in motion a number of watchmen's rattles, hidden under the eaves of the piazza.

All these were now set a-going, and their terrible din roused those of the neighborhood who had not before assembled around the house. At this moment Elizabeth Eliza met the chief engineer.

"You need not send for more help," he said; "we have all the engines in town here, and have stirred up all the towns in the neighborhood; there's no use in springing any more alarms. I can't find the fire yet, but we have water pouring all over the house."

Elizabeth Eliza waved her telegram in the air.

"We are only trying to send a telegram to my father and brother, who are in town," she endeavored to explain.

"If it is necessary," said the chief engineer, "you might send it down in one of the hackney carriages. I see a number standing before the door. We'd better begin to move the heavier furniture, and some of you women might fill the carriages with smaller things."

Mrs. Peterkin was ready to fall into hysterics. She controlled herself with a supreme power, and hastened to touch another knob.

Elizabeth Eliza corrected her telegram, and decided to take the advice of the chief engineer and went to the door to give her message to one of the hackmen, when she saw a telegraph boy appear. Her mother had touched the right knob. It was the fourth from the beginning; but the beginning was at the other end!

She went out to meet the boy, when, to her joy, she saw behind him her father and Agamemnon. She clutched her telegram, and hurried toward them.

Mr. Peterkin was bewildered. Was the house on fire? If so, where were the flames?

He saw the row of carriages. Was there a funeral, or a wedding? Who was dead? Who was to be married?

He seized the telegram that Elizabeth Eliza reached to him, and read it aloud.

"Come to us directly — the house is NOT on fire!"

The chief engineer was standing on the steps.

"The house not on fire!" he exclaimed. "What are we all summoned for?"

"It is a mistake," cried Elizabeth Eliza, wringing her hands. "We touched the wrong knob; we wanted the telegraph boy!"

"We touched all the wrong knobs," exclaimed Mrs. Peterkin, from the house.

The chief engineer turned directly to give counter-directions, with a few exclamations of disgust, as the bells of distant fire-engines were heard approaching.

Solomon John appeared at this moment, and proposed taking one of the carriages, and going for a doctor for his mother, for she was now nearly ready to fall into hysterics, and Agamemnon thought to send a telegram down by the boy, for the evening papers, to announce that the Peterkins' house had not been on fire.

The crisis of the commotion had reached its height. The beds of flowers, bordered with dark-colored leaves, were trodden down by the feet of the crowd that had assembled.

The chief engineer grew more and more indignant, as he sent his men to order back the fire-engines from the neighboring towns. The collection of boys followed the procession as it went away. The fire-brigade hastily removed covers from some of the furniture, restored the rest to their places, and took away their ladders. Many neighbors remained, but Mr. Peterkin hastened into the house to attend to Mrs. Peterkin.

Elizabeth Eliza took an opportunity to question her father, before he went in, as to the success of their visit to town.

"We saw all the patent-agents," answered Mr. Peterkin, in a hollow whisper. "Not one of them will touch the patent, or have anything to do with it."

Elizabeth Eliza looked at Agamemnon, as he walked silently into the house. She would not now speak to him of the patent; but she recalled some words of Solomon John. When they were discussing the patent he had said that many an inventor had grown gray before his discovery was acknowledged by the public. Others might reap the harvest, but it came, perhaps, only when he was going to his grave.

Elizabeth Eliza looked at Agamemnon reverently, and followed him silently into the house.

23

Agamemnon's Career

THERE had apparently been some mistake in Agamemnon's education. He had been to a number of colleges, indeed, but he had never completed his course in any one. He had continually fallen into some difficulty with the authorities. It was singular, for he was of an inquiring mind, and had always tried to find out what would be expected of him, but had never hit upon the right thing.

Solomon John thought the trouble might be in what they called the elective system, where you were to choose what study you might take. This had always bewildered Agamemnon a good deal.

"And how was a feller to tell," Solomon John had asked, "whether he wanted to study a thing before he tried it? It might turn out awful hard!"

Agamemnon had always been fond of reading, from his childhood up. He was at his book all day long. Mrs. Peterkin had imagined he would come out a great scholar, because she could never get him away from his books.

And so it was in his colleges; he was always to be found in the library, reading and reading. But they were always the wrong books.

For instance: the class were required to prepare themselves on the Spartan war. This turned Agamemnon's attention to the Fenians, and to study the subject he read up on "Charles O'Malley," and "Harry Lorrequer," and some later novels of that sort, which did not help him on the subject required, yet took up all his time, so that he found himself unfitted for anything else when the examinations came. In consequence he was requested to leave.

Agamemnon always missed in his recitations, for the same reason that Elizabeth Eliza did not get on in school, because he was always asked the questions he did not know. It seemed provoking; if the professors had only asked something else! But they always hit upon the very things he had not studied up.

Mrs. Peterkin felt this was encouraging, for Agamemnon knew the things they did not know in colleges. In colleges they were willing to take for students only those who already knew certain things. She thought Agamemnon might be a professor in a college for those students who didn't know those things.

"I suppose these professors could not have known a great deal," she added, "or they would not have asked you so many questions; they would have told you something."

Agamemnon had left another college on account of a mistake he had made with some of his classmates. They had taken a great deal of trouble to bring some wood from a distant wood-pile to make a bonfire with, under one of the professors' windows. Agamemnon had felt it would be a compliment to the professor.

It was with bonfires that heroes had been greeted on their return from successful wars. In this way beacon-lights had been kindled upon lofty heights, that had inspired mariners seeking their homes after distant adventures. As he plodded back and forward he imagined himself some hero of antiquity. He was reading "Plutarch's Lives" with deep interest. This had been recommended at a former college, and he was now taking it up in the midst of his French course. He fancied, even, that some future Plutarch was growing up in Lynn, perhaps, who would write of this night of suffering, and glorify its heroes.

For himself he took a severe cold and suffered from chilblains, in consequence of going back and forward through the snow, carrying the wood.

But the flames of the bonfire caught the blinds of the professor's room, and set fire to the building, and came near burning up the whole institution. Agamemnon regretted the result as much as his predecessor, who gave him his name, must have regretted that other bonfire, on the shores of Aulis, that deprived him of a daughter.

The result for Agamemnon was that he was requested to leave, after having been in the institution but a few months.

He left another college in consequence of a misunderstanding about the hour for morning prayers. He went every day regularly at ten o'clock, but found, afterward, that he should have gone at half-past six. This hour seemed to him and to Mrs. Peterkin unseasonable, at a time of year when the sun was not up, and he would have been obliged to go to the expense of candles.

Agamemnon was always willing to try another college, wherever he could be admitted. He wanted to attain knowledge, however it might be found. But, after going to five, and leaving each before the year was out, he gave it up.

He determined to lay out the money that would have been expended in a collegiate education in buying an Encyclopaedia, the most complete that he could find, and to spend his life studying it systematically. He would not content himself with merely reading it, but he would study into each subject as it came up, and perfect himself in that subject. By the time, then, that he had finished the Encyclopaedia he should have embraced all knowledge, and have experienced much of it.

The family were much interested in this plan of making practice of every subject that came up.

He did not, of course, get on very fast in this way. In the second column of the very first page he met with A as a note in music. This led him to the study of music. He bought a flute, and took some lessons, and attempted to accompany Elizabeth Eliza on the piano. This, of course, distracted him from his work on the Encyclopaedia. But he did not wish to return to A until he felt perfect in music. This required a long time.

Then in this same paragraph a reference was made; in it he was requested to "see Keys." It was necessary, then, to turn to "Keys." This was about the time the family were moving, which we have mentioned, when the difficult subject of keys came up, that suggested to him his own simple invention, and the hope of getting a patent for it. This led him astray, as inventions before have done with masterminds, so that he was drawn aside from his regular study.

The family, however, were perfectly satisfied with the career Agamemnon had chosen. It would help them all, in any path of life, if he should master the Encyclopaedia in a thorough way.

Mr. Peterkin agreed it would in the end be not as expensive as a college course, even if Agamemnon should buy all the different Encyclopaedias that appeared. There would be no "spreads" involved; no expense of receiving friends at entertainments in college; he could live at home, so that it would not be necessary to fit up another room, as at college. At all the times of his leaving he had sold out favorably to other occupants.

Solomon John's destiny was more uncertain. He was looking forward to being a doctor some time, but he had not decided whether to be allopathic or homoeopathic, or whether he could not better invent his own pills. And he could not understand how to obtain his doctor's degree.

For a few weeks he acted as clerk in a druggist's store. But he could serve only in the tooth-brush and soap department, because it was found he was not familiar enough with the Latin language to compound the drugs. He agreed to spend his evenings in studying the Latin grammar; but his course was interrupted by his being dismissed for treating the little boys too frequently to soda.

The little boys were going through the schools regularly. The family had been much exercised with regard to their education. Elizabeth Eliza felt that everything should be expected from them; they ought to take advantage from the family mistakes. Every new method that came up was tried upon the little boys. They had been taught spelling by all the different systems, and were just able to read, when Mr. Peterkin learned that it was now considered best that children should not be taught to read till they were ten years old.

Mrs. Peterkin was in despair. Perhaps, if their books were taken from them even then, they might forget what they had learned. But no, the evil was done; the brain had received certain impressions that could not be blurred over.

This was long ago, however. The little boys had since entered the public schools. They went also to a gymnasium, and a whittling school, and joined a class in music, and another in dancing; they went to some afternoon lectures for children, when there was no other school, and belonged to a walking-club. Still Mr. Peterkin was dissatisfied by  the slowness of their progress. He visited the schools himself, and found that they did not lead their classes. It seemed to him a great deal of time was spent in things that were not instructive, such as putting on and taking off their india-rubber boots.

Elizabeth Eliza proposed that they should be taken from school and taught by Agamemnon from the Encyclopaedia. The rest of the family might help in the education at all hours of the day. Solomon John could take up the Latin grammar; and she could give lessons in French.

The little boys were enchanted with the plan, only they did not want to have the study-hours all the time.

Mr. Peterkin, however, had a magnificent idea, that they should make their life one grand Object Lesson. They should begin at breakfast, and study everything put upon the table, — the material of which it was made, and where it came from. In the study of the letter A, Agamemnon had embraced the study of music, and from one meal they might gain instruction enough for a day.

"We shall have the assistance," said Mr. Peterkin, "of Agamemnon, with his Encyclopaedia."

Agamemnon modestly suggested that he had not yet got out of A, and in their first breakfast everything would therefore have to begin with A.

"That would not be impossible," said Mr. Peterkin. "There is Amanda, who will wait on table, to start with" —

"We could have 'am-and-eggs," suggested Solomon John.

Mrs. Peterkin was distressed. It was hard enough to think of anything for breakfast, and impossible if it all had to begin with one letter.

Elizabeth Eliza thought it would not be necessary. All they were to do was to ask questions, as in examination papers, and find their answers as they could. They could still apply to the Encyclopaedia, even if it were not in Agamemnon's alphabetical course.

Mr. Peterkin suggested a great variety. One day they would study the botany of the breakfast-table; another day, its natural history. The study of butter would include that of the cow. Even that of the butter-dish would bring in geology. The little boys were charmed at the idea of learning pottery from the cream-jug, and they were promised a potter's wheel directly.

"You see, my dear," said Mr. Peterkin to his wife, "before many weeks we shall be drinking our milk from jugs made by our children."

Elizabeth Eliza hoped for a thorough study.

"Yes," said Mr. Peterkin, "we might begin with botany. That would be near to Agamemnon alphabetically. We ought to find out the botany of butter. On what does the cow feed?"

The little boys were eager to go out and see.

"If she eats clover," said Mr. Peterkin, "we shall expect the botany of clover."

The little boys insisted that they were to begin the next day; that very evening they should go out and study the cow.

Mrs. Peterkin sighed, and decided she would order a simple breakfast. The little boys took their note-books and pencils, and clambered upon the fence, where they seated themselves in a row.

For there were three little boys. So it was now supposed. They were always coming in or going out, and it had been difficult to count them, and nobody was very sure how many there were.

There they sat, however, on the fence, looking at the cow. She looked at them with large eyes.

"She won't eat," they cried, "while we are looking at her!"

So they turned about, and pretended to look into the street, and seated themselves that way, turning their heads back, from time to time, to see the cow.

"Now she is nibbling a clover."

"No, that is a bit of sorrel."

"It's a whole handful of grass."

"What kind of grass?" they exclaimed.

It was very hard, sitting with their backs to the cow, and pretending to the cow that they were looking into  the street, and yet to be looking at the cow all the time, and finding out what she was eating; and the upper rail of the fence was narrow and a little sharp. It was very high, too, for some additional rails had been put on to prevent the cow from jumping into the garden or street.

Suddenly, looking out into the hazy twilight, Elizabeth Eliza saw six legs and six india-rubber boots in the air, and the little boys disappeared!

"They are tossed by the cow! The little boys are tossed by the cow!"

Mrs. Peterkin rushed for the window, but fainted on the way. Solomon John and Elizabeth Eliza were hurrying to the door, but stopped, not knowing what to do next. Mrs. Peterkin recovered herself with a supreme effort, and sent them out to the rescue.

But what could they do? The fence had been made so high, to keep the cow out, that nobody could get in. The boy that did the milking had gone off with the key of the outer gate, and perhaps with the key of the shed door. Even if that were not locked, before Agamemnon could get round by the wood-shed and cow-shed, the little boys might be gored through and through!

Elizabeth Eliza ran to the neighbors, Solomon John to the druggist's for plasters, while Agamemnon made his way through the dining-room to the wood-shed and outer-shed door. Mr. Peterkin mounted the outside of the fence, while Mrs. Peterkin begged him not to put himself in danger. He climbed high enough to view the scene. He held to the corner post and reported what he saw.

They were not gored. The cow was at the other end of the lot. One of the little boys was lying in a bunch of dark leaves. He was moving.

The cow glared, but did not stir. Another little boy was pulling his india-rubber boots out of the mud. The cow still looked at him.

Another was feeling the top of his head. The cow began to crop the grass, still looking at him.

Agamemnon had reached and opened the shed-door. The little boys were next seen running toward it.

A crowd of neighbors, with pitchforks, had returned meanwhile with Elizabeth Eliza. Solomon John had brought four druggists. But, by the time they had reached the house, the three little boys were safe in the arms of their mother!

"This is too dangerous a form of education," she cried; "I had rather they went to school."

"No!" they bravely cried. They were still willing to try the other way.

24

The Educational Breakfast

MRS. PETERKIN'S nerves were so shaken by the excitement of the fall of the three little boys into the enclosure where the cow was kept that the educational breakfast was long postponed. The little boys continued at school, as before, and the conversation dwelt as little as possible upon the subject of education.

Mrs. Peterkin's spirits, however, gradually recovered. The little boys were allowed to watch the cow at her feed. A series of strings was arranged by Agamemnon and Solomon John, by which the little boys could be pulled up, if they should again fall down into the enclosure. These were planned something like curtain-cords, and Solomon John frequently amused himself by pulling one of the little boys up or letting him down.

Some conversation did again fall upon the old difficulty of questions. Elizabeth Eliza declared that it was not always necessary to answer; that many who could did not answer questions, — the conductors of the railroads, for instance, who probably knew the names of all the stations on a road, but were seldom able to tell them.

"Yes," said Agamemnon, "one might be a conductor without even knowing the names of the stations, because you can't understand them when they do tell them!"

"I never know," said Elizabeth Eliza, "whether it is ignorance in them, or unwillingness, that prevents them from telling you how soon one station is coming, or how long you are to stop, even if one asks ever so many times. It would be so useful if they would tell."

Mrs. Peterkin thought this was carried too far in the horse-cars in Boston. The conductors had always left you as far as possible from the place where you wanted to stop; but it seemed a little too much to have the aldermen take it up, and put a notice in the cars, ordering the conductors "to stop at the farthest crossing."

Mrs. Peterkin was, indeed, recovering her spirits. She had been carrying on a brisk correspondence with Philadelphia, that she had imparted to no one, and at last she announced, as its result, that she was ready for a breakfast on educational principles.

A breakfast indeed, when it appeared! Mrs. Peterkin had mistaken the alphabetical suggestion, and had grasped the idea that the whole alphabet must be represented in one breakfast.

This, therefore, was the bill of fare: Apple-sauce, Bread, Butter, Coffee, Cream, Doughnuts, Eggs, Fish-balls, Griddles, Ham, Ice (on butter), Jam, Krout (sour), Lamb-chops, Morning Newspapers, Oatmeal, Pepper, Quince-marmalade, Rolls, Salt, Tea Urn, Veal-pie, Waffles, Yeast-biscuit.

Mr. Peterkin was proud and astonished. "Excellent!" he cried. "Every letter represented except Z." Mrs. Peterkin drew from her pocket a letter from the lady from Philadelphia. "She thought you would call it X-cellent for X, and she tells us," she read, "that if you come with a zest, you will bring the Z."

Mr. Peterkin was enchanted. He only felt that he ought to invite the children in the primary schools to such a breakfast; what a zest, indeed, it would give to the study of their letters!

It was decided to begin with Apple-sauce.

"How happy," exclaimed Mr. Peterkin, "that this should come first of all! A child might be brought up on apple-sauce till he had mastered the first letter of the alphabet, and could go on to the more involved subjects hidden in bread, butter, baked beans, etc."

Agamemnon thought his father hardly knew how much was hidden in the apple. There was all the story of William Tell and the Swiss independence. The little boys were wild to act William Tell, but Mrs. Peterkin was afraid of the arrows. Mr. Peterkin proposed they should begin by eating the apple-sauce, then discussing it, first botanically, next historically; or perhaps first historically, beginning with Adam and Eve, and the first apple.

Mrs. Peterkin feared the coffee would be getting cold, and the griddles were waiting. For herself, she declared she felt more at home on the marmalade, because the quinces came from grandfather's, and she had  seen them planted; she remembered all about it, and now the bush came up to the sitting-room window. She seemed to have heard him tell that the town of Quincy, where the granite came from, was named from them, and she never quite recollected why, except they were so hard, as hard as stone, and it took you almost the whole day to stew them, and then you might as well set them on again.

Mr. Peterkin was glad to be reminded of the old place at grandfather's. In order to know thoroughly about apples they ought to understand the making of cider. Now, they might some time drive up to grandfather's, scarcely twelve miles away, and see the cider made. Why, indeed, should not the family go this very day up to grandfather's and continue the education of the breakfast?

"Why not, indeed?" exclaimed the little boys. A day at grandfather's would give them the whole process of the apple, from the orchard to the cider-mill. In this way they could widen the field of study, even to follow in time the cup of coffee to Java.

It was suggested, too, that at grandfather's they might study the processes of maple syrup as involved in the griddle-cakes.

Agamemnon pointed out the connection between the two subjects: they were both the products of trees, — the apple-tree and the maple. Mr. Peterkin proposed that the lesson for the day should be considered the study of trees, and on the way they could look at other trees.

Why not, indeed, go this very day? There was no time like the present. Their breakfast had been so copious they would scarcely be in a hurry for dinner, and would, therefore, have the whole day before them.

Mrs. Peterkin could put up the remains of the breakfast for luncheon.

But how should they go? The carryall, in spite of its name, could hardly take the whole family, though they might squeeze in six, as the little boys did not take up much room.

Elizabeth Eliza suggested that she could spend the night at grandfather's. Indeed, she had been planning a visit there, and would not object to staying some days. This would make it easier about coming home, but it did not settle the difficulty in getting there.

Why not "Ride and Tie"?

The little boys were fond of walking; so was Mr. Peterkin; and Agamemnon and Solomon John did not object to their turn. Mrs. Peterkin could sit in the carriage, when it was waiting for the pedestrians to come up; or, she said, she did not object to a little turn of walking. Mr. Peterkin would start, with Solomon John and the little boys, before the rest, and Agamemnon should drive his mother and Elizabeth Eliza to the first stopping-place.

Then came up another question, —of Elizabeth Eliza's trunk. If she stayed a few days she would need to carry something. It might be hot, and it might be cold. Just  as soon as she carried her thin things she would need her heaviest wraps. You never could depend upon the weather. Even "Probabilities" got you no farther than to-day.

In an inspired moment Elizabeth Eliza bethought herself of the expressman. She would send her trunk by the express, and she left the table directly to go and pack it. Mrs. Peterkin busied herself with Amanda over the remains of the breakfast. Mr. Peterkin and Agamemnon went to order the horse and the expressman, and Solomon John and the little boys prepared themselves for a pedestrian excursion.

Elizabeth Eliza found it difficult to pack in a hurry; there were so many things she might want, and then again she might not. She must put up her music, because her grandfather had a piano; and then she bethought herself of Agamemnon's flute, and decided to pick out a volume or two of the Encyclopaedia. But it was hard to decide, all by herself, whether to take G for griddle-cakes, or M for maple syrup, or T for tree. She would take as many as she could make room for. She put up her work-box and two extra work-baskets, and she must take some French books she had never yet found time to read. This involved taking her French dictionary, as she doubted if her grandfather had one. She ought to put in a "Botany," if they were to study trees; but she could not tell which, so she would take all there were. She might as well take all her dresses, and it was no harm if one had too many wraps. When she had her trunk packed she found it over-full; it was difficult

to shut it. She had heard Solomon John set out from the front door with his father and the little boys, and Agamemnon was busy holding the horse at the side door, so there was no use in calling for help. She got upon the trunk; she jumped upon it; she sat down upon it, and, leaning over, found she could lock it! Yes, it was really locked.

But, on getting down from the trunk, she found her dress had been caught in the lid; she could not move away from it! What was worse, she was so fastened to the trunk that she could not lean forward far enough to turn the key back, to unlock the trunk and release herself! The lock had slipped easily, but she could not now get hold of the key in the right way to turn it back.

She tried to pull her dress away. No, it was caught too firmly. She called for help to her mother or Amanda, to come and open the trunk. But her door was shut. Nobody near enough to hear! She tried to pull the trunk toward the door, to open it and make herself heard; but it was so heavy that, in her constrained position, she could not stir it. In her agony she would have been willing to have torn her dress; but it was her travelling dress, and too stout to tear. She might cut it carefully. Alas, she had packed her scissors, and her knife she had lent to the little boys the day before! She called again. What silence there was in the house! Her voice seemed to echo through the room. At length, as she listened, she heard the sound of wheels.

Was it the carriage, rolling away from the side door? Did she hear the front door shut? She remembered then that Amanda was to "have the day." But she, Elizabeth Eliza, was to have spoken to Amanda, to explain to her to wait for the expressman. She was to have told her as she went downstairs. But she had not been able to go downstairs! And Amanda must have supposed that all the family had left, and she, too, must have gone, knowing nothing of the expressman. Yes, she heard the wheels! She heard the front door shut!

But could they have gone without her? Then she recalled that she had proposed walking on a little way with Solomon John and her father, to be picked up by Mrs. Peterkin, if she should have finished her packing in time. Her mother must have supposed that she had done so, — that she had spoken to Amanda, and started with the rest. Well, she would soon discover her mistake. She would overtake the walking party, and, not finding Elizabeth Eliza, would return for her. Patience only was needed. She had looked around for something to read; but she had packed up all her books. She had packed her knitting. How quiet and still it was! She tried to imagine where her mother would meet the rest of the family. They were good walkers, and they might have reached the two-mile bridge. But suppose they should stop for water beneath the arch of the bridge, as they often did, and the carryall pass over it without seeing them, her mother would not know but she was with them? And suppose her mother should decide to leave the horse at the place proposed for stopping and waiting for the first pedestrian party, and herself walk on, no one would be left to tell the rest when they should come up to the carryall. They might go on so, through the whole journey, without meeting, and she might not be missed till they should reach her grandfather's!

Horrible thought! She would be left here alone all day. The expressman would come, but the expressman would go, for he would not be able to get into the house!

She thought of the terrible story of Ginevra, of the bride who was shut up in her trunk, and forever! She was shut up on hers, and knew not when she should be released! She had acted once in the ballad of the "Mistletoe Bough." She had been one of the "guests," who had sung "Oh, the Mistletoe Bough!" and had looked up at it, and she had seen at the side-scenes how the bride had laughingly stepped into the trunk. But the trunk then was only a make-believe of some boards in front of a sofa, and this was a stern reality.

It would be late now before her family would reach her grandfather's. Perhaps they would decide to spend the night. Perhaps they would fancy she was coming by express. She gave another tremendous effort to move the trunk toward the door. In vain. All was still.

Meanwhile, Mrs. Peterkin sat some time at the door, wondering why Elizabeth Eliza did not come down. Mr. Peterkin had started on, with Solomon John and all the little boys. Agamemnon had packed the things into the carriage, — a basket of lunch, a change of shoes for Mr. Peterkin, some extra wraps, — everything that  Mrs. Peterkin could think of for the family comfort. Still Elizabeth Eliza did not come. "I think she must have walked on with your father," she said, at last; "you had better get in." Agamemnon now got in. "I should think she would have mentioned it," she continued; "but we may as well start on, and pick her up!" They started off. "I hope Elizabeth Eliza thought to speak to Amanda, but we must ask her when we come up with her."

But they did not come up with Elizabeth Eliza. At the turn beyond the village they found an envelope stuck up in an inviting manner against a tree. In this way they had agreed to leave missives for each other as they passed on. This note informed them that the walking party was going to take the short cut across the meadows, and would still be in front of them. They saw the party at last, just beyond the short cut; but Mr. Peterkin was explaining the character of the oak-tree to his children as they stood around a large specimen.

"I suppose he is telling them that it is some kind of a '*Quercus*,'" said Agamemnon, thoughtfully.

Mrs. Peterkin thought Mr. Peterkin would scarcely use such an expression; but she could see nothing of Elizabeth Eliza. Some of the party, however, were behind the tree, some were in front, and Elizabeth Eliza might be behind the tree. They were too far off to be shouted at. Mrs. Peterkin was calmed, and went on to the stopping-place agreed upon, which they reached before long. This had been appointed near Farmer Gordon's barn, that there might be somebody at hand whom they knew, in case there should be any difficulty in untying the horse. The plan had been that Mrs. Peterkin should always sit in the carriage, while the others should take turns for walking; and Agamemnon tied the horse to a fence, and left her comfortably arranged with her knitting. Indeed, she had risen so early to prepare for the alphabetical breakfast, and had since been so tired with preparations, that she was quite sleepy, and would not object to a nap in the shade, by the soothing sound of the buzzing of the flies. But she called Agamemnon back, as he started off for his solitary walk, with a perplexing question:—

"Suppose the rest all should arrive, how could they now be accommodated in the carryall? It would be too much for the horse! Why had Elizabeth Eliza gone with the rest without counting up? Of course, they must have expected that she—Mrs. Peterkin—would walk on to the next stopping-place!"

She decided there was no way but for her to walk on. When the rest passed her they might make a change. So she put up her knitting cheerfully. It was a little joggly in the carriage, she had already found, for the horse was restless from the flies, and she did not like being left alone. She walked on then with Agamemnon. It was very pleasant at first, but the sun became hot, and it was not long before she was fatigued. When they reached a hay-field she proposed going in to rest upon one of the hay-cocks. The largest and most shady was at the other end of the field, and they were seated there when the carryall passed them in the road. Mrs. Peterkin waved parasol and hat, and the party in the carryall returned their greetings; but they were too far apart to hear each other.

Mrs. Peterkin and Agamemnon slowly resumed their walk.

"Well, we shall find Elizabeth Eliza in the carryall," she said, "and that will explain all."

But it took them an hour or two to reach the carryall, with frequent stoppings for rest, and when they reached it no one was in it. A note was pinned up in the vehicle to say they had all walked on; it was "prime fun."

In this way the parties continued to dodge each other, for Mrs. Peterkin felt that she must walk on from the next station, and the carryall missed her again while she and Agamemnon stopped in a house to rest, and for a glass of water. She reached the carryall to find again that no one was in it. The party had passed on for the last station, where it had been decided all should meet at the foot of grandfather's hill, that they might all arrive at the house together. Mrs. Peterkin and Agamemnon looked out eagerly for the party all the way, as Elizabeth Eliza must be tired by this time; but Mrs. Peterkin's last walk had been so slow that the other party were far in advance and reached the stopping-place before them. The little boys were all rowed out on the stone fence, awaiting them, full of delight at having reached grandfather's. Mr. Peterkin came forward to meet them, and, at the same moment with Mrs. Peterkin, exclaimed: "Where is Elizabeth Eliza?" Each party looked eagerly at the other; no Elizabeth Eliza was to be seen.

Where was she? What was to be done? Was she left behind? Mrs. Peterkin was convinced she must have somehow got to grandfather's. They hurried up the hill. Grandfather and all the family came out to greet them, for they had been seen approaching. There was great questioning, but no Elizabeth Eliza!

It was sunset; the view was wide and fine. Mr. and Mrs. Peterkin stood and looked out from the north to the south. Was it too late to send back for Elizabeth Eliza? Where was she?

Meanwhile the little boys had been informing the family of the object of their visit, and while Mr. and Mrs. Peterkin were looking up and down the road, and Agamemnon and Solomon John were explaining to each other the details of their journeys, they had discovered some facts.

"We shall have to go back," they exclaimed. "We are too late! The maple syrup was all made last spring."

"We are too early; we shall have to stay two or three months, — the cider is not made till October."

The expedition was a failure! They could study the making of neither maple syrup nor cider, and Elizabeth Eliza was lost, perhaps forever! The sun went down, and Mr. and Mrs. Peterkin still stood to look up and down the road.

.   .   .   .

Elizabeth Eliza, meanwhile, had sat upon her trunk, as it seemed, for ages. She recalled all the terrible stories of prisoners, — how they had watched the growth of flowers through cracks in the pavement. She wondered how long she could live without eating. How thankful she was for her abundant breakfast!

At length she heard the door-bell. But who could go to the door to answer it? In vain did she make another effort to escape; it was impossible!

How singular! — there were footsteps. Some one was going to the door; some one had opened it. "They must be burglars." Well, perhaps that was a better fate — to be gagged by burglars, and the neighbors informed — than to be forever locked on her trunk. The steps approached the door. It opened, and Amanda ushered in the expressman.

Amanda had not gone. She had gathered, while waiting at the breakfast-table, that there was to be an expressman whom she must receive.

Elizabeth Eliza explained the situation. The expressman turned the key of her trunk and she was released!

What should she do next? So long a time had elapsed she had given up all hope of her family returning for her. But how could she reach them?

She hastily prevailed upon the expressman to take her along until she should come up with some of the family. At least she would fall in with either the walking party or the carryall, or she would meet them if they were on their return.

She mounted the seat with the expressman, and slowly they took their way, stopping for occasional parcels as they left the village.

But, much to Elizabeth Eliza's dismay, they turned off from the main road on leaving the village. She remonstrated, but the driver insisted he must go round by Millikin's to leave a bedstead. They went round by Millikin's, and then had further turns to make. Elizabeth Eliza explained that in this way it would be impossible for her to find her parents and family, and at last he proposed to take her all the way with her trunk. She remembered with a shudder that when she had first asked about her trunk he had promised it should certainly be delivered the next morning. Suppose they should have to be out all night? Where did express-carts spend the night? She thought of herself in a lone wood, in an express-wagon! She could scarcely bring herself to ask, before assenting, when he should arrive.

He guessed he could bring up before night.

And so it happened that as Mr. and Mrs. Peterkin in the late sunset were looking down the hill, wondering what they should do about the lost Elizabeth Eliza, they saw an express-wagon approaching. A female form sat upon the front seat.

"She has decided to come by express," said Mrs. Peterkin. "It is—it is—Elizabeth Eliza!"

25

The Peterkins at the "Carnival of Authors" in Boston

HE Peterkins were in quite a muddle (for them) about the carnival of authors, to be given in Boston. As soon as it was announced, their interests were excited, and they determined that all the family should go.

But they conceived a wrong idea of the entertainment, as they supposed that every one must go in costume. Elizabeth Eliza thought their lessons in the foreign languages would help them much in conversing in character.

As the carnival was announced early Solomon John thought there would be time to read up everything written by all the authors, in order to be acquainted with the characters they introduced. Mrs. Peterkin did not wish to begin too early upon the reading, for she was sure she should forget all that the different authors had written before the day came.

But Elizabeth Eliza declared that she should hardly have time enough, as it was, to be acquainted with all the authors. She had given up her French lessons, after taking six, for want of time, and had, indeed, concluded she had learned in them all she should need to know of that language. She could repeat one or two pages of phrases, and she was astonished to find how much she could understand already of what the French teacher said to her; and he assured her that when she went to Paris she could at least ask the price of gloves, or of some other things she would need, and he taught her, too, how to pronounce "*garçon*," in calling for more.

Agamemnon thought that different members of the family might make themselves familiar with different authors; the little boys were already acquainted with "Mother Goose." Mr. Peterkin had read the "Pickwick Papers," and Solomon John had actually seen Mr. Longfellow getting into a horse-car.

Elizabeth Eliza suggested that they might ask the Turk to give lectures upon the "Arabian Nights." Everybody else was planning something of the sort, to "raise funds" for some purpose, and she was sure they ought not to be behindhand. Mrs. Peterkin approved of this. It would be excellent if they could raise funds enough to pay for their own tickets to the carnival; then they could go every night.

Elizabeth Eliza was uncertain. She thought it was usual to use the funds for some object. Mr. Peterkin said that if they gained funds enough they might arrange a booth of their own, and sit in it, and take the carnival comfortably. But Agamemnon reminded him that none of the family were authors, and only authors had booths. Solomon John, indeed, had once started upon writing a book, but he was not able to think of anything to put in it, and nothing had occurred to him yet.

Mr. Peterkin urged him to make one more effort. If his book could come out before the carnival he could go as an author, and might have a booth of his own, and take his family.

But Agamemnon declared it would take years to become an author. You might indeed publish something, but you had to make sure that it would be read. Mrs. Peterkin, on the other hand, was certain that libraries were filled with books that never were read, yet authors had written them. For herself, she had not read half the books in their own library. And she was glad there was to be a Carnival of Authors, that she might know who they were.

Mr. Peterkin did not understand why they called them a "Carnival"; but he supposed they should find out when they went to it.

Mrs. Peterkin still felt uncertain about costumes. She proposed looking over the old trunks in the garret. They would find some suitable dresses there, and these would suggest what characters they should take. Elizabeth Eliza was pleased with this thought. She remembered an old turban of white mull muslin, in an old bandbox, and why should not her mother wear it?

Mrs. Peterkin supposed that she should then go as her own grandmother.

Agamemnon did not approve of this. Turbans are now worn in the East, and Mrs. Peterkin could go in some Eastern character. Solomon John thought she might be Cleopatra, and this was determined on. Among the treasures found were some old bonnets, of large size, with waving plumes. Elizabeth Eliza decided upon the largest of these.

She was tempted to appear as Mrs. Columbus, as Solomon John was to take the character of Christopher Columbus; but he was planning to enter upon the stage in a boat, and Elizabeth Eliza was a little afraid of sea-sickness, as he had arranged to be a great while finding the shore.

Solomon John had been led to take this character by discovering a coal-hod that would answer for a helmet; then, as Christopher Columbus was born in Genoa, he could use the phrases in Italian he had lately learned of his teacher.

As the day approached the family had their costumes prepared.

Mr. Peterkin decided to be Peter the Great. It seemed to him a happy thought, for the few words of Russian he had learned would come in play, and he was quite sure that his own family name made him kin to that of the great Czar. He studied up the life in the Encyclopaedia, and decided to take the costume of a ship-builder. He visited the navy-yard and some of the docks; but none of them gave him the true idea of dress for ship-building in Holland or St. Petersburg. But he found a picture of Peter the Great, representing him in a broad-brimmed hat. So he assumed one that he found at a costumer's, and with Elizabeth Eliza's black water-proof was satisfied with his own appearance.

Elizabeth Eliza wondered if she could not go with her father in some Russian character. She would have to lay aside her large bonnet, but she had seen pictures of Russian ladies, with fur muffs on their heads, and she might wear her own muff.

Mrs. Peterkin, as Cleopatra, wore the turban, with a little row of false curls in front, and a white embroidered muslin shawl crossed over her black silk dress. The little boys thought she looked much like the picture of their great-grandmother. But doubtless Cleopatra resembled this picture, as it was all so long ago, so the rest of the family decided.

Agamemnon determined to go as Noah. The costume, as represented in one of the little boys' arks, was simple.

His father's red-lined dressing gown, turned inside out, permitted it easily.

Elizabeth Eliza was now anxious to be Mrs. Shem, and make a long dress of yellow flannel, and appear with Agamemnon and the little boys. For the little boys were to represent two doves and a raven. There were feather-dusters enough in the family for their costumes, which would be then complete with their india-rubber boots.

Solomon John carried out in detail his idea of Christopher Columbus. He had a number of eggs boiled hard to take in his pocket, proposing to repeat, through the evening, the scene of setting the egg on its end. He gave up the plan of a boat, as it must be difficult to carry one into town; so he contented himself by practising the motion of landing by stepping up on a chair.

But what scene could Elizabeth Eliza carry out? If they had an ark, as Mrs. Shem she might crawl in and out of the roof constantly, if it were not too high. But Mr. Peterkin thought it as difficult to take an ark into town as Solomon John's boat.

The evening came. But with all their preparations they got to the hall late. The entrance was filled with a crowd of people, and, as they stopped at the cloak-room, to leave their wraps, they found themselves entangled with a number of people in costume coming out from a dressing-room below. Mr. Peterkin was much encouraged. They were thus joining the performers. The band was playing the "Wedding March" as they went upstairs to a door of the hall which opened upon one side of the stage. Here a procession was marching up the steps of the stage, all in costume, and entering behind the scenes.

"We are just in the right time," whispered Mr. Peterkin to his family; "they are going upon the stage; we must fall into line."

The little boys had their feather-dusters ready.

Some words from one of the managers made Mr. Peterkin understand the situation.

"We are going to be introduced to Mr. Dickens," he said.

"I thought he was dead!" exclaimed Mrs. Peterkin, trembling.

"Authors live forever!" said Agamemnon in her ear.

At this moment they were ushered upon the stage.

The stage manager glared at them, as he awaited their names for introduction, while they came up all unannounced, — a part of the programme not expected. But he uttered the words upon his lips, "Great Expectations"; and the Peterkin family swept across the stage with the rest: Mr. Peterkin costumed as Peter the Great, Mrs. Peterkin as Cleopatra, Agamemnon as Noah, Solomon John as Christopher Columbus, Elizabeth Eliza in yellow flannel as Mrs. Shem, with a large, old-fashioned bonnet on her head as Mrs. Columbus, and the little boys behind as two doves and a raven.

Across the stage, in face of all the assembled people, then following the rest down the stairs on the other side, in among the audience, they went; but into an audience not dressed in costume!

There were Ann Maria Bromwick and the Osbornes, — all the neighbors, — all as natural as though they were walking the streets at home, though Ann Maria did wear white gloves.

"I had no idea you were to appear in character," said Ann Maria to Elizabeth Eliza; "to what booth do you belong?"

"We are no particular author," said Mr. Peterkin.

"Ah, I see, a sort of varieties' booth," said Mr. Osborne.

"What is your character?" asked Ann Maria of Elizabeth Eliza.

"I have not quite decided," said Elizabeth Eliza. "I thought I should find out after I came here. The marshal called us 'Great Expectations.'"

Mrs. Peterkin was at the summit of bliss. "I have shaken hands with Dickens!" she exclaimed.

But she looked round to ask the little boys if they, too, had shaken hands with the great man, but not a little boy could she find.

They had been swept off in Mother Goose's train, which had lingered on the steps to see the Dickens reception, with which the procession of characters in costume had closed. At this moment they were dancing round the bar-berry bush, in a corner of the balcony in Mother Goose's quarters, their feather-dusters gaily waving in the air.

But Mrs. Peterkin, far below, could not see this, and con-soled herself with the thought, they should all meet on the stage in the grand closing tableau. She was bewildered by the crowds which swept her hither and thither. At last she found herself in the Whittier Booth, and sat a long time calmly there. As Cleopatra she seemed out of place, but as her own grandmother she answered well with its New England scenery.

Solomon John wandered about, landing in America when-ever he found a chance to enter a booth. Once before an admiring audience he set up his egg in the centre of the Goethe Booth, which had been deserted by its committee for the larger stage.

Agamemnon frequently stood in the background of scenes in the "Arabian Nights."

It was with difficulty that the family could be repressed

from going on the stage whenever the bugle sounded for the different groups represented there.

Elizabeth Eliza came near appearing in the "Dream of Fair Women," at its most culminating point.

Mr. Peterkin found himself with the "Cricket on the Hearth," in the Dickens Booth. He explained that he was Peter the Great, but always in the Russian language, which was never understood.

Elizabeth Eliza found herself, in turn, in all the booths. Every manager was puzzled by her appearance, and would send her to some other, and she passed along, always trying to explain that she had not yet decided upon her character.

Mr. Peterkin came and took Cleopatra from the Whittier Booth.

"I cannot understand," he said, "why none of our friends are dressed in costume, and why we are."

"I rather like it," said Elizabeth Eliza, "though I should be better pleased if I could form a group with some one."

The strains of the minuet began. Mrs. Peterkin was anxious to join the performers. It was the dance of her youth.

But she was delayed by one of the managers on the steps that led to the stage.

"I cannot understand this company," he said, distractedly.

"They cannot find their booth," said another.

"That is the case," said Mr. Peterkin, relieved to have it stated.

"Perhaps you had better pass into the corridor," said a polite marshal.

They did this, and, walking across, found themselves in the refreshment-room. "This is the booth for us," said Mr. Peterkin.

"Indeed it is," said Mrs. Peterkin, sinking into a chair, exhausted.

At this moment two doves and a raven appeared, — the little boys, who had been dancing eagerly in Mother Goose's establishment, and now came down for ice-cream.

"I hardly know how to sit down," said Elizabeth Eliza, "for I am sure Mrs. Shem never could. Still, as I do not know if I am Mrs. Shem, I will venture it."

Happily, seats were to be found for all, and they were soon arranged in a row, calmly eating ice-cream.

"I think the truth is," said Mr. Peterkin, "that we represent historical people, and we ought to have been fictitious characters in books. That is, I observe, what the others are. We shall know better another time."

"If we only ever get home," said Mrs. Peterkin, "I shall not wish to come again. It seems like being on the stage, sitting in a booth, and it is so bewildering, Elizabeth Eliza not knowing who she is, and going round and round in this way."

"I am afraid we shall never reach home," said Agamemnon, who had been silent for some time; "we may have to spend the night here. I find I have lost our checks for our clothes in the cloak-room!"

"Spend the night in a booth, in Cleopatra's turban!" exclaimed Mrs. Peterkin.

"We should like to come every night," cried the little boys.

"But to spend the night," repeated Mrs. Peterkin.

"I conclude the Carnival keeps up all night," said Mr. Peterkin.

"But never to recover our cloaks," said Mrs. Peterkin; "could not the little boys look round for the checks on the floors?"

She began to enumerate the many valuable things that they might never see again. She had worn her large fur cape of stone-marten, — her grandmother's, — that Elizabeth Eliza had been urging her to have made into a foot-rug. Now how she wished she had! And there were Mr. Peterkin's new overshoes, and Agamemnon had brought an umbrella, and the little boys had their mittens. Their india-rubber boots, fortunately, they had on, in the character of birds. But Solomon John had worn a fur cap, and Elizabeth Eliza a muff. Should they lose all these valuables entirely, and go home in the cold without them? No, it would be better to wait till everybody had gone, and then look carefully over the floors for the checks; if only the little boys could know where Agamemnon had been, they were willing to look. Mr. Peterkin was not sure as they would have time to reach the train. Still, they would need something to wear, and he could not tell the time. He had not brought his watch. It was a Waltham watch, and he thought it would not be in character for Peter the Great to wear it.

At this moment the strains of "Home, Sweet Home" were heard from the band, and people were seen preparing to go.

"All can go home, but we must stay," said Mrs. Peterkin, gloomily, as the well-known strains floated in from the larger hall.

A number of marshals came to the refreshment-room, looked at them, whispered to each other, as the Peterkins sat in a row.

"Can we do anything for you?" asked one at last. "Would you not like to go?" He seemed eager they should leave the room.

Mr. Peterkin explained that they could not go, as they had lost the checks for their wraps, and hoped to find their checks on the floor when everybody was gone. The marshal asked if they could not describe what they had worn, in which case the loss of the checks was not so important, as the crowds had now almost left, and it would not be difficult to identify their wraps. Mrs. Peterkin eagerly declared she could describe every article.

It was astonishing how the marshals hurried them through the quickly deserted corridors, how gladly they recovered their garments! Mrs. Peterkin, indeed, was disturbed by the eagerness of the marshals; she feared they had some pretext for getting the family out of the hall. Mrs. Peterkin was one of those who never consent to be forced to anything. She would not be compelled to go home, even with strains of music. She whispered her suspicions to Mr. Peterkin; but Agamemnon came hastily up to announce the time, which he had learned from the clock in the large hall. They must leave directly if they wished to catch the latest train, as there was barely time to reach it.

Then, indeed, was Mrs. Peterkin ready to leave. If they should miss the train! If she should have to pass the night in the streets in her turban! She was the first to lead the way, and, panting, the family followed her, just in time to take the train as it was leaving the station.

The excitement was not yet over. They found in the train many of their friends and neighbors, returning also from the Carnival; so they had many questions put to them which they were unable to answer. Still Mrs. Peterkin's turban was much admired, and indeed the whole appearance of the family; so that they felt themselves much repaid for their exertions.

But more adventures awaited them. They left the train with their friends; but as Mrs. Peterkin and Elizabeth Eliza were very tired, they walked very slowly, and Solomon John and the little boys were sent on with the pass-key to open the door. They soon returned with the startling intelligence that it was not the right key, and they could not

get in. It was Mr. Peterkin's office-key; he had taken it
by mistake, or he might have dropped the house-key in the
cloak-room of the Carnival.

"Must we go back?" sighed Mrs. Peterkin, in an exhausted
voice. More than ever did Elizabeth Eliza regret that Agamemnon's invention in keys had failed to secure a patent!

It was impossible to get into the house, for Amanda had
been allowed to go and spend the night with a friend, so
there was no use in ringing, though the little boys had tried it.

"We can return to the station," said Mr. Peterkin; "the
rooms will be warm, on account of the midnight train. We
can, at least, think what we shall do next."

At the station was one of the neighbors, proposing to
take the New York midnight train, for it was now after
eleven, and the train went through at half-past.

"I saw lights at the locksmith's over the way, as I passed,"
he said; "why do not you send over to the young man there?
He can get your door open for you. I never would spend the
night here."

Solomon John went over to "the young man," who agreed
to go up to the house as soon as he had closed the shop,
fit a key, and open the door, and come back to them on his
way home. Solomon John came back to the station, for it
was now cold and windy in the deserted streets. The family
made themselves as comfortable as possible by the stove,
sending Solomon John out occasionally to look for the young
man. But somehow Solomon John missed him; the lights
were out in the locksmith's shop, so he followed along to
the house, hoping to find him there. But he was not there!
He came back to report. Perhaps the young man had opened
the door and gone on home. Solomon John and Agamemnon
went back together, but they could not get in. Where was

the young man? He had lately come to town, and nobody knew where he lived, for on the return of Solomon John and Agamemnon it had been proposed to go to the house of the young man. The night was wearing on. The midnight train had come and gone. The passengers who came and went looked with wonder at Mrs. Peterkin, nodding in her turban, as she sat by the stove, on a corner of a long bench. At last the station-master had to leave, for a short rest. He felt obliged to lock up the station, but he promised to return at an early hour to release them.

"Of what use," said Elizabeth Eliza, "if we cannot even then get into our own house?"

Mr. Peterkin thought the matter appeared bad, if the locksmith had left town. He feared the young man might have gone in, and helped himself to spoons, and left. Only they should have seen him if he had taken the midnight train. Solomon John thought he appeared honest. Mr. Peterkin only ventured to whisper his suspicions, as he did not wish to arouse Mrs. Peterkin, who still was nodding in the corner of the long bench.

Morning did come at last. The family decided to go to their home; perhaps by some effort in the early daylight they might make an entrance.

On the way they met with the night-policeman, returning from his beat. He stopped when he saw the family.

"Ah! that accounts," he said; "you were all out last night, and the burglars took occasion to make a raid on your house.

I caught a lively young man in the very act; box of tools in his hand! If I had been a minute late he would have made his way in" —

The family then tried to interrupt — to explain —

"Where is he?" exclaimed Mr. Peterkin.

"Safe in the lock-up," answered the policeman.

"But he is the locksmith!" interrupted Solomon John.

"We have no key!" said Elizabeth Eliza; "if you have locked up the locksmith we can never get in."

The policeman looked from one to the other, smiling slightly when he understood the case.

"The locksmith!" he exclaimed; "he is a new fellow, and I did not recognize him, and arrested him! Very well, I will go and let him out, that he may let you in!" and he hurried away, surprising the Peterkin family with what seemed like insulting screams of laughter.

"It seems to me a more serious case than it appears to him," said Mr. Peterkin.

Mrs. Peterkin did not understand it at all. Had burglars entered the house? Did the policeman say they had taken spoons? And why did he appear so pleased? She was sure the old silver teapot was locked up in the closet of their room. Slowly the family walked towards the house, and, almost as soon as they, the policeman appeared with the released locksmith, and a few boys from the street, who happened to be out early.

The locksmith was not in very good humor, and took ill the jokes of the policeman. Mr. Peterkin, fearing he might not consent to open the door, pressed into his hand a large sum of money. The door flew open; the family could go in. Amanda arrived at the same moment. There was hope of breakfast. Mrs. Peterkin staggered towards the stairs. "I shall never go to another Carnival!" she exclaimed.

26

The Peterkins at the Farm

ES, at last they had reached the seaside, after much talking and deliberation, and summer after summer the journey had been constantly postponed.

But here they were at last, at the "Old Farm," so called, where seaside attractions had been praised in all the advertisements. And here they were to meet the Sylvesters, who knew all about the place, cousins of Ann Maria Bromwick. Elizabeth Eliza was astonished not to find them there, though she had not expected Ann Maria to join them till the very next day.

Their preparations had been so elaborate that at one time the whole thing had seemed hopeless; yet here they all were. Their trunks, to be sure, had not arrived; but the wagon was to be sent back for them, and, wonderful to tell, they had all their hand-baggage safe.

Agamemnon had brought his Portable Electrical Machine and Apparatus, and the volumes of the Encyclopaedia that might tell him how to manage it, and Solomon John had his photograph camera. The little boys had used their india-rubber boots as portmanteaux, filling them to the brim, and carrying one in each hand, — a very convenient way for travelling they considered it; but they found on arriving (when they wanted to put their boots directly on, for exploration round the house), that it was somewhat inconvenient to have to begin to unpack directly, and scarcely room enough could be found for all the contents in the small chamber allotted to them.

There was no room in the house for the electrical machine and camera. Elizabeth Eliza thought the other boarders were afraid of the machine going off; so an out-house was found for them, where Agamemnon and Solomon John could arrange them.

Mrs. Peterkin was much pleased with the old-fashioned porch and low-studded rooms, though the sleeping-rooms seemed a little stuffy at first.

Mr. Peterkin was delighted with the admirable order in which the farm was evidently kept. From the first moment he arrived he gave himself to examining the well-stocked stables and barns, and the fields and vegetable gardens, which were shown to him by a highly intelligent person, a Mr. Atwood, who devoted himself to explaining to Mr. Peterkin all the details of methods in the farming.

The rest of the family were disturbed at being so far from the sea, when they found it would take nearly all the afternoon to reach the beach. The advertisements had surely stated that the "Old Farm" was directly on the shore, and that sea-bathing would be exceedingly convenient; which was hardly the case if it took you an hour and a half to walk it.

Mr. Peterkin declared there were always such discrepancies between the advertisements of seaside places and the actual facts; but he was more than satisfied with the farm part, and was glad to remain and admire it, while the rest of the family went to find the beach, starting off in a wagon large enough to accommodate them, Agamemnon driving the one horse.

Solomon John had depended upon taking the photographs of the family in a row on the beach; but he decided not to take his camera out the first afternoon.

This was well, as the sun was already setting when they reached the beach.

"If this wagon were not so shaky," said Mrs. Peterkin, "we might drive over every morning for our bath. The road is very straight, and I suppose Agamemnon can turn on the beach."

"We should have to spend the whole day about it," said Solomon John, in a discouraged tone, "unless we can have a quicker horse."

"Perhaps we should prefer that," said Elizabeth Eliza, a little gloomily, "to staying at the house."

She had been a little disturbed to find there were not more elegant and fashionable-looking boarders at the farm, and she was disappointed that the Sylvesters had not arrived, who would understand the ways of the place. Yet, again, she was somewhat relieved, for if their trunks did not come till the next day, as was feared, she should have nothing but her travelling dress to wear, which would certainly answer for to-night.

She had been busy all the early summer in preparing her dresses for this very watering-place, and, as far as appeared, she would hardly need them, and was disappointed to have no chance to display them. But of course, when the Sylvesters and Ann Maria came, all would be different; but they would surely be wasted on the two old ladies she had seen, and on the old men who had lounged about the porch; there surely was not a gentleman among them.

Agamemnon assured her she could not tell at the seaside, as gentlemen wore their exercise dress, and took a pride in going around in shocking hats and flannel suits. Doubtless they would be dressed for dinner on their return.

On their arrival they had been shown to a room to have their meals by themselves, and could not decide whether they were eating dinner or lunch. There was a variety of meat, vegetables, and pie, that might come under either name; but Mr. and Mrs. Peterkin were well pleased.

"I had no idea we should have really farm-fare," Mrs. Peterkin said. "I have not drunk such a tumbler of milk since I was young."

Elizabeth Eliza concluded they ought not to judge from a first meal, as evidently their arrival had not been fully prepared for, in spite of the numerous letters that had been exchanged.

The little boys were, however, perfectly satisfied from the moment of their arrival, and one of them had stayed at the farm, declining to go to the beach, as he wished to admire the pigs, cows, and horses; and all the way over to the beach the other little boys were hopping in and out of the wagon, which never went too fast, to pick long mullein-stalks, for whips to urge on the reluctant horse with, or to gather huckleberries, with which they were rejoiced to find the fields were filled, although, as yet, the berries were very green.

They wanted to stay longer on the beach, when they finally reached it; but Mrs. Peterkin and Elizabeth Eliza insisted upon turning directly back, as it was not fair to be late to dinner the very first night.

On the whole the party came back cheerful, yet hungry. They found the same old men, in the same costume, standing against the porch.

"A little seedy, I should say," said Solomon John.

"Smoking pipes," said Agamemnon; "I believe that is the latest style."

"The smell of their tobacco is not very agreeable," Mrs. Peterkin was forced to say.

There seemed the same uncertainty on their arrival as to where they were to be put, and as to their meals.

Elizabeth Eliza tried to get into conversation with the old ladies, who were wandering in and out of a small sitting-room. But one of them was very deaf, and the other seemed to be a foreigner. She discovered from a moderately tidy maid, by the name of Martha, who seemed a sort of factotum, that there were other ladies in their rooms, too much of invalids to appear.

"Regular bed-ridden," Martha had described them, which Elizabeth Eliza did not consider respectful.

Mr. Peterkin appeared coming down the slope of the hill behind the house, very cheerful. He had made the tour of the farm, and found it in admirable order.

Elizabeth Eliza felt it time to ask Martha about the next meal, and ventured to call it supper, as a sort of compromise between dinner and tea. If dinner were expected she might offend by taking it for granted that it was to be "tea," and if they were unused to a late dinner they might be disturbed if they had only provided a "tea."

So she asked what was the usual hour for supper, and was surprised when Martha replied, "The lady must say," nodding to Mrs. Peterkin. "She can have it just when she wants, and just what she wants!"

This was an unexpected courtesy.

Elizabeth Eliza asked when the others had their supper.

"Oh, they took it a long time ago," Martha answered. "If the lady will go out into the kitchen she can tell what she wants."

"Bring us in what you have," said Mr. Peterkin, himself quite hungry. "If you could cook us a fresh slice of beefsteak that would be well."

"Perhaps some eggs," murmured Mrs. Peterkin.

"Scrambled," cried one of the little boys.

"Fried potatoes would not be bad," suggested Agamemnon.

"Couldn't we have some onions?" asked the little boy who had stayed at home, and had noticed the odor of onions when the others had their supper.

"A pie would come in well," said Solomon John.

"And some stewed cherries," said the other little boy.

Martha fell to laying the table, and the family was much pleased, when, in the course of time, all the dishes they had recommended appeared. Their appetites were admirable, and they pronounced the food the same.

"This is true Arab hospitality," said Mr. Peterkin, as he cut his juicy beefsteak.

"I know it," said Elizabeth Eliza, whose spirits began to rise. "We have not even seen the host and hostess."

She would, indeed, have been glad to find some one to tell her when the Sylvesters were expected, and why they had not arrived. Her room was in the wing, far from that of Mr. and Mrs. Peterkin, and near the aged deaf and foreign ladies, and she was kept awake for some time by perplexed thoughts.

She was sure the lady from Philadelphia, under such circumstances, would have written to somebody. But ought she to write to Ann Maria or the Sylvesters? And, if she

did write, which had she better write to? She fully determined to write, the first thing in the morning, to both parties.
But how should she address her letters? Would there be any
use in sending to the Sylvesters' usual address, which she
knew well by this time, merely to say they had not come?
Of course the Sylvesters would know they had not come.
It would be the same with Ann Maria. She might, indeed,
inclose her letters to their several postmasters. Postmasters
were always so obliging, and always knew where people were
going to, and where to send their letters. She might, at
least, write two letters, to say that they — the Peterkins —
had arrived, and were disappointed not to find the Sylvesters.
And she could add that their trunks had not arrived, and
perhaps their friends might look out for them on their way.
It really seemed a good plan to write. Yet another question
came up, as to how she would get her letters to the post-
office, as she had already learned it was at quite a distance,
and in a different direction from the station, where they were
to send the next day for their trunks.

She went over and over these same questions, kept awake
by the coughing and talking of her neighbors, the other
side of the thin partition.

She was scarcely sorry to be aroused from her uncomfortable sleep by the morning sounds of guinea-hens, pea-
cocks, and every other kind of fowl.

Mrs. Peterkin expressed her satisfaction at the early
breakfast, and declared she was delighted with such genuine
farm sounds.

They passed the day much as the afternoon before, reaching the beach only in time to turn round to come back for
their dinner, which was appointed at noon. Mrs. Peterkin
was quite satisfied. "Such a straight road, and the beach
such a safe place to turn round upon!"

Elizabeth Eliza was not so well pleased. A wagon had been sent to the station for their trunks, which could not be found; they were probably left at the Boston station, or, Mr. Atwood suggested, might have been switched off upon one of the White Mountain trains. There was no use to write any letters, as there was no way to send them. Elizabeth Eliza now almost hoped the Sylvesters would not come, for what should she do if the trunks did not come and all her new dresses? On her way to the beach she had been thinking what she should do with her new foulard and cream-colored surah if the Sylvesters did not come, and if their time was spent in only driving to the beach and back. But now, she would prefer that the Sylvesters would not come till the dresses and the trunks did. All she could find out, from inquiry, on returning, was, "that another lot was expected on Saturday." The next day she suggested: —

"Suppose we take our dinner with us to the beach, and spend the day." The Sylvesters and Ann Maria then would find them on the beach, where her travelling-dress would be quite appropriate. "I am a little tired," she added, "of going back and forward over the same road; but when the rest come we can vary it."

The plan was agreed to, but Mr. Peterkin and the little boys remained to go over the farm again.

They had an excellent picnic on the beach, under the shadow of a ledge of sand. They were just putting up their things when they saw a party of people approaching from the other end of the beach.

"I am glad to see some pleasant-looking people at last," said Elizabeth Eliza, and they turned to walk toward them.

As the other party drew near she recognized Ann Maria Bromwick! And with her were the Sylvesters, — so they proved to be, for she had never seen them before.

"What! you have come in our absence!" exclaimed Elizabeth Eliza.

"And we have been wondering what had become of you!" cried Ann Maria.

"I thought you would be at the farm before us," said Elizabeth Eliza to Mr. Sylvester, to whom she was introduced.

"We have been looking for you at the farm," he was saying to her.

"But we are at the farm," said Elizabeth Eliza.

"And so are we!" said Ann Maria.

"We have been there two days," said Mrs. Peterkin.

"And so have we, at the 'Old Farm,' just at the end of the beach," said Ann Maria.

"Our farm is old enough," said Solomon John.

"Whereabouts are you?" asked Mr. Sylvester.

Elizabeth Eliza pointed to the road they had come.

A smile came over Mr. Sylvester's face; he knew the country well.

"You mean the farm-house behind the hill, at the end of the road?" he asked.

The Peterkins all nodded affirmatively.

Ann Maria could not restrain herself, as broad smiles came over the faces of all the party.

"Why, that is the Poor-house!" she exclaimed.

"The town farm," Mr. Sylvester explained, deprecatingly.

The Peterkins were silent for a while. The Sylvesters tried not to laugh.

"There certainly were some disagreeable old men and women there!" said Elizabeth Eliza, at last.

"But we have surely been made very comfortable," Mrs. Peterkin declared.

"A very simple mistake," said Mr. Sylvester, continuing

his amusement. "Your trunks arrived all right at the 'Old Farm,' two days ago."

"Let us go back directly," said Elizabeth Eliza.

"As directly as our horse will allow," said Agamemnon.

Mr. Sylvester helped them into the wagon. "Your rooms are awaiting you," he said. "Why not come with us?"

"We want to find Mr. Peterkin before we do anything else," said Mrs. Peterkin.

They rode back in silence, till Elizabeth Eliza said, "Do you suppose they took us for paupers?"

"We have not seen any 'they,'" said Solomon John, "except Mr. Atwood."

At the entrance of the farm-yard Mr. Peterkin met them.

"I have been looking for you," he said. "I have just made a discovery."

"We have made it, too," said Elizabeth Eliza; "we are in the poor-house."

"How did you find it out?" Mrs. Peterkin asked of Mr. Peterkin.

"Mr. Atwood came to me, puzzled with a telegram that had been brought to him from the station, which he ought to have got two days ago. It came from a Mr. Peters, whom they were expecting here this week, with his wife and boys, to take charge of the establishment. He telegraphed to say he cannot come till Friday. Now, Mr. Atwood had supposed we were the Peterses, whom he had sent for the day we arrived, not having received this telegram."

"Oh, I see, I see!" said Mr. Peterkin; "and we did get into a muddle at the station!"

Mr. Atwood met them at the porch. "I beg pardon," he said. "I hope you have found it comfortable here, and shall be glad to have you stay till Mr. Peters' family comes."

At this moment wheels were heard. Mr. Sylvester had arrived, with an open wagon, to take the Peterkins to the "Old Farm."

Martha was waiting within the door, and said to Elizabeth Eliza, "Beg pardon, miss, for thinking you was one of the inmates, and putting you in that room. We thought it so kind of Mrs. Peters to take you off every day with the other gentlemen, that looked so wandering."

Elizabeth Eliza did not know whether to laugh or to cry.

Mr. Peterkin and the little boys decided to stay at the farm till Friday. But Agamemnon and Solomon John preferred to leave with Mr. Sylvester, and to take their electrical machine and camera when they came for Mr. Peterkin.

Mrs. Peterkin was tempted to stay another night, to be wakened once more by the guinea-hens. But Elizabeth Eliza bore her off. There was not much packing to be done. She shouted good-by into the ears of the deaf old lady, and waved her hand to the foreign one, and glad to bid farewell to the old men with their pipes, leaning against the porch.

"This time," she said, "it is not our trunks that were lost" —

"But we, as a family," said Mrs. Peterkin.

The Last of the Peterkins

Preface

THE following Papers contain the last records of the Peterkin Family, who unhappily ventured to leave their native land and have never returned. Elizabeth Eliza's Commonplace-Book has been found among the family papers, and will be published here for the first time. It is evident that she foresaw that the family were ill able to contend with the commonplace struggle of life; and we may not wonder that they could not survive the unprecedented, far away from the genial advice of friends, especially that of the lady from Philadelphia.

It is feared that Mr. and Mrs. Peterkin lost their lives after leaving Tobolsk, perhaps in some vast conflagration.

Agamemnon and Solomon John were probably sacrificed in some effort to join in or control the disturbances which arose in the distant places where they had established themselves—Agamemnon in Madagascar, Solomon John in Rustchuk.

The little boys have merged into men in some German university, while Elizabeth Eliza must have been lost in the mazes of the Russian language.

Elizabeth Eliza Writes a Paper

LIZABETH ELIZA joined the Circumambient Club with the idea that it would be a long time before she, a new member, would have to read a paper. She would have time to hear the other papers read, and to see how it was done; and she would find it easy when her turn came. By that time she would have some ideas; and long before she would be called upon, she would have leisure to sit down and write out something. But a year passed away, and the time was drawing near. She had, meanwhile, devoted herself to her studies, and had tried to inform herself on all subjects by way of preparation. She had consulted one of the old members of the Club as to the choice of subject.

"Oh, write about anything," was the answer, — "anything you have been thinking of."

Elizabeth Eliza was forced to say she had not been thinking lately. She had not had time. The family had moved, and there was always an excitement about something, that prevented her sitting down to think.

"Why not write out your family adventures?" asked the old member.

Elizabeth Eliza was sure her mother would think it made them too public; and most of the Club papers, she observed, had some thought in them. She preferred to find an idea.

So she set herself to the occupation of thinking. She went out on the piazza to think; she stayed in the house to think. She tried a corner of the china-closet. She tried thinking in the cars, and lost her pocketbook; she tried it in the garden, and walked into the strawberry bed. In the house and out of the house, it seemed to be the same, — she could not think of anything to think of. For many weeks she was seen sitting on the sofa or in the window, and nobody disturbed her. "She is thinking about her paper," the family would say, but she only knew that she could not think of anything.

Agamemnon told her that many writers waited till the last moment, when inspiration came which was much finer than anything studied. Elizabeth Eliza thought it would be terrible to wait till the last moment, if the inspiration should not come! She might combine the two ways, — wait till a few days before the last, and then sit down and write anyhow. This would give a chance for inspiration, while she would not run the risk of writing nothing.

She was much discouraged. Perhaps she had better give it up? But, no; everybody wrote a paper: if not now, she would have to do it sometime!

And at last the idea of a subject came to her! But it was as hard to find a moment to write as to think. The morning was noisy, till the little boys had gone to school; for they had begun again upon their regular course, with the plan of taking up the study of cider in October. And after the little boys had gone to school, now it was one thing, now it was another, — the china-closet to be cleaned, or one of the neighbors in to look at the sewing-machine. She tried after dinner, but would fall asleep. She felt that evening would be the true time, after the cares of day were over.

The Peterkins had wire mosquito-nets all over the house, —at every door and every window. They were as eager to keep out the flies as the mosquitoes. The doors were all furnished with strong springs, that pulled the doors to as soon as they were opened. The little boys had practised running in and out of each door, and slamming it after them. This made a good deal of noise, for they had gained great success in making one door slam directly after another, and at times would keep up a running volley of artillery, as they called it, with the slamming of the doors. Mr. Peterkin, however, preferred it to flies.

So Elizabeth Eliza felt she would venture to write of a summer evening with all the windows open.

She seated herself one evening in the library, between two large kerosene lamps, with paper, pen, and ink before her. It was a beautiful night, with the smell of the roses coming in through the mosquito-nets, and just the faintest odor of kerosene by her side. She began upon her work. But what was her dismay! She found herself immediately surrounded with mosquitoes. They attacked her at every point. They fell upon her hand as she moved it to the ink-stand; they hovered, buzzing, over her head; they planted themselves under the lace of her sleeve. If she moved her left hand to frighten them off from one point, another band fixed themselves upon her right hand. Not only did they flutter and sting, but they sang in a heathenish manner, distracting her attention as she tried to write, as she tried to waft them off. Nor was this all. Myriads of June-bugs and millers hovered round, flung themselves into the lamps, and made disagreeable funeral-pyres of themselves, tumbling noisily on her paper in their last unpleasant agonies. Occasionally one darted with a rush toward Elizabeth Eliza's head.

If there was anything Elizabeth Eliza had a terror of,

it was a June-bug. She had heard that they had a tendency to get into the hair. One had been caught in the hair of a friend of hers, who had long luxuriant hair. But the legs

of the June-bug were caught in it like fish-hooks, and it had to be cut out, and the June-bug was only extricated by sacrificing large masses of the flowing locks.

Elizabeth Eliza flung her handkerchief over her head.

Could she sacrifice what hair she had to the claims of literature? She gave a cry of dismay.

The little boys rushed in a moment to the rescue. They flapped newspapers, flung sofa-cushions; they offered to stand by her side with fly-whisks, that she might be free to write. But the struggle was too exciting for her, and the flying insects seemed to increase. Moths of every description — large brown moths, small, delicate white millers — whirled about her, while the irritating hum of the mosquito kept on more than ever. Mr. Peterkin and the rest of the family came in to inquire about the trouble. It was discovered that each of the little boys had been standing in the opening of a wire door for some time, watching to see when Elizabeth Eliza would have made her preparations and would begin to write. Countless numbers of dorbugs and winged creatures of every description had taken occasion to come in. It was found that they were in every part of the house.

"We might open all the blinds and screens," suggested Agamemnon, "and make a vigorous onslaught and drive them all out at once."

"I do believe there are more inside than out now," said Solomon John.

"The wire nets, of course," said Agamemnon, "keep them in now."

"We might go outside," proposed Solomon John, "and drive in all that are left. Then to-morrow morning, when they are all torpid, kill them and make collections of them."

Agamemnon had a tent which he had provided in case he should ever go to the Adirondacks, and he proposed using it for the night. The little boys were wild for this.

Mrs. Peterkin thought she and Elizabeth Eliza would prefer trying to sleep in the house. But perhaps Elizabeth Eliza would go on with her paper with more comfort out of doors.

A student's lamp was carried out, and she was established on the steps of the back piazza, while screens were all carefully closed to prevent the mosquitoes and insects from flying out. But it was of no use. There were outside still swarms of winged creatures that plunged themselves about her, and she had not been there long before a huge miller flung himself into the lamp and put it out. She gave up for the evening.

Still the paper went on. "How fortunate," exclaimed Elizabeth Eliza, "that I did not put it off till the last evening!" Having once begun, she persevered in it at every odd moment of the day. Agamemnon presented her with a volume of "Synonymes," which was of great service to her. She read her paper, in its various stages, to Agamemnon first, for his criticism, then to her father in the library, then to Mr. and Mrs. Peterkin together, next to Solomon John, and afterward to the whole family assembled. She was almost glad that the lady from Philadelphia was not in town, as she wished it to be her own unaided production. She declined all invitations for the week before the night of the club, and on the very day she kept her room with *eau sucrée*, that she might save her voice. Solomon John provided her with Brown's Bronchial Troches when the evening came, and Mrs. Peterkin advised a handkerchief over her head, in case of June-bugs. It was, however, a cool night. Agamemnon escorted her to the house.

The Club met at Ann Maria Bromwick's. No gentlemen were admitted to the regular meetings. There were what Solomon John called "occasional annual meetings," to which they were invited, when all the choicest papers of the year were re-read.

Elizabeth Eliza was placed at the head of the room, at

a small table, with a brilliant gas-jet on one side. It was so cool the windows could be closed. Mrs. Peterkin, as a guest, sat in the front row.

This was her paper, as Elizabeth Eliza read it, for she frequently inserted fresh expressions: —

The Sun

It is impossible that much can be known about it. This is why we have taken it up as a subject. We mean the sun that lights us by day and leaves us by night. In the first place, it is so far off. No measuring-tapes could reach it; and both the earth and the sun are moving about so, that it would be difficult to adjust ladders to reach it, if we could. Of course, people have written about it, and there are those who have told us how many miles off it is. But it is a very large number, with a great many figures in it; and though it is taught in most if not all of our public schools, it is a chance if any one of the scholars remembers exactly how much it is.

It is the same with its size. We cannot, as we have said, reach it by ladders to measure it; and if we did reach it, we should have no measuring-tapes large enough, and those that shut up with springs are difficult to use in a high place. We are told, it is true, in a great many of the school-books, the size of the sun; but, again, very few of those who have learned the number have been able to remember it after they have recited it, even if they remembered it then. And almost all of the scholars have lost their school-books, or have neglected to carry them home, and so they are not able to refer to them, — I mean, after leaving school. I must say that is the case with me, I should say with us, though it was different. The older ones gave their school-books to the younger ones, who took them back to school to lose them, or who have destroyed them when there were no younger ones to go to school. I should say there are such families. What I mean is, the fact that in some families there are no younger children to take off the school-books. But even then they are put away on upper shelves, in closets or in attics, and seldom found if wanted, — if then, dusty.

Of course, we all know of a class of persons called astronomers, who might be able to give us information on the subject in hand, and who probably do furnish what information is found in school-books. It should be observed, however, that these astronomers carry on their observations always in the night. Now it is well known that the sun does not shine in the night. Indeed, that is one of the peculiarities of the night, that there is no sun to light us, so we have to go to bed as long as there is nothing else we can do without its light, unless we use lamps, gas, or kerosene, which is very well for the evening, but would be expensive all night long; the same with candles. How, then, can we depend upon their statements, if not made from their own observation, — I mean, if they never saw the sun?

We cannot expect that astronomers should give us any valuable information with regard to the sun, which they never see, their occupation compelling them to be up at night. It is quite likely that they never see it; for we should not expect them to sit up all day as well as all night, as, under such circumstances, their lives would not last long.

Indeed, we are told that their name is taken from the word *aster*, which means "star"; the word is "aster — know — more." This, doubtless, means that they know more about the stars than other things. We see, therefore, that their knowledge is confined to the stars, and we cannot trust what they have to tell us of the sun.

There are other asters which should not be mixed up with

these, — we mean those growing by the wayside in the fall of the year. The astronomers, from their nocturnal habits, can scarcely be acquainted with them; but as it does not come within our province, we will not inquire.

We are left, then, to seek our own information about the sun. But we are met with a difficulty. To know a thing, we must look at it. How can we look at the sun? It is so very bright that our eyes are dazzled in gazing upon it. We have to turn away, or they would be put out, — the sight, I mean. It is true, we might use smoked glass, but that is apt to come off on the nose. How, then, if we cannot look at it, can we find out about it? The noonday would seem to be the better hour, when it is the sunniest; but, besides injuring the eyes, it is painful to the neck to look up for a long time. It is easy to say that our examination of this heavenly body should take place at sunrise, when we could look at it more on a level, without having to endanger the spine. But how many people are up at sunrise? Those who get up early do it because they are compelled to, and have something else to do than look at the sun.

The milkman goes forth to carry the daily milk, the ice-man to leave the daily ice. But either of these would be afraid of exposing their vehicles to the heating orb of day, — the milkman afraid of turning the milk, the ice-man timorous of melting his ice, — and they probably avoid those directions where they shall meet the sun's rays. The student, who might inform us, has been burning the midnight oil. The student is not in the mood to consider the early sun.

There remains to us the evening, also, — the leisure hour of the day. But, alas! our houses are not built with an adaptation to this subject. They are seldom made to look toward the sunset. A careful inquiry and close observation, such as have been called for in preparation of this paper, have developed the fact that not a single house in this town faces the sunset! There may be windows looking that way, but in such a case there is always a barn between. I can testify to this from personal observations, because, with my brothers, we have walked through the several streets of this town with notebooks, carefully noting every house looking upon the sunset, and have found none from which the sunset could be studied. Sometimes it was the next house, sometimes a row of houses, or its own wood-house, that stood in the way.

Of course, a study of the sun might be pursued out of doors. But in summer, sunstroke would be likely to follow; in winter, neuralgia and cold. And how could you consult your books, your dictionaries, your encyclopaedias? There seems to be no hour of the day for studying the sun. You might go to the East to see it at its rising, or to the West to gaze upon its setting, but — you don't.

Here Elizabeth Eliza came to a pause. She had written five different endings, and had brought them all, thinking, when the moment came, she would choose one of them. She was pausing to select one, and inadvertently said, to close the phrase, "you don't." She had not meant to use the expression, which she would not have thought sufficiently imposing, — it dropped out unconsciously, — but it was received as a close with rapturous applause.

She had read slowly, and now that the audience applauded at such a length, she had time to feel she was much exhausted and glad of an end. Why not stop there, though there were some pages more? Applause, too, was heard from the outside. Some of the gentlemen had come, — Mr. Peterkin, Agamemnon, and Solomon John, with others, — and demanded admission.

"Since it is all over, let them in," said Ann Maria Bromwick.

Elizabeth Eliza assented, and rose to shake hands with her applauding friends.

Elizabeth Eliza's Commonplace-Book

am going to jot down, from time to time, any suggestions that occur to me that will be of use in writing another paper, in case I am called upon. I might be asked unexpectedly for certain occasions, if anybody happened to be prevented from coming to a meeting.

I have not yet thought of a subject, but I think that is not of as much consequence as to gather the ideas. It seems as if the ideas might suggest the subject, even if the subject does not suggest the ideas.

Now, often a thought occurs to me in the midst, perhaps, of conversation with others; but I forget it afterwards, and spend a great deal of time in trying to think what it was I was thinking of, which might have been very valuable.

I have indeed, of late, been in the habit of writing such thoughts on scraps of paper, and have often left the table to record some idea that occurred to me; but, looking up the paper and getting ready to write it, the thought has escaped me.

Then again, when I have written it, it has been on the backs of envelopes or the off sheet of a note, and it has been lost, perhaps thrown into the scrap-basket. Amanda is a little careless about such things; and, indeed, I have before encouraged her in throwing away old envelopes, which do not seem of much use otherwise, so perhaps she is not to blame.

.   .   .   .   .   .

The more I think of it, the more does it seem to me there would be an advantage if everybody should have the same number to their houses, — of course not everybody, but everybody acquainted. It is so hard to remember all the numbers; the streets you are not so likely to forget. Friends might combine to have the same number. What made me think of it was that we do have the same number as the Easterlys. To be sure, we are out of town, and they are in Boston; but it makes it so convenient, when I go into town to see the Easterlys, to remember that their number is the same as ours.

Agamemnon has lost his new silk umbrella. Yet the case was marked with his name in full, and the street address and the town. Of course he left the case at home, going out in the rain. He might have carried it with the address in his pocket, yet this would not have helped after losing the umbrella. Why not have a pocket for the case in the umbrella?

In shaking the dust from a dress, walk slowly backwards. This prevents the dust from falling directly on the dress again.

On Carving Duck. — It is singular that I can never get so much off the breast as other people do.

Perhaps I have it set on wrong side up.

I wonder why they never have catalogues for libraries arranged from the last letter of the name instead of the first.

There is our Italian teacher whose name ends with a "j," which I should remember much easier than the first letter, being so odd.

I cannot understand why a man should want to marry his wife's deceased sister. If she is dead, indeed, how can he? And if he has a wife, how wrong! I am very glad there is a law against it.

It is well, in prosperity, to be brought up as though you were living in adversity; then, if you have to go back to adversity, it is all the same.

On the other hand, it might be as well, in adversity, to act as though you were living in prosperity; otherwise, you would seem to lose the prosperity either way.

Solomon John has invented a new extinguisher. It is to represent a Turk smoking a pipe, which is to be hollow, and lets the smoke out. A very pretty idea!

A bee came stumbling into my room this morning, as it has done every spring since we moved here, — perhaps not the same bee. I think there must have been a family bee-line across this place before ever a house was built here, and the bees are trying for it every year.

Perhaps we ought to cut a window opposite.

There's room enough in the world for me and thee; go thou and trouble some one else, — as the man said when he put the fly out of the window.

Ann Maria thinks it would be better to fix upon a subject first; but then she has never yet written a paper herself, so she does not realize that you have to have some thoughts before you can write them. She should think, she says, that I would write about something that I see. But of what use is it for me to write about what everybody is seeing, as long as they can see it as well as I do?

The paper about emergencies read last week was one of the best I ever heard; but, of course, it would not be worth while for me to write the same, even if I knew enough.

.   .   .   .

My commonplace-book ought to show me what to do for common things; and then I can go to lectures, or read the "Rules of Emergencies" for the uncommon ones.

Because, as a family, I think we are more troubled about what to do on the common occasions than on the unusual ones. Perhaps because the unusual things don't happen to us, or very seldom; and for the uncommon things, there is generally some one you can ask.

I suppose there really is not as much danger about these uncommon things as there is in the small things, because they don't happen so often, and because you are more afraid of them.

I never saw it counted up, but I conclude that more children tumble into mud-puddles than into the ocean or Niagara Falls, for instance. It was so, at least, with our little boys; but that may have been partly because they never saw the ocean till last summer, and have never been to Niagara. To be sure, they had seen the harbor from the top of Bunker Hill Monument, but there they could not fall in. They might have fallen off from the top of the monument, but did not. I am sure, for our little boys, they have never had the remarkable things happen to them. I suppose because they were so dangerous that they did not try them, like firing at marks and rowing boats. If they had used guns, they might have shot themselves or others; but guns have never been allowed in the house. My father thinks it is dangerous to have them. They might go off unexpected. They would require us to have gunpowder and shot in the house, which would be dangerous. Amanda, too, is a little careless. And we never shall forget the terrible time when the "fulminating paste" went off one Fourth of July. It showed what might happen even if you did not keep gunpowder in the house.

To be sure, Agamemnon and Solomon John are older now, and might learn the use of fire-arms; but even then they might shoot the wrong person — the policeman or some friends coming into the house — instead of the burglar.

And I have read of safe burglars going about. I don't know whether it means that it is safe for them or for us; I hope it is the latter. Perhaps it means that they go without fire-arms, making it safer for them.

.   .   .   .

I have the "Printed Rules for Emergencies," which will be of great use, as I should be apt to forget which to do for which. I mean I should be quite likely to do for burns and scalds what I ought to do for cramp. And when a person is choking, I might sponge from head to foot, which is what I ought to do to prevent a cold.

But I hope I shall not have a chance to practise. We have never had a case of a broken leg, and it would hardly be worth while to break one on purpose.

Then we have had no cases of taking poison, or bites from mad dogs, perhaps partly because we don't keep either poison or dogs; but then our neighbors might, and we ought to be prepared. We do keep cats, so that we do not need to have poison for the rats; and in this way we avoid both dangers, — from the dogs going mad, and from eating the poison by mistake instead of the rats.

To be sure, we don't quite get rid of the rats, and need a trap for the mice; but if you have a good family cat it is safer.

About window-curtains — I mean the drapery ones — we

have the same trouble in deciding every year. We did not put any in the parlor windows when we moved, only window-shades, because there were so many things to be done, and we wanted time to make up our minds as to what we would have.

But that was years ago, and we have not decided yet, though we consider the subject every spring and fall.

The trouble is, if we should have heavy damask ones like the Bromwicks', it would be very dark in the winter, on account of the new, high building opposite.

Now, we like as much light as we can get in the winter, so we have always waited till summer, thinking we would have some light muslin ones, or else of the new laces. But in summer we like to have the room dark, and the sun does get round in the morning quite dazzling on the white shades. (We might have dark-colored shades, but there would be the same trouble of its being too dark in the winter.)

We seem to need the heavy curtains in summer and the light curtains in winter, which would look odd. Besides, in winter we do need the heavy curtains to shut out the draughts, while in summer we like all the air we can get.

I have been looking for material that shall shut out the air and yet let in the light, or else shut out the light and let in the air; or else let in the light when you want it, and not when you don't. I have not found it yet; but there are so many new inventions that I dare say I shall come across it in time. They seem to have invented everything except a steamer that won't go up and down as well as across.

I never could understand about averages. I can't think why people are so fond of taking them, — men generally. It seems to me they tell anything but the truth. They try to tell what happens every evening, and they don't tell one evening right.

There was our Free Evening Cooking-school. We had a class of fourteen girls; and they admired it, and liked nothing better, and attended regularly. But Ann Maria made out the report according to the average of attendance on the whole number of nights in the ten weeks of the school, one evening a week; so she gave the numbers $12\frac{3}{5}$ each night.

Now the fact was, they all came every night except one, when there was such a storm, nobody went, — not even the teacher, nor Ann Maria, nor any of us. It snowed and it hailed and the wind blew, and our steps were so slippery Amanda could not go out to put on ashes; ice even on the upper steps. The janitor, who makes the fire, set out to go; but she was blown across the street into the gutter. She did succeed in getting in to Ann Maria's, who said it was foolish to attempt it, and that nobody would go; and I am not sure but she spent the night there, — at Ann Maria's, I mean. Still, Ann Maria had to make up the account of the number of evenings of the whole course.

But it looks, in the report, as though there were never the whole fourteen there, and as though $1\frac{2}{5}$ of a girl stayed away every night, when the facts are we did not have a single absence, and the whole fourteen were there every night, except the night there was no school; and I have been told they all had on their things to come that night, but their mothers would not let them, — those that had mothers, — and they would have been blown away if they had come.

It seems to me the report does not present the case right, on account of the averages.

I think it is indeed the common things that trouble one to decide about, as I have said, since for the remarkable ones one can have advice. The way we do on such occasions is to ask our friends, especially the lady from Philadelphia.

Whatever we should have done without her, I am sure I cannot tell, for her advice is always inestimable. To be sure, she is not always here; but there is the daily mail (twice from her to Boston), and the telegraph, and to some places the telephone.

But for some common things there is not time for even the telephone.

Yesterday morning, for instance, going into Boston in the early train, I took the right side for a seat, as is natural, though I noticed that most of the passengers were crowding into the seats on the other side. I found, as we left the station, that I was on the sunny side, which was very uncomfortable. So I made up my mind to change sides, coming out. But, unexpectably, I stayed in till afternoon at Mrs. Easterly's. It seems she had sent a note to ask me (which I found at night all right, when I got home), as Mr. Easterly was away. So I did not go out till afternoon. I did remember my determination to change sides in going out, and as I took the right going in, not to take the right going out. But then I remembered, as it was afternoon, the sun would have changed; so if the right side was wrong in the morning, it would be right in the afternoon. At any rate, it would be safe to take the other side. I did observe that most of the people took the opposite side, the left side; but I supposed they had not stopped to calculate.

When we came out of the station and from under the bridges, I found I was sitting in the sun again, the same way as in the morning, in spite of all my reasoning. Ann Maria, who had come late and taken the last seat on the other side, turned round and called across to me, "Why do you always take the sunny side? Do you prefer it?" I was sorry not to explain it to her, but she was too far off.

It might be safe to do what most of the other people do, when you cannot stop to inquire; but you cannot always tell, since very likely they may be mistaken. And then if they have taken all the seats, there is not room left for you. Still, this time, in coming out, I had reached the train in plenty of season, and might have picked out my seat, but then there was nobody there to show where most of the people would go. I might have changed when I saw where most would go; but I hate changing, and the best seats were all taken.

My father thinks it would be a good plan for Amanda to go to the Lectures on Physics. She has lived with us a great many years, and she still breaks as many things as she did at the beginning.

Dr. Murtrie, who was here the other night, said he learned when quite a boy, from some book on Physics, that if he placed some cold water in the bottom of a pitcher, before pouring in boiling-hot water, it would not break. Also, that in washing a glass or china pitcher in very hot water, the outside and inside should be in hot water, or, as he said, should feel the hot water at the same time. I don't quite understand exactly how, unless the pitcher has a large mouth, when it might be put in sideways.

He told the reasons, which, being scientific, I cannot remember or understand.

If Amanda had known about this, she might have saved a great deal of valuable glass and china. Though it has not always been from hot water, the breaking, for I often think she has not the water hot enough; but often from a whole tray-full sliding out of her hand, as she was coming up-stairs, and everything on it broke.

But Dr. Murtrie said if she had learned more of the Laws of Physics she would not probably so often tip over the waiter.

The trouble is, however, remembering at the right time. She might have known the law perfectly well, and forgotten it just on the moment, or her dress coming in the way may have prevented.

Still, I should like very well myself to go to the Lectures on Physics. Perhaps I could find out something about scissors, — why it is they do always tumble down, and usually, though so heavy, without any noise, so that you do not know that they have fallen. I should say they had no law, because sometimes they are far under the sofa in one direction, or hidden behind the leg of the table in another, or perhaps not even on the floor, but buried in the groove at the back of the easy-chair, and you never find them till you have the chair covered again. I do feel always in the back of the chair now; but Amanda found mine, yesterday, in the groove of the sofa.

It is possible Elizabeth Eliza may have taken the remaining sheets of her commonplace-book abroad with her. We have not been able to recover them.

The Peterkins Practise Travelling

LONG ago Mrs. Peterkin had been afraid of the Mohammedans, and would have dreaded to travel among them; but since the little boys had taken lessons of the Turk, and she had become familiar with his costume and method of sitting, she had felt less fear of them as a nation.

To be sure, the Turk had given but few lessons, as, soon after making his engagement, he had been obliged to go to New York to join a tobacconist's firm. Mr. Peterkin had not regretted his payment for instruction in advance; for the Turk had been very urbane in his manners, and had always assented to whatever the little boys or any of the family had said to him.

Mrs. Peterkin had expressed a desire to see the famous Cleopatra's Needle which had been brought from Egypt. She had heard it was something gigantic for a needle, and it would be worth a journey to New York. She wondered at their bringing it such a distance, and would have supposed that some of Cleopatra's family would have objected to it if they were living now.

Agamemnon said that was the truth; there was no one left to object; they were all mummies under ground, with such heavy pyramids over them that they would not easily rise to object.

Mr. Peterkin feared that all the pyramids would be

brought away in time. Agamemnon said there were a great many remaining in Egypt. Still, he thought it would be well to visit Egypt soon, before they were all brought away, and nothing but the sand left. Mrs. Peterkin said she would be almost as willing to travel to Egypt as to New York, and it would seem more worth while to go so far to see a great many than to go to New York only for one needle.

"That would certainly be a needless expense," suggested Solomon John.

Elizabeth Eliza was anxious to see the Sphinx. Perhaps it would answer some of the family questions that troubled them day after day.

Agamemnon felt it would be a great thing for the education of the little boys. If they could have begun with the Egyptian hieroglyphics before they had learned their alphabet, they would have begun at the right end. Perhaps it was not too late now to take them to Egypt, and let them begin upon its old learning. The little boys declared it was none too late. They could not say the alphabet backward now, and could never remember whether *u* came before *v;* and the voyage would be a long one, and before they reached Egypt, very likely they would have forgotten all.

It was about this voyage that Mrs. Peterkin had much doubt. What she was afraid of was getting in and out of the ships and boats. She was afraid of tumbling into the water between, when she left the wharf. Elizabeth Eliza agreed with her mother in this, and began to calculate how many times they would have to change between Boston and Egypt.

There was the ferry-boat across to East Boston would make two changes; one more to get on board the steamer; then Liverpool — no, to land at Queenstown would make two more, — four, five changes; Liverpool, six. Solomon John brought the map, and they counted up. Dover, seven;

Calais, eight; Marseilles, nine; Malta, if they landed, ten, eleven; and Alexandria, twelve changes.

Mrs. Peterkin shuddered at the possibilities, not merely for herself, but for the family. She could fall in but once, but by the time they should reach Egypt, how many would be left out of a family of eight? Agamemnon began to count up the contingencies. Eight times twelve would make ninety-six chances (8 x 12 = 96). Mrs. Peterkin felt as if all might be swept off before the end could be reached.

Solomon John said it was usual to allow more than one chance in a hundred. People always said "one in a hundred," as though that were the usual thing expected. It was not at all likely that the whole family would be swept off.

Mrs. Peterkin was sure they would not want to lose one; they could hardly pick out which they could spare, she felt certain. Agamemnon declared there was no necessity for such risks. They might go directly by some vessel from Boston to Egypt.

Solomon John thought they might give up Egypt, and content themselves with Rome. "All roads lead to Rome"; so it would not be difficult to find their way.

But Mrs. Peterkin was afraid to go. She had heard you must do as the Romans did if you went to Rome; and there were some things she certainly should not like to do that they did. There was that brute who killed Caesar! And she should not object to the long voyage. It would give them time to think it all over.

Mr. Peterkin thought they ought to have more practise in travelling, to accustom themselves to emergencies. It would be fatal to start on so long a voyage and to find they were not prepared. Why not make their proposed excursion to the cousins at Gooseberry Beach, which they had been planning all summer? There they could practise getting in and out of a boat, and accustom themselves to the air of the sea. To be sure, the cousins were just moving up from the sea-shore, but they could take down a basket of luncheon, in order to give no trouble, and they need not go into the house.

Elizabeth Eliza had learned by heart, early in the summer, the list of trains, as she was sure they would lose the slip their cousins had sent them; and you never could find the paper that had the trains in when you wanted it. They must take the 7 A.M. train into Boston in time to go across to the station for the Gooseberry train at 7:45, and they would have to return from Gooseberry Beach by a 3:30 train. The cousins would order the "barge" to meet them on their arrival, and to come for them at 3 P.M., in time for the return train, if they were informed the day before. Elizabeth Eliza wrote them a postal card, giving them the information that they would take the early train. The "barge" was the name of the omnibus that took passengers to and from the Gooseberry station. Mrs. Peterkin felt that its very name was propitious to this Egyptian undertaking.

The day proved a fine one. On reaching Boston, Mrs. Peterkin and Elizabeth Eliza were put into a carriage with the luncheon-basket to drive directly to the station. Elizabeth Eliza was able to check the basket at the baggage-station, and to buy their "go-and-return" tickets before the arrival of the rest of the party, which appeared, however, some minutes before a quarter of eight. Mrs. Peterkin counted the little boys. All were there. This promised well for Egypt. But their joy was of short duration. On presenting their tickets at the gate of entrance, they were stopped. The Gooseberry train had gone at 7:35! The Mattapan train was now awaiting its passengers. Impossible! Elizabeth Eliza had repeated 7:45 every morning through the summer. It must be the Gooseberry train. But the conductor would not yield. If they wished to go to Mattapan they could go; if to Gooseberry, they must wait till the 5 P.M. train.

Mrs. Peterkin was in despair. Their return train was 3:30; how could 5 P.M. help them?

Mr. Peterkin, with instant decision, proposed they should try something else. Why should not they take their luncheon-basket across some ferry? This would give them practise. The family hastily agreed to this. What could be better? They went to the baggage-office, but found their basket had gone in the 7:35 train! They had arrived in time, and could have gone too. "If we had only been checked!" exclaimed Mrs. Peterkin. The baggage-master, showing a tender interest, suggested that there was a train for Plymouth at eight, which would take them within twelve miles of Gooseberry Beach, and they might find "a team" there to take them across. Solomon John and the little boys were delighted with the suggestion.

"We could see Plymouth Rock," said Agamemnon.

But hasty action would be necessary. Mr. Peterkin quickly procured tickets for Plymouth, and no official objected to their taking the 8 A.M. train. They were all safely in the train. This had been a test expedition; and each of the party had taken something, to see what would be the proportion of things lost to those remembered. Mr. Peterkin had two umbrellas, Agamemnon an atlas and spyglass, and the little boys were taking down two cats in a basket. All were safe.

"I am glad we have decided upon Plymouth," said Mr. Peterkin. "Before seeing the pyramids of Egypt we certainly ought to know something of Plymouth Rock. I should certainly be quite ashamed, when looking at their great obelisks, to confess that I had never seen our own Rock."

The conductor was attracted by this interesting party. When

Mr. Peterkin told him of their mistake of the morning, and that they were bound for Gooseberry Beach, he advised them to stop at Kingston, a station nearer the beach. They would have but four miles to drive, and a reduction could be effected on their tickets. The family demurred. Were they ready now to give up Plymouth? They would lose time in going there. Solomon John, too, suggested it would be better, chronologically, to visit Plymouth on their return from Egypt, after they had seen the earliest things.

This decided them to stop at Kingston.

But they found here no omnibus nor carriage to take them to Gooseberry. The station-master was eager to assist them and went far and near in search of some sort of wagon. Hour after hour passed away, the little boys had shared their last peanut, and gloom was gathering over the family, when Solomon John came into the station to say there was a photographer's cart on the other side of the road. Would not this be a good chance to have their photographs taken for their friends before leaving for Egypt? The idea reanimated the whole party, and they made their way to the cart, and into it, as the door was open. There was, however, no photographer there.

Agamemnon tried to remember what he had read of photography. As all the materials were there, he might take the family's picture. There would indeed be a difficulty in introducing his own. Solomon John suggested they might arrange the family group, leaving a place for him. Then, when all was ready, he could put the curtain over the box, take his place hastily, then pull away the curtain by means of a string. And Solomon John began to look around for a string while the little boys felt in their pockets.

Agamemnon did not exactly see how they could get the curtain back. Mr. Peterkin thought this of little importance.

They would all be glad to sit some time after travelling so long. And the longer they sat the better for the picture, and perhaps somebody would come along in time to put back the curtain. They began to arrange the group. Mr. and Mrs. Peterkin were placed in the middle, sitting down. Elizabeth Eliza stood behind them, and the little boys knelt in front with the basket of cats. Solomon John and Agamemnon were also to stand behind, Agamemnon leaning over his father's shoulder. Solomon John was still looking around for a string when the photographer himself appeared. He was much surprised to find a group all ready for him. He had gone off that morning for a short holiday, but was not unwilling to take the family, especially when he heard they were soon going to Egypt. He approved of the grouping made by the family, but suggested that their eyes should not all be fixed upon the same spot. Before the pictures were finished, the station-master came to announce that two carriages were found to take the party to Gooseberry Beach.

"There is no hurry," said Mr. Peterkin. "Let the pictures be finished; they have made us wait, we can keep them waiting as long as we please."

The result, indeed, was very satisfactory. The photographer pronounced it a remarkably fine group. Elizabeth Eliza's eyes were lifted to the heavens perhaps a little too high. It gave her a rapt expression not customary with her; but Mr. Peterkin thought she might look in that way in the presence of the Sphinx. It was necessary to have a number of copies, to satisfy all the friends left behind when they should go to Egypt; and it certainly would not be worth while to come again so great a distance for more.

It was therefore a late hour when they left Kingston. It took some time to arrange the party in two carriages. Mr. Peterkin ought to be in one, Mrs. Peterkin in the other; but it was difficult to divide the little boys, as all wished to take charge of the cats. The drive, too, proved longer than was expected, — six miles instead of four.

When they reached their cousin's door, the "barge" was already standing there.

"It has brought our luncheon-basket!" exclaimed Solomon John.

"I am glad of it," said Agamemnon, "for I feel hungry enough for it."

He pulled out his watch. It was three o'clock!

This was indeed the "barge," but it had come for their return. The Gooseberry cousins, much bewildered that the family did not arrive at the time expected, had forgotten to send to countermand it. And the "barge" driver, supposing the family had arrived by the other station, had taken occasion to bring up the lunch-basket, as it was addressed to the Gooseberry cousins. The cousins flocked out to meet them. "What had happened? What had delayed them? They were glad to see them at last."

Mrs. Peterkin, when she understood the state of the case, insisted upon getting directly into the "barge" to return, although the driver said there would be a few moments to spare. Some of the cousins busied themselves in opening the luncheon-basket, and a part led the little boys and Agamemnon and Solomon John down upon the beach in front of the house; there would be a few moments for a glance at the sea. Indeed, the little boys ventured in their India-rubber boots to wade in a little way, as the tide was low. And Agamemnon and Solomon John walked to look at a boat that was drawn up on the beach, and got into it and out of it for practice, till they were all summoned back to the house.

It was indeed time to go. The Gooseberry cousins had

got out the luncheon, and had tried to persuade the family to spend the night. Mrs. Peterkin declared this would be impossible. They never had done such a thing. So they went off, eating their luncheon as they went, the little boys each with a sandwich in one hand and a piece of cake in the other.

Mrs. Peterkin was sure they should miss the train or lose some of the party. No, it was a great success; for all, and more than all, were found in the train: slung over the arm of one of the little boys was found the basket containing the cats. They were to have left the cats, but in their haste had brought them away again.

This discovery was made in a search for the tickets which Elizabeth Eliza had bought, early in the morning, to go and return; they were needed now for return. She was sure she had given them to her father. Mrs. Peterkin supposed that Mr. Peterkin must have changed them for the Kingston tickets. The little boys felt in their pockets, Agamemnon and Solomon John in theirs. In the excitement, Mrs. Peterkin insisted upon giving up her copy of their new photograph, and could not be satisfied till the conductor had punched it. At last the tickets were found in the outer lappet of Elizabeth Eliza's hand-bag. She had looked for them in the inner part.

It was after this that Mr. Peterkin ventured to pronounce the whole expedition a success. To be sure, they had not passed the day at the beach, and had scarcely seen their cousins; but their object had been to practise travelling, and surely they had been travelling all day. Elizabeth Eliza had seen the sea, or thought she had. She was not sure — she had been so busy explaining to the cousins and showing the photographs. Agamemnon was sorry she had not walked with them to the beach, and tried getting in and out of the boat. Elizabeth Eliza regretted this. Of course it was not the same as getting into a boat on the sea, where it would be wobbling more, but the step must have been higher from the sand. Solomon John said there was some difficulty. He had jumped in, but was obliged to take hold of the side in getting out.

The little boys were much encouraged by their wade into the tide. They had been a little frightened at first when the splash came, but the tide had been low. On the whole, Mr. Peterkin continued, things had gone well. Even the bringing back of the cats might be considered a good omen. Cats were worshipped in Egypt, and they ought not to have tried to part with them. He was glad they had brought the cats. They gave the little boys an interest in feeding them while they were waiting at the Kingston station.

Their adventures were not quite over, as the station was crowded when they reached Boston. A military company had arrived from the South and was received by a procession. A number of distinguished guests also were expected, and the Peterkins found it difficult to procure a carriage. They had determined to take a carriage, so that they might be sure to reach their own evening train in season.

At last Mr. Peterkin discovered one that was empty, standing at the end of a long line. There would be room for Mrs. Peterkin, Elizabeth Eliza, himself, and the little boys, and Agamemnon and Solomon John agreed to walk behind in order to keep the carriage in sight. But they were much disturbed when they found they were going at so slow a pace. Mr. Peterkin called to the coachman in vain. He soon found that they had fallen into the line of the procession, and the coachman was driving slowly on behind the other carriages. In vain Mr. Peterkin tried to attract the driver's attention. He put his head out of one window after another, but only to receive the cheers of the populace ranged along the sidewalk.

He opened the window behind the coachman and pulled his coat. But the cheering was so loud that he could not make himself heard. He tried to motion to the coachman to turn down one of the side streets, but in answer the driver pointed out with his whip the crowds of people. Mr. Peterkin, indeed, saw it would be impossible to make their way through the throng that filled every side street which they crossed. Mrs. Peterkin looked out of the back window for Agamemnon and Solomon John. They were walking side by side, behind the carriage, taking off their hats, and bowing to the people cheering on either side.

"They are at the head of a long row of men, walking two by two," said Mrs. Peterkin.

"They are part of the procession," said Elizabeth Eliza.

"We are part of the procession," Mr. Peterkin answered.

"I rather like it," said Mrs. Peterkin, with a calm smile, as she looked out of the window and bowed in answer to a cheer.

"Where do you suppose we shall go?" asked Elizabeth Eliza.

"I have often wondered what became of a procession," said Mr. Peterkin. "They are always going somewhere, but I never could tell where they went to."

"We shall find out!" exclaimed the little boys, who were filled with delight, looking now out of one window, now out of the other.

"Perhaps we shall go to the armory," said one.

This alarmed Mrs. Peterkin. Sounds of martial music were now heard, and the noise of the crowd grew louder. "I think you ought to ask where we are going," she said to Mr. Peterkin.

"It is not for us to decide," he answered calmly. "They have taken us into the procession. I suppose they will show us the principal streets, and will then leave us at our station."

This, indeed, seemed to be the plan. For two hours more the Peterkins, in their carriage, and Agamemnon and Solomon John, afoot, followed on. Mrs. Peterkin looked out upon rows and rows of cheering people. The little boys waved their caps.

"It begins to be a little monotonous," said Mrs. Peterkin, at last.

"I am afraid we have missed all the trains," said Elizabeth Eliza, gloomily. But Mr. Peterkin's faith held to the last, and was rewarded. The carriage reached the square in which stood the railroad station. Mr. Peterkin again seized the lapels of the coachman's coat and pointed to the station, and he was able to turn his horses in that direction. As they left the crowd, they received a parting cheer. It was with difficulty that Agamemnon and Solomon John broke from the ranks.

"That was a magnificent reception!" exclaimed Mr. Peterkin, wiping his brow, after paying the coachman twice his fee. But Elizabeth Eliza said, —

"But we have lost all the trains, I am sure."

They had lost all but one. It was the last.

"And we have lost the cats!" the little boys suddenly exclaimed. But Mrs. Peterkin would not allow them to turn back in search of them.

The Peterkins' Excursion for Maple Sugar

IT was, to be sure, a change of plan to determine to go to Grandfather's for a maple-sugaring instead of going to Egypt! But it seemed best. Egypt was not given up, — only postponed. "It has lasted so many centuries," sighed Mr. Peterkin, "that I suppose it will not crumble much in one summer more."

The Peterkins had determined to start for Egypt in June, and Elizabeth Eliza had engaged her dressmaker for January; but after all their plans were made, they were told that June was the worst month of all to go to Egypt in, — that they would arrive in mid-summer, and find the climate altogether too hot, — that people who were not used to it died of it. Nobody thought of going to Egypt in summer; on the contrary, everybody came away. And what was worse, Agamemnon learned that not only the summers were unbearably hot, but there really was no Egypt in summer, — nothing to speak of, — nothing but water; for there was a great inundation of the river Nile every summer, which completely covered the country, and it would be difficult to get about except in boats.

Mr. Peterkin remembered he had heard something of the sort, but he did not suppose it had been kept up with the modern improvements.

Mrs. Peterkin felt that the thing must be very much

exaggerated. She could not believe the whole country would be covered, or that everybody would leave; as summer was surely the usual time for travel, there must be strangers there, even if the natives left. She would not be sorry if there were fewer savages. As for the boats, she supposed after their long voyage they would all be used to going about in boats; and she had thought seriously of practising, by getting in and out of the rocking-chair from the sofa.

The family, however, wrote to the lady from Philadelphia, who had travelled in Egypt, and whose husband knew everything about Egypt that could be known, — this is, everything that had already been dug up, though he could only guess at what might be brought to light next.

The result was a very earnest recommendation not to leave for Egypt till the autumn. Travellers did not usually reach there before December, though October might be pleasant on account of the fresh dates.

So the Egypt plan was reluctantly postponed; and, to make amends for the disappointment to the little boys, an excursion for maple syrup was proposed instead.

Mr. Peterkin considered it almost a necessity. They ought to acquaint themselves with the manufactures of their own new country before studying those of the oldest in the world. He had been inquiring into the products of Egypt at the present time, and had found sugar to be one of their staples. They ought, then, to understand the American methods and compare them with those of Egypt. It would be a pretty attention, indeed, to carry some of the maple sugar to the principal dignitaries of Egypt.

But the difficulties in arranging an excursion proved almost as great as for going to Egypt. Sugar-making could not come off until it was warm enough for the sun to set the sap stirring. On the other hand, it must be cold enough for snow, as you could only reach the woods on snow-sleds. Now, if there were sun enough for the sap to rise, it would melt the snow; and if it were cold enough for sledding it must be too cold for the syrup. There seemed an impossibility about the whole thing. The little boys, however, said there always had been maple sugar every spring, — they had eaten it; why shouldn't there be this spring?

Elizabeth Eliza insisted gloomily that this was probably old sugar they had eaten, — you never could tell in the shops.

Mrs. Peterkin thought there must be fresh sugar occasionally, as the old would have been eaten up. She felt the same about chickens. She never could understand why there were only the old, tough ones in the market, when there were certainly fresh young broods to be seen around the farm-houses every year. She supposed the market-men had begun with the old, tough fowls, and so they had to go on so. She wished they had begun the other way; and she had done her best to have the family eat up the old fowls, hoping they might, some day, get down to the young ones.

As to the uncertainty about the weather, she suggested they should go to Grandfather's the day before. But how can you go the day before, when you don't yet know the day?

All were much delighted, therefore, when Hiram appeared with the wood-sled, one evening, to take them, as early as possible the next day, to their grandfather's. He reported that the sap had started, the kettles had been on some time, there had been a light snow for sleighing, and to-morrow promised to be a fine day. It was decided that he should take the little boys and Elizabeth Eliza early, in the wood-sled; the other would follow later, in the carry-all.

Mrs. Peterkin thought it would be safer to have some of the party go on wheels, in case of a general thaw the the next day.

A brilliant sun awoke them in the morning. The wood-sled was filled with hay, to make it warm and comfortable, and an arm-chair was tied in for Elizabeth Eliza. But she was obliged to go first to visit the secretary of the Circumambient Society, to explain that she should not be present at their evening meeting. One of the rules of this society was to take always a winding road when going upon society business, as the word "circumambient" means "compassing about." It was one of its laws to copy Nature as far as possible, and a straight line is never seen in Nature. Therefore she could not send a direct note to say she should not be present; she could only hint it in general conversation with the secretary; and she was obliged to take a roundabout way to reach the secretary's house, where the little boys called for her in her wood-sled.

What was her surprise to find eight little boys instead of three! In passing the schoolhouse they had picked up five of their friends, who had reached the school door a full hour before the time. Elizabeth Eliza thought they ought to inquire if their parents would be willing they should go, as they all expected to spend the night at Grandfather's. Hiram thought it would require too much time to stop for the consent of ten parents; if the sun kept on at this rate, the snow would be gone before they should reach the woods. But the little boys said most of the little boys lived in a row, and Elizabeth Eliza felt she ought not to take the boys away for all night without their parents' knowledge. The consent of two mothers and two fathers was gained, and Mr. Dobson was met in the street, who said he would tell the other mother. But at each place they were obliged to stop for additional tippets and great-coats and india-rubber boots for the little boys. At the Harrimans', too, the Harriman girls insisted on dressing up the wood-sled with evergreens, and made one of the boys bring their last Christmas-tree, that was leaning up against the barn, to set it up in the back of the sled, over Elizabeth Eliza. All this made considerable delay; and when they reached the high-road again, the snow was indeed fast melting. Elizabeth Eliza was inclined to turn back, but Hiram said they would find the sleighing better farther up among the hills. The arm-chair joggled about a good deal, and the Christmas-tree creaked behind her; and Hiram was obliged to stop occasionally and tie in the chair and the tree more firmly.

But the warm sun was very pleasant, the eight little boys were very lively, and the sleigh-bells jingled gayly as they went on.

It was so late when they reached the wood-road that Hiram decided they had better not go up the hill to their grandfather's, but turn off into the woods.

"Your grandfather will be there by this time," he declared.

Elizabeth Eliza was afraid the carry-all would miss them, and thought they had better wait. Hiram did not like to wait longer, and proposed that one or two of the little boys should stop to show the way. But it was so difficult to decide which little boys should stay that he gave it up. Even to draw lots would take time. So he explained that there was a lunch hidden somewhere in the straw; and the little boys thought it an admirable time to look it up, and it was decided to stop in the sun at the corner of the road. Elizabeth Eliza felt a little jounced in the arm-chair, and was glad of a rest; and the little boys soon discovered an ample lunch, —just what might have been expected from Grandfather's, —apple-pie and doughnuts, and plenty of them! "Lucky we brought so many little boys!" they exclaimed.

Hiram, however, began to grow impatient.

"There'll be no snow left," he exclaimed, "and no afternoon for the syrup!"

But far in the distance the Peterkin carry-all was seen slowly approaching through the snow, Solomon John waving a red handkerchief. The little boys waved back, and Hiram ventured to enter upon the wood-road, but at a slow pace, as Elizabeth Eliza still feared that by some accident the family might miss them.

It was with difficulty that the carry-all followed in the deep but soft snow, in among the trunks of the trees and over piles of leaves hidden in the snow. They reached at last the edge of a meadow; and on the high bank above it stood a row of maples, a little shanty by the side, a slow smoke proceeding from its chimney. The little boys screamed with delight, but there was no reply. Nobody there!

"The folks all gone!" exclaimed Hiram; "then we must be late." And he proceeded to pull out a large silver watch from a side pocket. It was so large that he seldom was at the pains to pull it out, as it took time; but when he had succeeded at last, and looked at it, he started.

"Late, indeed! It is four o'clock, and we were to have been here by eleven; they have given you up."

The little boys wanted to force in the door; but Hiram said it was no use, — they wouldn't understand what to do, and he should have to see to the horses, — and it was too late, and it was likely they had carried off all the syrup. But he thought a minute, as they all stood in silence and gloom; and then he guessed they might find some sugar at Deacon Spear's, close by, on the back road, and that would be better than nothing. Mrs. Peterkin was pretty cold, and glad not to wait in the darkening wood; so the eight little boys walked through the wood-path, Hiram leading the way; and slowly the carry-all followed.

They reached Deacon Spear's at length; but only Mrs. Spear was home. She was very deaf, but could explain that the family had taken all their syrup to the annual festival.

"We might go to the festival," exclaimed the little boys.

"It would be very well," said Mrs. Peterkin, "to eat our fresh syrup there."

But Mrs. Spear could not tell where the festival was to be, as she had not heard; perhaps they might know at Squire Ramsay's. Squire Ramsay's was on their way to Grandfather's, so they stopped there; but they learned that the "Squire's folks had all gone with their syrup to the festival," but the man who was chopping wood did not know where the festival was to be.

"They'll know at your grandfather's," said Mrs. Peterkin, from the carry-all.

"Yes, go on to your grandfather's," advised Mr. Peterkin, "for I think I felt a drop of rain." So they made the best of their way to Grandfather's.

At the moment they reached the door of the house, a party of young people whom Elizabeth Eliza knew came by in sleighs. She had met them all when visiting at her grandfather's.

"Come along with us," they shouted; "we are all going down to the sugar festival."

"That is what we have come for," said Mr. Peterkin.

"Where is it?" asked Solomon John.

"It is down your way," was the reply.

"It is in your own New Hall," said another. "We have sent down all our syrup. The Spears and Ramsays and Doolittles have gone on with theirs. No time to stop; there's good sleighing on the old road."

There was a little consultation with the grandfather. Hiram said that he could take them back with the wood-sled, when he heard there was sleighing on the old road; and it was decided that the whole party should go in the wood-sled, with the exception of Mr. Peterkin, who would follow on with the carry-all. Mrs. Peterkin would take on the arm-chair, and cushions were put in for Elizabeth Eliza, and more apple-pie for all. No more drops of rain appeared, though the clouds were thickening over the setting sun.

"All the way back again," sighed Mrs. Peterkin, "when we might have stayed at home all day, and gone quietly out to the New Hall!" But the little boys thought the sledding all day was great fun, — and the apple-pie! "And we did see the kettle through the cracks of the shanty!"

"It is odd the festival should be held at the New Hall," said Elizabeth Eliza; "for the secretary did say something about the society meeting there to-night, being so far from the centre of the town."

This hall was so called because it was once a new hall, built to be used for lectures, assemblies, and entertainments of this sort, for the convenience of the inhabitants who had collected about some flourishing factories.

"You can go to your own Circumambient Society, then!" exclaimed Solomon John.

"And in a truly circumambient manner," said Agamemnon; and he explained to the little boys that they could now understand the full meaning of the word, for surely Elizabeth Eliza had taken the most circumambient way of reaching the place by coming away from it.

"We little thought, when we passed it early this morning," said Elizabeth Eliza, "that we should come back to it for our maple sugar."

"It is odd the secretary did not tell you they were going to join the sugar festival," said Mrs. Peterkin.

"It is one of the rules of the society," said Elizabeth Eliza, "that the secretary never tells anything directly. She only hinted at the plan of the New Hall."

"I don't see how you can find enough to talk about," said Solomon John.

"We can tell of things that never have happened," said Elizabeth Eliza, "or that are not likely to happen, and wonder what would have happened if they had happened."

They arrived at the festival at last, but very late, and glad to find a place that was warm. There was a stove at each end of the hall, and an encouraging sound and smell from the simmering syrup. There were long tables down the hall, on which were placed, in a row, first a bowl of snow, then a pile of saucers and spoons, then a plate of pickles, intended to whet the appetite for more syrup; another of bread, then another bowl of snow, and so on. Hot syrup was to be poured on the snow and eaten as candy.

The Peterkin family were received at this late hour with a wild enthusiasm. Elizabeth Eliza was an especial heroine, and was made directly the president of the evening. Everybody said that she had best earned the distinction; for had she not come to the meeting by the longest way possible, by going away from it? The secretary declared that the principles of the society had been completely carried out. She had always believed that if left to itself, information would spread itself in a natural instead of a forced way.

"Now, in this case, if I had written twenty-nine notifications to this meeting, I should have wasted just so much of my time. But the information has disseminated naturally. Ann Maria said what a good plan it would be to have the Circumambients go to the sugaring at the New Hall. Everybody said it would be a good plan. Elizabeth Eliza came and spoke of the sugaring, and I spoke of the New Hall."

"But if you had told Elizabeth Eliza that all the maple syrup was to be brought here —" began Mrs. Peterkin.

"We should have lost our excursion for maple syrup," said Mr. Peterkin.

Later, as they reached home in the carry-all (Hiram having gone back with the wood-sled), Mr. and Mrs. Peterkin, after leaving little boys at their homes all along the route, found none of their own to get out at their own door. They must have joined Elizabeth Eliza, Agamemnon, and Solomon John in taking a circuitous route home with the rest of the Circumambients.

"The little boys will not be at home till midnight," said Mrs. Peterkin, anxiously. "I do think this is carrying the thing too far, after such a day!"

"Elizabeth Eliza will feel that she has acted up to the principles of the society," said Mr. Peterkin, "and we have done our best; for, as the little boys said, 'we did see the kettle.'"

The Peterkins "At Home"

IGHT not something be done by way of farewell before leaving for Egypt? They did not want to give another tea-party, and could not get in all at dinner. They had had charades and a picnic. Elizabeth Eliza wished for something unusual, that should be remembered after they had left for Egypt. Why should it not be a fancy ball? There never had been one in the place.

Mrs. Peterkin hesitated. Perhaps for that reason they ought not to attempt it. She liked to have things that other people had. She however objected most to the "ball" part. She could indeed still dance a minuet, but she was not sure she could get on in the "Boston dip."

The little boys said they would like the "fancy" part and "dressing up." They remembered their delight when they browned their faces for Hindus, at their charades, just for a few minutes; and what fun it would be to wear their costumes through a whole evening! Mrs. Peterkin shook her head; it was days and days before the brown had washed out of their complexions.

Still, she too was interested in the "dressing up." If they should wear costumes, they could make them of things that might be left behind, that they had done wearing, if they could only think of the right kind of things.

Mrs. Peterkin, indeed, had already packed up, although they were not to leave for two months, for she did not want to be hurried at the last. She and Elizabeth Eliza went on different principles in packing.

Elizabeth Eliza had been told that you really needed very little to travel with, — merely your travelling dress and a black silk. Mrs. Peterkin, on the contrary, had heard it was best to take everything you had, and then you need not spend your time shopping in Paris. So they had decided upon adopting both ways. Mrs. Peterkin was to take her "everything," and already had all the shoes and stockings she should need for a year or two. Elizabeth Eliza, on the other hand, prepared a small valise. She consoled herself with the thought that if she should meet anything that would not go into it, she could put it in one of her mother's trunks.

It was resolved to give the fancy ball.

Mr. Peterkin early determined upon a character. He decided to be Julius Caesar. He had a bald place on the top of his head, which he was told resembled that of the great Roman; and he concluded that the dress would be a simple one to get up, requiring only a sheet for a toga.

Agamemnon was inclined to take the part which his own name represented, and he looked up the costume of the Greek king of men. But he was dissatisfied with the representation given of him in Dr. Schliemann's "Mykenae." There was a picture of Agamemnon's mask, but very much battered. He might get a mask made in that pattern, indeed, and the little boys were delighted with the idea of battering it. Agamemnon would like to wear a mask, then he would have no trouble in keeping up his expression. But Elizabeth Eliza objected to the picture in Dr. Schliemann's book; she did not like it for Agamemnon, — it was too slanting in the eyes. So it was decided he should take the part of Nick Bottom, in "Midsummer Night's Dream." He could then wear the ass's head, which would have the same advantage as a mask, and would conceal his own face entirely. Then he could be making up any face he pleased in the ass's head, and would look like an ass without any difficulty, while his feet would show he was not one. Solomon John thought that they might make an ass's head if they could get a pattern, or could see the real animal and form an idea of the shape. Barnum's Circus would be along in a few weeks, and they could go on purpose to study the donkeys, as there usually was more than one donkey in the circus. Agamemnon, however, in going with a friend to a costumer's in Boston, found an ass's head already made.

The little boys found in an illustrated paper an accurate description of the Hindu snake-charmer's costume, and were so successful in their practice of shades of brown for the complexion, that Solomon John decided to take the part of Othello, and use some of their staining fluid.

There was some discussion as to consulting the lady from Philadelphia, who was in town.

Solomon John thought they ought to practise getting on by themselves, for soon the Atlantic would lie between her and them. Mrs. Peterkin thought they could telegraph. Elizabeth Eliza wanted to submit to her two or three questions about the supper, and whether, if her mother were Queen Elizabeth, they could have Chinese lanterns. Was China invented at that time? Agamemnon was sure China was one of the oldest countries in the world and did exist, though perhaps Queen Elizabeth did not know it.

Elizabeth Eliza was relieved to find that the lady from Philadelphia thought the question not important. It would be impossible to have everything in the house to correspond with all the different characters, unless they selected some period to represent, such as the age of Queen Elizabeth. Of course, Elizabeth Eliza would not wish to do this when her father was to be Julius Caesar.

The lady from Philadelphia advised Mrs. Peterkin to send for Jones the "caterer" to take charge of the supper. But his first question staggered her. How many did she expect?

They had not the slightest idea. They had sent invitations to everybody. The little boys proposed getting the directory of the place, and marking out the people they didn't know and counting up the rest. But even if this would give the number of invitations, it would not show how many would accept; and then there was no such directory. They could not expect answers, as their invitations were cards with "At Home" on them. One answer had come from a lady, that she too would be "at home" with rheumatism. So they only knew there was one person who would not come. Elizabeth Eliza had sent in Circumambient ways to all the members of that society, — by the little boys, for instance, who were sure to stop at the base-ball grounds, or somewhere, so a note was always delayed by them. One Circumambient note she sent by mail, purposely omitting the "Mass.," so that it went to the Dead-Letter Office, and came back six weeks after the party.

But the Peterkin family were not alone in commotion. The whole town was in excitement, for "everybody" had been invited. Ann Maria Bromwick had a book of costumes that she lent to a few friends, and everybody borrowed dresses or lent them, or went into town to the costumer's. Weeks passed in preparation. "What are you going to wear?" was the only question exchanged; and nobody answered, as nobody would tell.

At length the evening came, — a beautiful night in late summer, warm enough to have had the party out-of-doors;

but the whole house was lighted up and thrown open, and Chinese lanterns hung in the portico and on the pillars of the piazzas.

At an early hour the Peterkins were arrayed in their costumes. The little boys had their legs and arms and faces browned early in the day, and wore dazzingly white full trousers and white turbans.

Elizabeth Eliza had prepared a dress as Queen Elizabeth; but Solomon John was desirous that she should be Desdemona, and she gave up her costume to her mother. Mrs. Peterkin therefore wore a red wig which Ann Maria had found at a costumer's, a high ruff, and an old-fashioned brocade. She was not sure that it was proper for Queen Elizabeth to wear spectacles; but Queen Elizabeth must have been old enough, as she lived to be seventy. As for Elizabeth Eliza, in recalling the fact that Desdemona was smothered by pillows, she was so impressed by it that she decided she could wear the costume of a sheet-and-pillowcase party. So she wore a white figured silk that had been her mother's wedding-dress, and over it draped a sheet as a large mantle, and put a pillow-case upon her head, and could represent Desdemona not quite smothered. But Solomon John wished to carry out the whole scene at the end.

As they stood together, all ready to receive, in the parlor at the appointed hour, Mr. Peterkin suddenly exclaimed, —

"This will never do! We are not the Peterkins, — we are distinguished guests! We cannot receive."

"We shall have to give up the party," said Mrs. Peterkin.

"Or our costumes," groaned Agamemnon from his ass's head.

"We must go out, and come in as guests," said Elizabeth Eliza, leading the way to a back door, for guests were already thronging in, and up the front stairs. They passed out by a piazza, through the hedge of hollyhocks, toward the front of the house. Through the side windows of the library they could see the company pouring in. The black attendant was showing them upstairs; some were coming down, in doubt whether to enter the parlors, as no one was there. The wide middle entrance hall was lighted brilliantly; so were the parlors on one side and the library on the other.

But nobody was there to receive! A flock of guests was assembling, — peasant girls, Italian, German, and Norman; Turks, Greeks, Persians, fish-wives, brigands, chocolate-women, Lady Washington, Penelope, Red Riding-hood, Joan of Arc, nuns, Amy Robsart, Leicester, two or three Mary Stuarts, Neapolitan fisherboys, pirates of Penzance and elsewhere, — all lingering, some on the stairs, some going up, some coming down.

Charles I. without his head was entering the front door (a short gentleman, with a broad ruff drawn neatly together on top of his own head, which was concealed in his doublet below).

Three Hindu snake-charmers leaped wildly in and out among the throng, flinging about dark, crooked sticks for snakes.

There began to be a strange, deserted air about the house. Nobody knew what to do, where to go!

"Can anything have happened to the family?"

"Have they gone to Egypt?" whispered one.

No ushers came to show them in. A shudder ran through the whole assembly, the house seemed so uninhabited; and some of the guests were inclined to go away. The Peterkins saw it all through the long library-windows.

"What shall we do?" said Mr. Peterkin. "We have said *we* should be 'At Home.'"

"And here we are, all out-of-doors among the hollyhocks," said Elizabeth Eliza.

"There are no Peterkins to 'receive,'" said Mr. Peterkin, gloomily.

"We might go in and change our costumes," said Mrs. Peterkin, who already found her Elizabethan ruff somewhat stiff; "but, alas! I could not get at my best dress."

"The company is filling all the upper rooms," said Elizabeth Eliza; "we cannot go back."

At this moment the little boys returned from the front door, and in a subdued whisper explained that the lady from Philadelphia was arriving.

"Oh, bring her here!" said Mrs. Peterkin. And Solomon John hastened to meet her.

She came, to find a strange group half lighted by the Chinese lanterns. Mr. Peterkin, in his white toga, with a green wreath upon his head, came forward to address her in a noble manner, while she was terrified by the appearance of Agamemnon's ass's head, half hidden among the leaves.

"What shall we do?" exclaimed Mr. Peterkin. "There are no Peterkins; yet we have sent cards to everybody that they are 'At Home!'"

The lady from Philadelphia, who had been allowed to come without costume, considered for a moment. She looked through the windows to the seething mass now crowding the entrance hall. The Hindu snake-charmers gambolled about her.

"*We* will receive as the Peterkin family!" she exclaimed. She inquired for a cap of Mrs. Peterkin's, with a purple satin bow, such as she had worn that very morning. Amanda was found by a Hindu, and sent for it and for a purple cross-over shawl that Mrs. Peterkin was wont to wear. The daughters of the lady from Philadelphia put on some hats of the little boys and their india-rubber boots. Hastily they went in through the back door and presented themselves, just as some of the wavering guests had decided to leave the house, it seeming so quiet and sepulchral.

The crowd now flocked into the parlors. The Peterkins themselves left the hollyhocks and joined the company that was entering; Mr. Peterkin, as Julius Caesar, leading in Mrs. Peterkin, as Queen Elizabeth. Mrs. Peterkin hardly knew what to do, as she passed the parlor door; for one of the Osbornes, as Sir Walter Raleigh, flung a velvet cloak before her. She was uncertain whether she ought to step on it, especially as she discovered at that moment that she had forgotten to take off her rubber overshoes, which she had put on to go through the garden. But as she stood hesitating, the lady from Philadelphia, as Mrs. Peterkin, beckoned her forward, and she walked over the ruby velvet as though it were a door-mat.

For another surprise stunned her, — there were three Mrs. Peterkins! Not only Mrs. Bromwick, but their opposite neighbor, had induced Amanda to take dresses of Mrs. Peterkin's from the top of the trunks, and had come in at the same moment with the lady from Philadelphia, ready to receive. She stood in the middle of the bow-window at the back of the room, the two others in the corners. Ann Maria Bromwick had the part of Elizabeth Eliza, and Agamemnon too was represented; and there were many sets of "little boys" in india-rubber boots, going in and out with the Hindu snake-charmers.

Mr. Peterkin had studied up his Latin grammar a little, in preparation for his part of Julius Caesar. Agamemnon had reminded him that it was unnecessary, as Julius Caesar in Shakespeare spoke in English. Still he now found himself using with wonderful ease Latin phrases such as "E pluribus unum," "lapsus Linguae," and "sine qua non," where they seemed to be appropriate.

Solomon John looked well as Othello, although by some he was mistaken for an older snake-charmer, with his brown complexion, glaring white trousers, and white shirt. He wore a white lawn turban that had belonged to his great-grandmother. His part, however, was more understood when he was with Elizabeth Eliza as Desdemona; for they occasionally formed a tableau, in which he pulled the pillow-case completely over her head.

Agamemnon was greeted with applause as Nick Bottom. He sang the song of the "ousel cock," but he could not make himself heard. At last he found a "Titania" who listened to him.

But none of the company attempted to carry out the parts represented by their costumes. Charles I. soon conversed with Oliver Cromwell and with the different Mary Stuarts, who chatted gaily, as though executions were every-day occurrences.

At first there was a little awkwardness. Nuns stood as quiet as if in their convent cells, and brave brigands hid themselves behind the doors; but as the different guests began to surprise each other, the sounds of laughter and talking increased. Every new-comer was led up to each several Mrs. Peterkin.

Then came a great surprise, — a band of music sounded from the piazza. Some of the neighbors had sent in the town band, as a farewell tribute. This added to the excitement of the occasion. Strains of dance-music were heard, and dancing was begun. Sir Walter Raleigh led out Penelope, and Red Riding-hood without fear took the arm of the fiercest brigand for a round dance.

The various groups wandered in and out. Elizabeth Eliza studied the costumes of her friends, and wished she had tried each one of them. The members of the Circumambient

Society agreed that it would be always well to wear costumes at their meetings. As the principles of the society enforced a sort of uncertainty, if you always went in a different costume you would never have to keep up your own character. Elizabeth Eliza thought she should enjoy this. She had all her life been troubled with uncertainties and questions as to her own part of "Elizabeth Eliza," wondering always if she were doing the right thing. It did not seem to her that other people had such a bother. Perhaps they had simpler parts. They always seemed to know when to speak and when to be silent, while she was always puzzled as to what she should do as Elizabeth Eliza. Now, behind her pillow-case, she could look on and do nothing; all that was expected of her was to be smothered now and then. She breathed freely and enjoyed herself, because for the evening she could forget the difficult role of Elizabeth Eliza.

Mrs. Peterkin was bewildered. She thought it a good occasion to study how Mrs. Peterkin should act; but there were three Mrs. Peterkins. She found herself gazing first at one, then at another. Often she was herself called Mrs. Peterkin.

At supper-time the bewilderment increased. She was led in by the Earl of Leicester, as principal guest. Yet it was to her own dining-room, and she recognized her own forks and spoons among the borrowed ones, although the china was different (because their own set was not large enough to go round for so much company). It was all very confusing. The dance-music floated through the air. Three Mrs. Peterkins hovered before her, and two Agamemnons; for the ass's head proved hot and heavy, and Agamemnon was forced to hang it over his arm as he offered coffee to Titania. There seemed to be two Elizabeth Elizas, for Elizabeth Eliza had thrown back her pillow-case in order to eat her fruit-ice.

Mr. Peterkin was wondering how Julius Caesar would have managed to eat his salad with his fork, before forks were invented, and then he fell into a fit of abstraction, planning to say "Vale" to the guests as they left, but anxious that the word should not slip out before the time. Eight little boys and three Hindu snake-charmers were eating copiously of frozen pudding. Two Joans of Arc were talking to Charles I., who had found his head. All things seemed doubled to Mrs. Peterkin as they floated before her.

"Was she eating her own supper or somebody's else? Were they Peterkins, or were they not?"

Strains of dance-music sounded from the library. Yes, they were giving a fancy ball! The Peterkins were "At Home" for the last time before leaving for Egypt!

6

Mrs. Peterkin in Egypt

HE family had taken passage in the new line for Bordeaux. They supposed they had; but would they ever reach the vessel in New York? The last moments were terrific. In spite of all their careful arrangements, their planning and packing of the last year, it seemed, after all, as if everything were left for the very last day. There were presents for the family to be packed, six steamerbags for Mrs. Peterkin, half a dozen satchels of salts-bottles for Elizabeth Eliza, Apollinaris water, lunch-baskets. All these must be disposed of.

On the very last day Elizabeth Eliza went into Boston to buy a bird, as she had been told she would be less likely to be sea-sick if she had a bird in a cage in her stateroom. Both she and her mother disliked the singing of caged birds, especially of canaries; but Mrs. Peterkin argued that they would be less likely to be homesick, as they never had birds at home. After long moments of indecision, Elizabeth Eliza determined upon two canary-birds, thinking she might let them fly as they approached the shore of Portugal, and they would then reach their native islands. This matter detained her till the latest train, so that on her return from Boston to their quiet suburban home, she found the whole family assembled in the station, ready to take the through express train to New York.

She did not have time, therefore, to go back to the house for her own things. It was now locked up and the key intrusted to the Bromwicks; and all the Bromwicks and the rest of the neighbors were at the station, ready to bid them goodby. The family had done their best to collect all her scattered bits of baggage; but all through her travels, afterward, she was continually missing something she had left behind, that she would have packed and had intended to bring.

They reached New York with half a day on their hands; and during this time Agamemnon fell in with some old college friends, who were going with a party to Greece to look up the new excavations. They were to leave the next day in a steamer for Gibraltar. Agamemnon felt that here was the place for him, and hastened to consult his family. Perhaps he could persuade them to change their plans and take passage with the party for Gibraltar. But he reached the pier just as the steamer for Bordeaux was leaving the shore. He was late, and was left behind! Too late to consult them, too late even to join them! He examined his map, however, — one of his latest purchases, which he carried in his pockets, — and consoled himself with the fact that on reaching Gibraltar he could soon communicate with his family at Bordeaux, and he was easily reconciled to his fate.

It was not till the family landed at Bordeaux that they discovered the absence of Agamemnon. Every day there had been some of the family unable to come on deck, — sea-sick below. Mrs. Peterkin never left her berth and constantly sent messages to the others to follow her example, as she was afraid some one of them would be lost overboard. Those who were on deck from time to time were always different ones, and the passage was remarkably quick; while, from the tossing of the ship, as they met rough weather, they were all too miserable to compare notes or count their numbers.

Elizabeth Eliza especially had been exhausted by the voyage. She had not been many days sea-sick, but the incessant singing of the birds had deprived her of sleep. Then the necessity of talking French had been a great tax upon her. The other passengers were mostly French, and the rest of the family constantly appealed to her to interpret their wants, and explain them to the *garçon* once every day at dinner. She felt as if she never wished to speak another word in French; and the necessity of being interpreter at the hotel at Bordeaux, on their arrival, seemed almost too much for her. She had even forgotten to let her canary-birds fly when off shore in the Bay of Biscay, and they were still with her, singing incessantly, as if they were rejoicing over an approach to their native shores. She thought now she must keep them till their return, which they were already planning.

The little boys, indeed, would like to have gone back on the return trip of the steamer. A son of the steward told them that the return cargo consisted of dried fruits and raisins; that every stateroom, except those occupied with passengers, would be filled with boxes of raisins and jars of grapes; that these often broke open in the passage, giving a great opportunity for boys.

But the family held to their Egypt plan, and were cheered by making the acquaintance of an English party. At the *table d'hôte* Elizabeth Eliza by chance dropped her fork into her neighbor's lap. She apologized in French; her neighbor answered in the same language, which Elizabeth Eliza understood so well that she concluded she had at last met with a true Parisian, and ventured on more conversation, when suddenly they both found they were talking in English, and Elizabeth Eliza exclaimed, "I am so glad to meet an American," at the moment that her companion was saying, "Then you are an Englishwoman!"

From this moment Elizabeth Eliza was at ease, and indeed both parties were mutually pleased. Elizabeth Eliza's new friend was one of a large party, and she was delighted to find that they too were planning a winter in Egypt. They were waiting till a friend should have completed her "cure" at Pau, and the Peterkins were glad also to wait for the appearance of Agamemnon, who might arrive in the next steamer.

One of the little boys was sure he had heard Agamemnon's voice the morning after they left New York, and was certain he must have been on board the vessel. Mr. Peterkin was not so sure. He now remembered that Agamemnon had not been at the dinner-table the very first evening; but then neither Mrs. Peterkin nor Solomon John was able to be present, as the vessel was tossing in a most uncomfortable manner, and nothing but dinner could have kept the little boys at table. Solomon John knew that Agamemnon had not been in his own stateroom during the passage, but he himself had seldom left it, and it had been always planned that Agamemnon should share that of a fellow-passenger.

However this might be, it would be best to leave Marseilles with the English party by the "P. & O." steamer. This was one of the English "Peninsular and Oriental" line, that left Marseilles for Alexandria, Egypt, and made a return trip directly to Southampton, England. Mr. Peterkin thought it might be advisable to take "go-and-return" tickets, coming back to Southampton; and Mrs. Peterkin liked the idea of no change of baggage, though she dreaded the longer voyage. Elizabeth Eliza approved of this return trip in the P. & O. steamer, and decided it would give a good opportunity to dispose of her canary-birds on her return.

The family therefore consoled themselves at Marseilles with the belief that Agamemnon would appear somehow. If not, Mr. Peterkin thought he could telegraph him from

Marseilles, if he only knew where to telegraph to. But at Marseilles there was great confusion at the Hôtel de Noailles; for the English party met other friends, who persuaded them to take route together by Brindisi. Elizabeth Eliza was anxious to continue with her new English friend, and Solomon John was delighted with the idea of passing through the whole length of Italy. But the sight of the long journey, as she saw it on the map in the guide-book, terrified Mrs. Peterkin. And Mr. Peterkin had taken their tickets for the Marseilles line. Elizabeth Eliza still dwelt upon the charm of crossing under the Alps, while this very idea alarmed Mrs. Peterkin.

On the last morning the matter was still undecided. On leaving the hotel, it was necessary for the party to divide and take two omnibuses. Mr. and Mrs. Peterkin reached the steamer at the moment of departure, and suddenly Mrs. Peterkin found they were leaving the shore. As they crossed the broad gangway to reach the deck, she had not noticed they had left the pier; indeed, she had supposed that the steamer was one she saw out in the offing, and that they would be obliged to take a boat to reach it. She hurried from the group of travellers whom she had followed to find Mr. Peterkin reading from his guide-book to the little boys an explanation that they were passing the Château d'If, from which the celebrated historical character the Count of Monte Cristo had escaped by flinging himself into the sea.

"Where is Elizabeth Eliza? Where is Solomon John?" Mrs. Peterkin exclaimed, seizing Mr. Peterkin's arm. Where indeed? There was a pile of the hand-baggage of the family, but not that of Elizabeth Eliza, not even the bird-cage. "It was on the top of the other omnibus," exclaimed Mrs. Peterkin. Yes, one of the little boys had seen it on the pavement of the court-yard of the hotel, and had carried it to the omnibus in which Elizabeth Eliza was sitting. He had seen her through the window.

"Where is that other omnibus?" exclaimed Mrs. Peterkin, looking vaguely over the deck, as they were fast retreating from the shore. "Ask somebody what became of that other omnibus!" she exclaimed. "Perhaps they have gone with the English people," suggested Mr. Peterkin; but he went to the officers of the boat, and attempted to explain in French that one half of his family had been left behind. He was relieved to find that the officers could understand his French, though they did not talk English. They declared, however, it was utterly impossible to turn back. They were already two minutes and a half behind time on account of waiting for a party who had been very long in crossing the gangway.

Mr. Peterkin returned gloomily with the little boys to Mrs. Peterkin. "We cannot go back," he said, "we must content ourselves with going on; but I conclude we can telegraph from Malta. We can send a message to Elizabeth Eliza and Solomon John, telling them that they can take the next Marseilles P. & O. steamer in ten days, or that they can go back to Southampton for the next boat, which leaves at the end of this week. And Elizabeth Eliza may decide upon this," Mr. Peterkin concluded, "on account of passing so near the Canary Isles."

"She will be glad to be rid of the birds," said Mrs. Peterkin, calming herself.

These anxieties, however, were swallowed up in new trials. Mrs. Peterkin found that she must share her cabin (she found it was called "cabin," and not "stateroom," which bothered her and made her feel like Robinson Crusoe), — her cabin she must share with some strange ladies, while Mr. Peterkin and the little boys were carried to another part of the ship. Mrs. Peterkin remonstrated, delighted to find that her English was understood, though it was not listened to. It was explained to her that every family was divided in this way, and that she would meet Mr. Peterkin and the little boys at mealtimes in the large *salon* — on which all the cabins opened — and on deck; and she was obliged to content herself with this. Whenever they met their time was spent in concocting a form of telegram to send from Malta. It would be difficult to bring it into the required number of words, as it would be necessary to suggest three different plans to Elizabeth Eliza and Solomon John. Besides the two they had already discussed, there was to be considered the possibility of their having joined the English party. But Mrs. Peterkin was sure they must have gone back first to the Hôtel de Noailles, to which they could address their telegram.

She found, meanwhile, the ladies in her cabin very kind and agreeable. They were mothers returning to India, who had been home to England to leave their children, as they were afraid to expose them longer to the climate of India. Mrs. Peterkin could have sympathetic talks with them over their family photographs. Mrs. Peterkin's family-book was, alas! in Elizabeth Eliza's hand-bag. It contained the family photographs, from early childhood upward, and was a large volume, representing the children at every age.

At Malta, as he supposed, Mr. Peterkin and the little boys landed, in order to send their telegram. Indeed, all of the gentlemen among the passengers, and some of the ladies, gladly went on shore to visit the points of interest that could be seen in the time allotted. The steamer was to take in coal, and would not leave till early the next morning.

Mrs. Peterkin did not accompany them. She still had her fears about leaving the ship and returning to it, although it had been so quietly accomplished at Marseilles.

The party returned late at night, after Mrs. Peterkin had

gone to her cabin. The next morning, she found the ship was in motion, but she did not find Mr. Peterkin and the little boys at the breakfast-table as usual. She was told that the party who went on shore had all been to the opera, and had returned at a late hour to the steamer, and would naturally be late at breakfast. Mrs. Peterkin went on deck to await them, and look for Malta as it seemed to retreat in the distance. But the day passed on, and neither Mr. Peterkin nor either of the little boys appeared! She tried to calm herself with the thought that they must need sleep; but all the rest of the passengers appeared, relating their different adventures. At last she sent the steward to inquire for them. He came back with one of the officers of the boat, much disturbed, to say that they could not be found; they must have been left behind. There was great excitement, and deep interest expressed for Mrs. Peterkin. One of the officers was very surly, and declared he could not be responsible for the inanity of passengers. Another was more courteous. Mrs. Peterkin asked if they could not go back, — if, at least, she could not be put back. He explained how this would be impossible, but that the company would telegraph when they reached Alexandria.

Mrs. Peterkin calmed herself as well as she could, though indeed she was bewildered by her position. She was to land in Alexandria alone, and the landing she was told would be especially difficult. The steamer would not be able to approach the shore; the passengers would go down the sides of the ship, and be lifted off the steps, by Arabs, into a felucca (whatever that was) below. She shuddered at the prospect. It was darker than her gloomiest fancies had pictured. Would it not be better to remain in the ship, go back to Southampton, perhaps meet Elizabeth Eliza there, picking up Mr. Peterkin at Malta on the way? But at this moment

she discovered that she was not on a "P. & O." steamer, —
it was a French steamer of the "Messagerie" line; they had
stopped at Messina, and not at Malta. She could not go back
to Southampton, so she was told by an English colonel on
his way to India. He indeed was very courteous, and advised her to "go to an hotel" at Alexandria with some of
the ladies, and send her telegrams from there. To whom,
however, would she wish to send a telegram?

"Who is Mr. Peterkin's banker?" asked the Colonel. Alas!
Mrs. Peterkin did not know. He had at first selected a banker
in London, but had afterward changed his mind and talked
of a banker in Paris; and she was not sure what was his final
decision. She had known the name of the London banker,
but had forgotten it, because she had written it down, and
she never did remember the things she wrote down in her
book. That was her old memorandum-book, and she had left
it at home because she had brought a new one for her travels.
She was sorry now she had not kept the old book. This,
however, was not of so much importance, as it did not contain the name of the Paris banker; and this she had never
heard. "Elizabeth Eliza would know"; but how could she
reach Elizabeth Eliza?

Some one asked if there were not some friend in America
to whom she could appeal, if she did not object to using the
ocean telegraph.

"There is a friend in America," said Mrs. Peterkin, "to
whom we all of us do go for advice, and who always does
help us. She lives in Philadelphia."

"Why not telegraph to her for advice?" asked her friends.

Mrs. Peterkin gladly agreed that it would be the best plan.
The expense of the cablegram would be nothing in compari-
son with the assistance the answer would bring.

Her new friends then invited her to accompany them to

their hotel in Alexandria, from which she could send her despatch. The thought of thus being able to reach her hand across the sea to the lady from Philadelphia gave Mrs. Peterkin fresh courage, — courage even to make the landing. As she descended the side of the ship and was guided down the steps, she closed her eyes that she might not see herself lifted into the many-oared boat by the wild-looking Arabs, of whom she had caught a glimpse from above. But she could not close her ears; and as they approached the shore, strange sounds almost deafened her. She closed her eyes again, as she was lifted from the boat and heard the wild yells and shrieks around her. There was a clashing of brass, a jingling of bells, and the screams grew more and more terrific. If she did open her eyes, she saw wild figures gesticulating, dark faces, gay costumes, crowds of men and boys, donkeys, horses, even camels, in the distance. She closed her eyes once more as she was again lifted. Should she now find herself on the back of one of those high camels? Perhaps for this she came to Egypt. But when she looked round again, she found she was leaning back in a comfortable open carriage, with a bottle of salts at her nose. She was in the midst of a strange whirl of excitement; but all the party were bewildered, and she had scarcely recovered her composure when they reached the hotel.

Here a comfortable meal and rest somewhat restored them. By the next day a messenger from the boat brought her the return telegram from Messina. Mr. Peterkin and family, left behind by the "Messagerie" steamer, had embarked the next day by steamer, probably for Naples.

More anxious than ever was Mrs. Peterkin to send her despatch. It was too late the day of their arrival; but at an early hour next day it was sent, and after a day had elapsed, the answer came: —

"All meet at the Sphinx."

Everything now seemed plain. The words were few but clear. Her English friends were going directly to Cairo, and she accompanied them.

After reaching Cairo, the whole party were obliged to rest awhile. They would indeed go with Mrs. Peterkin on her first visit to the Sphinx, as to see the Sphinx and ascend the pyramid formed part of their programme. But many delays occurred to detain them, and Mrs. Peterkin had resolved to carry out completely the advice of the telegram. She would sit every day before the Sphinx. She found that as yet there was no hotel exactly in front of the Sphinx, nor indeed on that side of the river, and she would be obliged to make the excursion of nine miles there and nine miles back, each day. But there would always be a party of travellers whom she could accompany. Each day she grew more and more accustomed to the bewildering sights and sounds about her, and more and more willing to intrust herself to the dark-colored guides. At last, chafing at so many delays, she decided to make the expedition without her new friends. She had made some experiments in riding upon a donkey, and found she was seldom thrown, and could not be hurt by the slight fall.

And so, one day, Mrs. Peterkin sat alone in front of the Sphinx, — alone, as far as her own family and friends were concerned, and yet not alone indeed. A large crowd of guides sat around this strange lady who proposed to spend the day in front of the Sphinx. Clad in long white robes, with white turbans crowning their dark faces, they gazed into her eyes with something of the questioning expression with which she herself was looking into the eyes of the Sphinx.

There were other travellers wandering about. Just now her own party had collected to eat their lunch together;

but they were scattered again, and she sat with a circle of Arabs about her, the watchful dragoman lingering near.

Somehow the Eastern languor must have stolen upon her, or she could not have sat so calmly, not knowing where a single member of her family was at that moment. And she had dreaded Egypt so; had feared separation; had even been a little afraid of the Sphinx, upon which she was now looking as at a protecting angel. But they all were to meet at the Sphinx!

If only she could have seen where the different members of the family were at that moment, she could not have sat so quietly. She little knew that a tall form, not far away (following some guides down into the lower halls of a lately excavated temple), with a blue veil wrapped about a face shielded with smoke-colored spectacles, was that of Elizabeth Eliza herself, from whom she had been separated two weeks before.

She little knew that at this moment Solomon John was standing looking over the edge of the Matterhorn, wishing he had not come up so high. But such a gay young party had set off that morning from the hotel that he had supposed it an easy thing to join them; and now he would fain go back, but was tied to the rest of his party with their guide preceding them, and he must keep on and crawl up behind them, still farther, on hands and knees.

Agamemnon was at Mycenae, looking down into an open pit.

Two of the little boys were roasting eggs in the crater of Mount Vesuvius.

And she would have seen Mr. Peterkin comfortably reclining in a gondola, with one of the little boys, in front of the palaces of Venice.

But none of this she saw; she only looked into the eyes of the Sphinx.

7

Mrs. Peterkin Faints on the Great Pyramid

EET at the Sphinx!" Yes; these were the words that the lady from Philadelphia had sent in answer to the several telegrams that had reached her from each member of the Peterkin family. She had received these messages while staying in a remote country town, but she could communicate with the cable line by means of the telegraph office at a railway station. The intelligent operator, seeing the same date affixed at the close of each message, "took in," as she afterward expressed it, that it was the date of the day on which the message was sent; and as this was always prefixed to every despatch, she did not add it to the several messages. She afterward expressed herself as sorry for the mistake, and declared it should not occur another time.

Elizabeth Eliza was the first at the appointed spot, as her route had been somewhat shorter than the one her mother had taken. A wild joy had seized her when she landed in Egypt, and saw the frequent and happy use of the donkey as a beast of travel. She had never ventured to ride at home, and had always shuddered at the daring of the women who rode at the circuses, and closed her eyes at their performances. But as soon as she saw the little Egyptian donkeys, a mania for riding possessed her. She was so tall that she could scarcely, under any circumstances, fall from them, while she could mount them with as much ease as she could the arm of the sofa at home, and most of the animals seemed as harmless. It is true, the donkey-boys gave her the wrong word to use when she might wish to check the pace of her donkey, and mischievously taught her to avoid the soothing phrase of *beschwesch*, giving her instead one that should goad the beast she rode to its highest speed; but Elizabeth Eliza was so delighted with the quick pace that she was continually urging her donkey onward, to the surprise and delight of each fresh attendant donkey-boy. He would run at a swift pace after her, stopping sometimes to pick up a loose slipper, if it were shuffled off from his foot in his quick run, but always bringing up even in the end.

Elizabeth Eliza's party had made a quick journey by the route from Brindisi, and, proceeding directly to Cairo, had stopped at a small French hotel not very far from Mrs. Peterkin and her party. Every morning at an early hour Elizabeth Eliza made her visit to the Sphinx, arriving there always the first one of her own party, and spending the rest of the day in explorations about the neighborhood.

Mrs. Peterkin, meanwhile, set out each day at a later hour, arriving in time to take her noon lunch in front of the Sphinx, after which she indulged in a comfortable nap and returned to the hotel before sunset.

A week — indeed, ten days — passed in this way. One morning, Mrs. Peterkin and her party had taken the ferry-boat to cross the Nile. As they were leaving the boat on the other side, in the usual crowd, Mrs. Peterkin's attention was arrested by a familiar voice. She turned, to see a tall young man who, though he wore a red fez upon his head and a scarlet wrap around his neck, certainly resembled Agamemnon. But this Agamemnon was talking Greek, with gesticulations. She was so excited that she turned to follow him through the crowd, thus separating herself from the rest of the party. At once she found herself surrounded by a mob of Arabs, in every kind of costume, all screaming and yelling in the manner to which she was becoming accustomed. Poor Mrs. Peterkin plaintively protested in English, exclaiming, "I should prefer a donkey!" but the Arabs could not understand her strange words. They had, however, struck the ear of the young man in the red fez whom she had been following. He turned, and she gazed at him. It was Agamemnon!

He, meanwhile, was separated from his party, and hardly knew how to grapple with the urgent Arabs. His recently acquired Greek did not assist him, and he was advising his mother to yield and mount one of the steeds, while he followed on another, when, happily, the dragoman of her party appeared. He administered a volley of rebukes to the persistent Arabs, and bore Mrs. Peterkin to her donkey. She was thus carried away from Agamemnon, who was also mounted upon a donkey by his companions. But their destination was the same; and though they could hold no conversation on the way, Agamemnon could join his mother as they approached the Sphinx.

But he and his party were to ascend the pyramid before going on to the Sphinx, and he advised his mother to do the same. He explained that it was a perfectly easy thing to do. You had only to lift one of your feet up quite high, as though you were going to step on the mantelpiece, and an Arab on each side would lift you to the next step. Mrs. Peterkin was sure she could not step up on their mantelpieces at home. She never had done it, — she never had even tried to. But Agamemnon reminded her that those in their own house were very high, — "old colonial"; and meanwhile she found herself carried along with the rest of the party.

At first the ascent was delightful to her. It seemed as if she were flying. The powerful Nubian guides, one on each side, lifted her jauntily up, without her being conscious of motion. Having seen them daily for some time past, she was now not much afraid of these handsome athletes, with their polished black skins, set off by dazzling white garments. She called out to Agamemnon, who had preceded her, that it was charming; she was not at all afraid. Every now and then she stopped to rest on the broad cornice made by each retreating step. Suddenly, when she was about half-way up, as she leaned back against the step above, she found herself panting and exhausted. A strange faintness came over her. She was looking off over a beautiful scene: through the wide Libyan desert the blue Nile wound between borders of green edging, while the picturesque minarets of Cairo, on the opposite side of the river, and the sand in the distance beyond, gleamed with a red and yellow light beneath the rays of the noonday sun.

But the picture danced and wavered before her dizzy sight. She sat there alone; for Agamemnon and the rest had passed on, thinking she was stopping to rest. She seemed deserted, save by the speechless black statues, one on either side, who, as she seemed to be fainting before their eyes, were looking at her in some anxiety. She saw dimly these wild men gazing at her. She thought of Mungo Park, dying with the African women singing about him. How little she had ever dreamed, when she read that account in her youth, and gazed at the savage African faces in the picture, that she might be left to die in the same way alone, in a strange land — and on the side of a pyramid! Her guides were kindly. One of them took her shawl to wrap about her, as she seemed to be shivering; and as a party coming down from the top had a jar of water, one of her Nubians moistened a handkerchief with water and laid it upon her head. Mrs. Peterkin had closed her eyes, but she opened them again, to see the black figures in their white draperies still standing by her. The travellers coming down paused a few minutes to wonder and give counsel, then passed on, to make way for another party following them. Again Mrs. Peterkin closed her eyes, but once more opened them at hearing a well-known shout, — such a shout as only one of the Peterkin family could give, — one of the little boys!

Yes, he stood before her, and Agamemnon was behind; they had met on top of the pyramid.

The sight was indeed a welcome one to Mrs. Peterkin, and revived her so that she even began to ask questions: "Where had he come from? Where were the other little boys? Where was Mr. Peterkin?" No one could tell where the other little boys were. And the sloping side of the pyramid, with a fresh party waiting to pass up and the guides eager to go down, was not just the place to explain the long, confused story. All that Mrs. Peterkin could understand was that Mr. Peterkin was now, probably, inside the pyramid, beneath her very feet! Agamemnon had found this solitary "little boy" on top of the pyramid, accompanied by a guide and one of the party that he and his father had joined on leaving Venice. At the foot of the pyramid there had been some dispute in the party as to whether they should first go up the pyramid, or down inside, and in the altercation the party was divided; the little boy had been sure that his father meant to go up first, and so he had joined the guide who went up. But where was Mr. Peterkin? Probably in the inner-most depths of the pyramid below. As soon as Mrs. Peterkin understood this, she was eager to go down, in spite of her late faintness; even to tumble down would help her to meet Mr. Peterkin the sooner. She was lifted from stone to stone by the careful

Nubians. Agamemnon had already emptied his pocket of coins, in supplying backsheesh to his guide, and all were anxious to reach the foot of the pyramid and find the dragoman, who could answer the demands of the others.

Breathless as she was, as soon as she had descended, Mrs. Peterkin was anxious to make for the entrance to the inside. Before, she had declared that nothing would induce her to go into the pyramid. She was afraid of being lost in its stairways and shut up forever as a mummy. But now she forgot all her terrors; she must find Mr. Peterkin at once!

She was the first to plunge down the narrow stairway after the guide, and was grateful to find the steps so easy to descend. But they presently came out into a large, open room, where no stairway was to be seen. On the contrary, she was invited to mount the shoulders of a burly Nubian, to reach a large hole half-way up the side-wall (higher than any mantelpiece), and to crawl through this hole along the passage till she should reach another stairway. Mrs. Peterkin paused. Could she trust these men? Was not this a snare to entice her into one of these narrow passages? Agamemnon was far behind. Could Mr. Peterkin have ventured into this treacherous place?

At this moment a head appeared through the opening above, followed by a body. It was that of one of the native guides. Voices were heard coming through the passage: one voice had a twang to it that surely Mrs. Peterkin had heard before. Another head appeared now, bound with a blue veil, while the eyes were hidden by green goggles. Yet Mrs. Peterkin could not be mistaken, — it was — yes, it was the head of Elizabeth Eliza!

It seemed as though that were all, it was so difficult to bring forward any more of her. Mrs. Peterkin was screaming from below, asking if it were indeed Elizabeth Eliza, while excitement at recognizing her mother made it more difficult for Elizabeth Eliza to extricate herself. But travellers below and behind urged her on, and with the assistance of the guides, she pushed forward and almost fell into the arms of her mother. Mrs. Peterkin was wild with joy as Agamemnon and his brother joined them.

"But Mr. Peterkin!" at last exclaimed their mother. "Did you see anything of your father?"

"He is behind," said Elizabeth Eliza. "I was looking for the body of Chufu, the founder of the pyramid, — for I have longed to be the discoverer of his mummy, — and I found instead — my father!"

Mrs. Peterkin looked up, and at that moment saw Mr. Peterkin emerging from the passage above. He was carefully planting one foot on the shoulder of a stalwart Nubian guide. He was very red in the face, from recent exertion, but he was indeed Mr. Peterkin. On hearing the cry of Mrs. Peterkin, he tottered, and would have fallen but for the support of the faithful guide.

The narrow place was scarcely large enough to hold their joy. Mrs. Peterkin was ready to faint again with her great excitement. She wanted to know what had become of the other little boys, and if Mr. Peterkin had heard from Solomon John. But the small space was becoming more and more crowded. The dragomans from the different parties with which the Peterkins were connected came to announce their several luncheons, and insisted upon their leaving the pyramid.

Mrs. Peterkin's dragoman wanted her to go on directly to the Sphinx, and she still clung to the belief that only then would there be a complete reunion of the family. Yet she could not separate herself from the rest. They could not let her go, and they were all hungry, and she herself felt the need of food.

But with the confusion of so many luncheons, and so much explanation to be gone through with, it was difficult to get an answer to her questions.

Elizabeth Eliza and her father were involved in a discussion as to whether they should have met if he had not gone into the queen's chamber in the pyramid. For if he had not gone to the queen's chamber he would have left the inside of the pyramid before Mrs. Peterkin reached it, and would have missed her, as he was too fatigued to make the ascent. And Elizabeth Eliza, if she had not met her father, had planned going back to the king's chamber in another search for the body of Chufu, in which case she would have been too late to meet her mother. Mrs. Peterkin was not much interested in this discussion; it was enough that they had met. But she could not get answers to what she considered more important questions; while Elizabeth Eliza, though delighted to meet again her father and mother and brothers, and though interested in the fate of the missing ones, was absorbed in the Egyptian question; and the mingling of all their interests made satisfactory intercourse impracticable.

Where was Solomon John? What had become of the body of Chufu? Had Solomon John been telegraphed to? When had Elizabeth Eliza seen him last? Was he Chufu or Shufu, and why Cheops? and where were the other little boys?

Mr. Peterkin attempted to explain that he had taken a steamer from Messina to the south of Italy, and a southern route to Brindisi. By mistake he had taken the steamer *from* Alexandria, on its way to Venice, instead of the one that was leaving Brindisi for Alexandria at the same hour. Indeed, just as he had discovered his mistake, and had seen the other steaming off by his side in the other direction, too late he fancied he saw the form of Elizabeth Eliza on deck, leaning over the taffrail (if it was a taffrail). It was a tall lady, with a blue veil wound around her hat. Was it possible? Could he have been in time to reach Elizabeth Eliza? His explanation only served to increase the number of questions. Mrs. Peterkin had many more. How had Agamemnon reached them? Had he come to Bordeaux with them? But Agamemnon and Elizabeth Eliza were now discussing with others the number of feet that the Great Pyramid measured. The remaining members of all the parties, too, whose hunger and thirst were now fully satisfied, were ready to proceed to the Sphinx, which only Mrs. Peterkin and Elizabeth Eliza had visited.

Side by side on their donkeys, Mrs. Peterkin attempted to learn something from Mr. Peterkin about the other little boys. But his donkey proved restive: now it bore him on in swift flight from Mrs. Peterkin; now it would linger behind. His words were jerked out only at intervals. All that could be said was that they were separated; the little boys wanted to go to Vesuvius, but Mr. Peterkin felt they must hurry to Brindisi. At a station where the two trains parted—one for Naples, the other for Brindisi—he found suddenly, too late, that they were not with him; they must have gone on to Naples. But where were they now?

8

The Last of the Peterkins

THE expedition up the Nile had taken place successfully. The Peterkin family had reached Cairo again, — at least, its scattered remnant was there, and they were now to consider what next.

Mrs. Peterkin would like to spend her life in the dahabieh,[1] though she could not pronounce its name, and she still felt the strangeness of the scenes about her. However, she had only to look out upon the mud villages on the bank to see that she was in the veritable "Africa" she had seen pictured in the geography of her childhood. If further corroboration were required, had she not, only the day before, when accompanied by no one but a little donkey-boy, shuddered to meet a strange Nubian, attired principally in hair that stood out from his savage face in frizzes at least half a yard long?

But oh the comforts of no trouble in housekeeping on board the dahabieh! Never to know what they were to have for dinner, nor to be asked what they would like, and yet always to have a dinner you could ask chance friends to, knowing all would be perfectly served! Some of the party with whom they had engaged their dahabieh had even brought canned baked beans from New England, which seemed to make their happiness complete.

[1] A boat used for transportation on the Nile.

"Though we see beans here," said Mrs. Peterkin, "they are not 'Boston beans'!"

She had fancied she would have to live on stuffed ostrich (ostrich stuffed with iron filings, that the books tell of), or fried hippopotamus, or boiled rhinoceros. But she met with none of these, and day after day was rejoiced to find her native turkey appearing on the table, with pigeons and chickens (though the chickens, to be sure, were scarcely larger than the pigeons), and lamb that was really not more tough than that of New Hampshire and the White Mountains.

If they dined with the Arabs, there was indeed a kind of dark molasses-gingerbread-looking cake, with curds in it, that she found it hard to eat. "But *they* like it," she said complacently.

The remaining little boy, too, smiled over his pile of ripe bananas, as he thought of the quarter-of-a-dollar-a-half-dozen green ones at that moment waiting at the corners of the streets at home. Indeed, it was a land for boys. There were the dates, both fresh and dried, — far more juicy than those learned at school; and there was the gingerbread-nut tree, the dôm palm, that bore a nut tasting "like baker's gingerbread that has been kept a few days in the shop," as the remaining little boy remarked. And he wished for his brothers when the live dinner came on board their boat, at the stopping-places, in the form of good-sized sheep struggling on the shoulders of stout Arabs, or an armful of live hens and pigeons.

All the family (or as much of it as was present) agreed with Mrs. Peterkin's views. Amanda at home had seemed quite a blessing, but at this distance her services, compared with the attentions of their Maltese dragoman and the devotion of their Arab servants, seemed of doubtful value, and even Mrs. Peterkin dreaded returning to her tender mercies.

"Just imagine inviting the Russian Count to dinner at home — and Amanda!" exclaimed Elizabeth Eliza.

"And he came to dinner at least three times a week on board the boat," said the remaining little boy.

"The Arabs are so convenient about carrying one's umbrellas and shawls," said Elizabeth Eliza. "How I should miss Hassan in picking up my blue veil!"

The family recalled many anecdotes of the shortcomings of Amanda, as Mrs. Peterkin leaned back upon her divan and wafted a fly-whisk. Mr. Peterkin had expended large sums in telegrams from every point where he found the telegraph in operation; but there was no reply from Solomon John, and none from the two little boys.

By a succession of telegrams they had learned that no one had fallen into the crater of Vesuvius in the course of the last six months, not even a little boy. This was consoling.

By letters from the lady from Philadelphia, they learned that she had received Solomon John's telegram from Geneva at the time she heard from the rest of the family, and one signed "L. Boys" from Naples. But neither of these telegrams gave an address for return answers, which she had, however, sent to Geneva and Naples, with the fatal omission by the operator (as she afterward learned) of the date, as in other telegrams.

Mrs. Peterkin therefore disliked to be long away from the Sphinx, and their excursion up the Nile had been shortened on this account. All the Nubian guides near the pyramids had been furnished with additional backsheesh and elaborate explanations from Mr. Peterkin as to how they should send him information if Solomon John and the little boys should turn up at the Sphinx, — for all the family agreed they would probably appear in Egypt together.

Mrs. Peterkin regretted not having any photographs to

leave with the guides; but Elizabeth Eliza, alas! had lost at Brindisi the hand-bag that contained the family photograph-book.

Mrs. Peterkin would have liked to take up her residence near the Sphinx for the rest of the year. But every one warned her that the heat of an Egyptian summer would not allow her to stay at Cairo, — scarcely even on the sea-shore, at Alexandria.

How thankful was Mrs. Peterkin, a few months after, when the war in Egypt broke out, that her wishes had not been yielded to! For many nights she could not sleep, picturing how they all might have been massacred by the terrible mob in Alexandria.

Intelligence of Solomon John led them to take their departure.

One day, they were discussing at the *table d'hôte* their letters from the lady from Philadelphia, and how they showed that Solomon John had been at Geneva.

"Ah, there was his mistake!" said Elizabeth Eliza. "The Doolittles left Marseilles with us, and were to branch off for Geneva, and we kept on to Genoa, and Solomon John was always mistaking Genoa for Geneva, as we planned our route. I remember there was a great confusion when they got off."

"I always mix up Geneva and Genoa," said Mrs. Peterkin. "I feel as if they were the same."

"They are quite different," said Elizabeth Eliza; "and Genoa lay in our route, while Geneva took him into Switzerland."

An English gentleman, on the opposite side of the table, then spoke to Mr. Peterkin.

"I beg pardon," he said. "I think I met one of your name in Athens. He attracted our attention because he went every day to the same spot, and he told us he expected to meet his family there, — that he had an appointment by telegraph —"

"In Athens!" exclaimed Mrs. Peterkin.

"Was his name Solomon John?" asked Elizabeth Eliza.

"Were there two little boys?" inquired Mrs. Peterkin.

"His initials were the same as mine," replied the Englishman, — "S.J.P., — for some of his luggage came by mistake into my room, and that is why I spoke of it."

"Is there a Sphinx in Athens?" Mrs. Peterkin inquired.

"There used to be one there," said Agamemnon.

"I beg your pardon," said the Englishman, "but that Sphinx never was in Athens."

"But Solomon John may have made the mistake, — we all make our mistakes," said Mrs. Peterkin, tying her bonnet-strings, as if ready to go to meet Solomon John at that moment.

"The Sphinx was at Thebes in the days of Oedipus," said the Englishman. "No one would expect to find it anywhere in Greece at the present day."

"But was Solomon John inquiring for it?" asked Mr. Peterkin.

"Indeed, no!" answered the Englishman; "he went every day to the Pnyx, a famous hill in Athens, where his telegram had warned him he should meet his friends."

"The Pnyx!" exclaimed Mr. Peterkin; "and how do you spell it?"

"P-n-y-x!" cried Agamemnon, — "the same letters as in Sphinx!"

"All but the *s* and the *h* and the *y*," said Elizabeth Eliza.

"I often spell Sphinx with a *y* myself," said Mr. Peterkin.

"And a telegraph-operator makes such mistakes!" said Agamemnon.

"His telegram had been forwarded to him from Switzerland," said the Englishman; "it had followed him into the dolomite region, and must have been translated many times." "And of course they could not all have been expected to keep the letters in the right order," said Elizabeth Eliza. "And were there two little boys with him?" repeated Mrs. Peterkin.

No; there were no little boys. But further inquiries satisfied the family that Solomon John must be awaiting them in Athens. And how natural the mistake! Mrs. Peterkin said that if she had known of a Pnyx, she should surely have looked for the family there.

Should they then meet Solomon John at the Pnyx, or summon him to Egypt? It seemed safer to go directly to Athens, especially as Mr. Peterkin and Agamemnon were anxious to visit that city.

It was found that a steamer would leave Alexandria next day for Athens, by way of Smyrna and Constantinople. This was a roundabout course; but Mr. Peterkin was impatient to leave, and was glad to gain more acquaintance with the world. Meanwhile they could telegraph their plans to Solomon John, as the English gentleman could give them the address of his hotel.

And Mrs. Peterkin did not shrink from another voyage. Her experience on the Nile had made her forget her sufferings in crossing the Atlantic, and she no longer dreaded entering another steamboat. Their delight in river navigation, indeed, had been so great that the whole family had listened with interest to the descriptions given by their Russian fellow-traveller of steamboat navigation on the Volga — "the most beautiful river in the world," as he declared. Elizabeth Eliza and Mr. Peterkin were eager to try it, and Agamemnon remarked that such a trip would give them an opportunity to visit the renowned fair at Nijninovgorod. Even Mrs. Peterkin had consented to this expedition, provided they should meet Solomon John and the other little boys.

She started, therefore, on a fresh voyage without any dread, forgetting that the Mediterranean, if not so wide as the Atlantic, is still a sea, and often as tempestuous and uncomfortably "choppy." Alas! she was soon to be awakened from her forgetfulness: the sea was the same old enemy.

As they passed up among the Ionian Isles, and she heard Agamemnon and Elizabeth Eliza and their Russian friend (who was accompanying them to Constantinople) talking of the old gods of Greece, she fancied that they were living still, and that Neptune and the classic waves were wreaking their vengeance on them, and pounding and punishing them for venturing to rule them with steam. She was fairly terrified. As they entered Smyrna she declared she would never enter any kind of a boat again, and that Mr. Peterkin must find some way by which they could reach home by land.

How delightful it was to draw near the shore, on a calm afternoon, — even to trust herself to the charge of the boatmen in leaving the ship, and to reach land once more and meet the tumult of voices and people! Here were the screaming and shouting usual in the East, and the same bright array of turbans and costumes in the crowd awaiting them. But a well-known voice reached them, and from the crowd rose a well-known face. Even before they reached the land they had recognized its owner. With his American dress, he looked almost foreign in contrast to the otherwise universal Eastern color. A tall figure on either side seemed, also, each to have a familiar air.

Were there three Solomon Johns?

No; it was Solomon John and the two other little boys—

but grown so that they were no longer little boys. Even Mrs. Peterkin was unable to recognize them at first. But the tones of their voices, their ways, were as natural as ever. Each had a banana in his hand, and pockets stuffed with oranges.

Questions and answers interrupted each other in a most confusing manner: —

"Are you the little boys?"

"Where have you been?"

"Did you go to Vesuvius?"

"How did you get away?"

"Why didn't you come sooner?"

"Our india-rubber boots stuck in the hot lava."

"Have you been there all this time?"

"No; we left them there."

"Have you had fresh dates?"

"They are all gone now, but the dried ones are better than those squeezed ones we have at home."

"How you have grown!"

"Why didn't you telegraph?"

"Why did you go to Vesuvius, when Papa said he couldn't?"

"Did you, too, think it was Pnyx?"

"Where have you been all winter?"

"Did you roast eggs in the crater?"

"When did you begin to grow?"

The little boys could not yet thoroughly explain themselves; they always talked together and in foreign languages, interrupting each other, and never agreeing as to dates.

Solomon John accounted for his appearance in Smyrna by explaining that when he received his father's telegram in Athens, he decided to meet them at Smyrna. He was tired of waiting at the Pnyx. He had but just landed, and came near missing his family, and the little boys too, who had reached Athens just as he was leaving it. None of the family wished now to continue their journey to Athens, but they had the advice and assistance of their Russian friend in planning to leave the steamer at Constantinople; they would, by adopting this plan, be *en route* for the proposed excursion to the Volga.

Mrs. Peterkin was overwhelmed with joy at having all her family together once more; but with it a wave of homesickness surged over her. They were all together; why not go home?

It was found that there was a sailing-vessel bound absolutely for Maine, in which they might take passage. No more separation; no more mistakes; no more tedious study of guide-books; no more weighing of baggage. Every trunk and bag, every Peterkin, could be placed in the boat, and safely landed on the shores of home. It was a temptation, and at one time Mrs. Peterkin actually pleaded for it.

But there came a throbbing in her head, a swimming in her eyes, a swaying of the very floor of the hotel. Could she bear it, day after day, week after week? Would any of them be alive? And Constantinople not seen, nor steam-navigation on the Volga!

And so new plans arose, and wonderful discoveries were made, and the future of the Peterkin family was changed forever.

In the first place a strange stout gentleman in spectacles had followed the Peterkin family to the hotel, had joined in the family councils, and had rendered valuable service in negotiating with the officers of the steamer for the cancellation of their through tickets to Athens. He dined at the same table, and was consulted by the (formerly) little boys.

Who was he?

They explained that he was their "preceptor." It appeared that after they parted from their father, the little boys had become mixed up with some pupils who were being taken by their preceptor to Vesuvius. For some time he had not noticed that his party (consisting of boys of their own age) had been enlarged; and after finding this out, he had concluded they were the sons of an English family with whom he had been corresponding. He was surprised that no further intelligence came with them, and no extra baggage. They had, however, their hand-bags; and after sending their telegram to the lady from Philadelphia, they assured him that all would be right. But they were obliged to leave Naples the very day of despatching the telegram, and left no address to which an answer could be sent. The preceptor took them, with his pupils, directly back to his institution in Gratz, Austria, from which he had taken them on this little excursion.

It was not till the end of the winter that he discovered that his youthful charges — whom he had been faithfully instructing, and who had found the gymnasium and invigorating atmosphere so favorable to growth — were not the sons of his English correspondent, whom he had supposed, from their explanations, to be travelling in America.

He was, however, intending to take his pupils to Athens in the spring, and by this time the little boys were able to explain themselves better in his native language. They assured him they should meet their family in the East, and the preceptor felt it safe to take them upon the track proposed.

It was now that Mr. Peterkin prided himself upon the plan he had insisted upon before leaving home. "Was it not well," he exclaimed, "that I provided each of you with a bag of gold, for use in case of emergency, hidden in the lining of your handbags?"

This had worked badly for Elizabeth Eliza, to be sure, who had left hers at Brindisi; but the little boys had been able to pay some of their expenses, which encouraged the preceptor to believe he might trust them for the rest. So much pleased were all the family with the preceptor that they decided that all three of the little boys should continue under his instructions, and return with him to Gratz. This decision made more easy the other plans of the family.

Both Agamemnon and Solomon John had decided they would like to be foreign consuls. They did not much care where, and they would accept any appointment; and both, it appeared, had written on the subject to the Department at Washington. Agamemnon had put in a plea for a vacancy at Madagascar, and Solomon John hoped for an opening at Rustchuk, Turkey; if not there, at Aintab, Syria. Answers were expected, which were now telegraphed for, to meet them in Constantinople.

Meanwhile Mr. Peterkin had been consulting the preceptor and the Russian Count about a land-journey home. More and more Mrs. Peterkin determined she could not and would not trust herself to another voyage, though she consented to travel by steamer to Constantinople. If they went as far as Nijninovgorod, which was now decided upon, why could they not presevere through "Russia in Asia"?

Their Russian friend at first shook his head at this, but at last agreed that it might be possible to go on from Novgorod comfortably to Tobolsk, perhaps even from there to Yakoutsk, and then to Kamtschatka.

"And cross at Behring's Strait!" exclaimed Mrs. Peterkin. "It looks so narrow on the map."

"And then we are in Alaska," said Mr. Peterkin.

"And at home," exclaimed Mrs. Peterkin, "and no more voyages."

But Elizabeth Eliza doubted about Kamtschatka and Behring's Strait, and thought it would be very cold. "But we can buy furs on our way," insisted Mrs. Peterkin. "And if you do not find the journey agreeable," said their Russian friend, "you can turn back from Yakoutsk, even from Tobolsk, and come to visit us."

Yes — *us!* For Elizabeth Eliza was to marry the Russian Count!

He had been in a boat that was behind them on the Nile, had met them often, had climbed the ruins with them, joined their excursions, and had finally proposed at Edfu.

Elizabeth Eliza had then just written to consult the lady from Philadelphia with regard to the offer of a German professor they had met, and she could give no reply to the Count.

Now, however, it was necessary to make a decision. She had meanwhile learned a few words of Russian. The Count spoke English moderately well, made himself understood better than the Professor, and could understand Elizabeth Eliza's French. Also the Count knew how to decide questions readily, while the Professor had to consider both sides before he could make up his mind.

Mrs. Peterkin objected strongly at first. She could not even pronounce the Russian's name. "How should she be able to speak to him, or tell anybody whom Elizabeth Eliza had married?" But finally the family all gave their consent, won by the attention and devotion of Elizabeth Eliza's last admirer.

The marriage took place in Constantinople, not at Santa Sophia, as Elizabeth Eliza would have wished, as that was under a Mohammedan dispensation. A number of American residents were present, and the preceptor sent for his other pupils in Athens. Elizabeth Eliza wished there was time to invite the lady from Philadelphia to be present, and Ann Maria Bromwick. Would the name be spelled right in the newspapers? All that could be done was to spell it by telegraph as accurately as possible, as far as they themselves knew how, and then leave the papers to do their best (or their worst) in their announcements of the wedding "at the American Consulate, Constantinople, Turkey. No cards."

The last that was ever heard of the Peterkins, Agamemnon was on his way to Madagascar, Solomon John was at Rustchuk, and the little boys at Gratz; Mr. and Mrs. Peterkin, in a comfortable sledge, were on their way from Tobolsk to Yakoutsk; and Elizabeth Eliza was passing her honeymoon in the neighborhood of Moscow.

LUCRETIA PEABODY HALE (1820–1900) was descended from two of New England's most illustrious families and grew up surrounded by Boston's nineteenth-century intelligentsia. Her father, Nathan Hale, was publisher of *The Boston Daily Advertiser*; her uncle Edward Everett was a United States Senator and later president of Harvard; and her brother Edward Everett Hale was a well-known Unitarian clergyman and abolitionist. Hale was educated at progressive schools and, from a young age, helped her father with various editorial tasks at his paper. By the time she was in her twenties, she was able to support herself by writing for several publications, including *The Atlantic Monthly*. Hale liked to amuse her young friends and relations with tales of the antic Peterkin family, and when *Our Folks*, a popular children's magazine, issued a call for fiction that was not just morally improving, she sent some of her stories in. "The Lady Who Put Salt in Her Coffee" was published in 1868 and proved an instant success; stories continued to appear for nine years and were collected in two volumes. Hale was also active in charity and politics, overcoming fierce opposition, from her brother Charles among others, to be elected as the first woman member of the Boston School Committee.